Advance Praise for *The Year Marjorie Moore Learned to Live*

"Grotheim writes unflinchingly about life's letdowns—and how we come back from them—with infectious humor. She has crafted a character to whom we can all relate, and whom we love not only in spite of her imperfections, but because of them."
—Kera Yonker, founder of Final Word

"Grotheim's sharp writing had me guffawing out loud at times at Margie's witty internal monologue, wholeheartedly rooting for her wanderlust, then in the next breath feeling compelled to grab Margie by the shoulders and shake her. Deeply observational, the novel unpeels layers of addiction—to spending, to substances, to risk, to attention from others—making the reader ponder how to extract more joy, spark, light, and color from our everyday lives. Grotheim is a fresh voice in contemporary fiction."
—Heidi K. Brown, author of *The Introverted Lawyer*

"A riveting, modern-day *House of Mirth*. Marjorie Moore, our lovable Texas screw-up, makes one bad decision after another. The book is merciless: scathingly funny, achingly full of heart—and impossible to put down."
 —Olivia Dunn, English Professor at Skimore College

"Grotheim is a promising young talent whose characters come alive on the page. Her portrayal of Margie's mid-life crisis is perfectly captured in thoughtful prose, and the building tensions and well-paced storytelling make it a compelling read."
—Scott Weeks, author of *A Familiar Face* and *Purgatory NY*

"*The Year Marjorie Moore Learned to Live* is a book that can teach us all how to live and remind us that what we experience is, in many ways, up to us. While taking us on a laugh-out-loud fun but cringe-worthy ride of a life about to implode, Grotheim brings us to a point of our own decision about what we value."
—Lisa Kohn, author of *To The Moon And Back*

THE YEAR
MARJORIE
MOORE
LEARNED
TO LIVE

THE YEAR MARJORIE MOORE LEARNED TO LIVE

CHRISTIE GROTHEIM

Heliotrope Books
New York

ISBN: 978-1-942762-46-1

Cover Design by Christie Grotheim
Interior designed and typeset by Naomi Rosenblatt

For Niklas

"People do not seem to realize that their opinion of the world is also a confession of character."

—RALPH WALDO EMERSON

PROLOGUE

When Marjorie Moore emerged from the dark cocoon of her mother's womb, suddenly bathed in a sea of light, the fresh air against her skin making her tiny body tingle, she was sure she'd felt a primitive sense of pure freedom. It was high noon on August 16, 1978, and a real scorcher. People say it's impossible to remember but Margie swears she does; maybe she dreamed it, but it's a vision, a feeling, locked somewhere deep in her subconscious.

Days before, she had become claustrophobic as the space inside her mother's belly grew tighter and more cramped. When she made her exit—and her grand entrance—she let out a terrific scream, not because of the warm, cozy place she had left behind, but in order to test her strength, her independence, the power of her lungs. When she had proven her point, her face relaxed into a calm, contented expression, revealing her full cherub lips and the gleam of a smile in her eyes.

As she looked on curiously while the doctor clipped the umbilical cord, she could not foresee that she would be chained to circumstance, emotionally bound long after the physical connection was cut. Of course, her perceptions were primal and her newly-formed mind was not yet cognizant enough to register any of this, other than the whisper of a memory.

The next thing she felt was being swaddled by the sun, brilliant beams stretching down to her as she was carried out of the hospital in a second-hand car seat, the sweltering Texas heat toasting her face and hands nicely after the overly-cool air conditioning in the stark hospital room. Of this there is a photo somewhere, but she is sure she can remember the pleasure she felt being placed into the car, as soothing as a sauna, while her parents drove her home to their modest double-wide trailer house.

Everyone had said she'd had the most adorable laugh as a baby, enveloping her body and soul like a little seizure. It delighted her aunts, her neighbors, and her mother, who'd captured it on Super 8 film. But as she grew, more often she cried, becoming more unsatisfied, more demanding with each passing year. Her parents told her the first word she learned was not Momma, not Dadda, but "more." As she developed into a young child and then an adolescent, Margie had wanted—had needed—more, and as such, often felt she ended up with less.

So when exactly did she begin to discern that she had drawn the short end of the stick? Was there a certain moment in time when she began to feel that what she had wasn't good enough, and therefore neither was she? When she grew fearful and insecure?

Was it when as a two-year-old she recognized that something wasn't right with the glazed look in her father's eyes? That during those times, which was often, he was rough and unpredictable, and that when he stumbled and slurred she didn't feel safe. That her mother would shout at him, send him to bed, and then speak extra softly to her, holding her a little too tightly. That although it was her father who wasn't in control, she was the one who felt unstable. That she had loved him deeply, since birth, but as she grew older had learned not to trust him entirely.

Or maybe it was when she cried in hunger only to have a wet washcloth stuffed in her mouth to suck on. Or worse, when her brother came along later, and they stuffed a washcloth in his mouth, invoking the sour taste, making her nearly gag at the memory. When they left the room she would dig through the cabinets for cereal, and feed him what she could find: cornflakes or small bits of bread torn off from a stale loaf. Not knowing what solid foods he was capable of eating, she always sat with him until he swallowed the last bite and normal breathing resumed.

Or it might have been in the nursery at church. When some of the volunteer helpers—godly women, no less—looked at her in discernible disgust when she was dropped off with an already dirty diaper. She wondered how old she might have been, probably at least three; old enough to be potty-trained, according to the ladies, and also old enough to feel flushed with humiliation. Poor kid, they said, doesn't deserve this. Disgusting, irresponsible, they snickered among themselves. Trashy. Margie didn't yet know what these words meant, but her mind held onto the words to replay back to her when she did know, and wouldn't let them go even as an adult.

She has a clear memory from when she was about seven of her parents buying her a brand-new doll for her birthday. But instead of the pretty one she had asked for, it was a knockoff with a disturbing frozen smile poorly painted on its cheap plastic face, and as such Margie purposely left the doll outside as thunder loomed and lightning cracked, abandoning her in the rain. She left her there all summer, at the base of a scraggly pine, until she was covered in dirt and mold, small sprouts shooting up from her lumpy arms and legs. Hoping, probably, her parents would find the doll and see a parallel. When that never happened, and she herself rediscovered the discarded doll, she felt bad about what she'd done. Yet Margie instinctively blamed first her parents—for buying the wrong doll in the first place—and then the storm for the damage done.

As a child if she could have looked into the future, she might not have liked what she would see. Might have been disappointed, once again, and on a grander scale. And if it had been possible to peer further, to look more closely, she would see it was in her fortieth year that her life would change—though not at all in the ways she had originally hoped.

JANUARY

Margie was scrolling through her Facebook feed killing time while nursing a glass of cold red wine, two shrinking ice cubes bobbing around within, clinking against the edges when she took a gulp. Still slightly pruney after a long bath, she was on the sofa in her bathrobe waiting for Jack and the kids to return from a movie. She was annoyed by the feed, slightly irked that no one was sharing anything of interest. In fact, it was probably sheer boredom that was stirring up a restless energy within her, an energy with a dark edge, its persistence making her contemplate popping a pill. She certainly had plenty to choose from in her medicine cabinet, with even more stockpiled in bottles and baggies in the back of her nightstand, to restock, refill or replace the ones in the bathroom on an as-need basis.

She immediately reprimanded herself. Ambien and Xanax were sleep aids, not to be used for pure pleasure and the dreamy high it would produce—and before the kids came home—well it was unthinkable. But she had thought it. Her day, now evolving into evening, had been tedious and tiresome, a combination that created an itch she couldn't seem to scratch, gnawing at her insides, which must be why she was having this sudden desire for a drug. It was probably nothing more than a passing craving. Yet she wondered if this yearning was an indication of addiction, or as she often told herself, she was only using the pills to deal with her horrible insomnia. Yes, it was early, not even nine p.m., but she knew she would suffer from it later, as many women did. So it could be considered a treatment, even preventative, and therefore completely harmless—and totally normal.

Just then a Pinterest picture posted by a friend caught her eye and captured her attention, overpowering and then purging the thought of meds from her mind. It was a gorgeous chandelier made of multicolored glass, or was it beads? She zoomed in to see. She was the master of enlarging an image to the perfect point just before pixelation, whether it was to analyze a friend's newborn baby to decide if it was actually cute before commenting, to search for crow's feet to see how well a companion was aging, or to hone in on an important detail such as this. Now she leaned in towards the screen, straining to see, then pulled back hoping to regain focus, too comfortable—and too stubborn—to admit she needed her reading glasses. She found the light fixture funky, bohemian and chic, and unlike anything she'd seen. She liked what she saw, and clicked on it to pin it to her own page.

When Margie had first begun to see Pinterest pins infiltrating her Facebook feed, she was a little peeved. And the more she clicked around on her friends' pages, the more irritated she became. Not at their greedy desire and unapologetic consumerism; that she could relate to. The truth was she felt robbed. After all, she had invented the concept, had already been pinning things for years, cutting out pictures from magazines— things she wanted, things she *needed*—and taping them up in intricate collages all around her house.

Take her kitchen, for example. A large section of the entryway wall was covered with overlapping images of her ideal kitchen, photos she had painstakingly chosen from various interior design magazines: *Town & Country, Architectural Digest,* and her personal favorite, *Elle Decor.* The montage included stainless steel appliances, a country-style cooking island, multi-colored mixing dishes—even though she rarely cooked— and a premium-grade Italian cappuccino maker.

She had taste—that much was clear—even if she was limited as to what she could do financially. The clippings were the first things visitors would see when they entered, like makeshift wallpaper on the once-white walls, before actually stepping into the dining area. She would show guests what it was supposed to be like, tell them that she was frustrated, apologizing for the imperfect aspects, the disarray, like she did when her new friend Katie had come over for the first time six months ago.

"I'm sorry about the unfinished cupboards. We want to paint them white eventually, and mount the paper towel holder, of course. I mean it's a work in progress, obviously. But look, here are the pendant lights I want to get and this is my dream sofa, and I fully intend to purchase each and every item in these photos, but progress has been slow...for monetary reasons," she had explained.

There was nothing terribly wrong with the house to an outsider's eye. It was a big two-story house on a smallish plot, sandwiched between many others with similar façades, the entire block seeming to share the same brick supplier. The focal point was a grand front door with etched glass in the center, somewhat showy and yet somehow not as solid as one would imagine. Crossing the threshold, guests would enter the great room, an open living area with high ceilings and a partial view of the dining room and kitchen, and a hall that led to two bedrooms and a bathroom, with an oversized jacuzzi tub wedged in where its photo had once existed.

Upon closer inspection, one would find that more effort had been put in to the exterior than the interior, with no crown moldings and not much detail, the walls mostly undecorated other than the random collages scattered throughout. The upstairs had that much-lived-in yet unfinished look: carpet worn but doors unpainted, with round holes where knobs should be, and included a guest bedroom, currently being used for storage and unpacked boxes, a cluttered laundry-office-weight room, and a toy-strewn play area for the children.

Yet somehow their toys still made their way into all the other rooms, stuffed animals dropped mid-way down the stairs, a baton angled across the bathroom floor, tiny plastic building blocks left scattered in the living room. How she despised their sharp edges. As she made her way now to the kitchen counter to refill her wine glass she stepped on a bony Barbie doll, snapping its head off. She scooped up the body parts and brought the whole bottle back with her to the couch, to avoid injuring herself on the next trip, knowing she would need to refill again sooner rather than later. As she struggled to pop the head back on she felt herself growing more irritable, fully aware that a pill would solve that problem instantly. She looked at her watch; shouldn't the movie be over already? She felt trapped in her head, trapped in her home—even trapped on the couch—and as such she continued to sit and stew, the tender arch of her foot throbbing.

No, Margie hadn't envisioned living in this incomplete house, in an incomplete neighborhood. She lived in Prairie Mound, a suburb of a suburb, near the suburb where she had grown up—but farther away from, rather than closer to, Dallas itself. When she married Jack he had just finished building the house, and he refused to move—even though he knew she didn't care for the area. She had imagined herself living downtown, or in some bigger city altogether. She considered herself a city girl at heart, but had never really had the chance to prove the theory.

It seemed to her that in the ever-expanding outer limits of the metroplex, the only criteria of a town was having a newly built highway leading to an intersection with a Starbucks and a supermarket. And some of the highways intended to connect the outer 'burbs were left unfinished—missing the integral entrance and exit ramps and forsaken in a field—due to lack of funding, she assumed, or lack of interest.

One of the abandoned freeways nearby cut across the barren landscape and then rose up to a sloping incline, perhaps intended as an overpass, and ended abruptly in the middle of nowhere, at a height that would be a deadly drop, a backhoe up and left behind with its arm outstretched toward the sky. Sometimes when she saw it, it gave her the eerie feeling that she herself was incomplete, that her life had somehow been suspended mid-flow, and that she too was reaching for something.

Marrying Jack after only a short period of dating had felt wild and spontaneous at the time, though in hindsight she could see that it just sort of happened. She had dated better-looking men, but he had an animal magnetism that the others had been lacking. She met him when he was mowing the lawn of her soon-to-be ex-boyfriend, with whom she had moved in two years prior. After Jack cut the grass each month while the almost ex was at work, they cultivated a relationship over cold lemonade on hot summer days. He was a good listener, and she gave him an earful.

Margie's relationship had been in decline; she had recently learned that her boyfriend had cheated on her.

"It was with Darla, you know, Darla Dingwall, that slut-puppy who used to work at the Blockbuster in high school? And she used to be a friend of mine. I mean, what a two-faced bitch!" Margie had said. In such a small town they knew many of the same people. "Why would he choose her, of all people, with her painted-on jeans—her nickname used to be camel-toe, I kid you not. Well, it's insulting on so many levels." She laughed loudly to lighten the mood. But Jack seemed to sense the pain behind her eyes.

"What an asshole. He's a complete idiot," Jack had said.

Jack had a warm smile and wide-set blue eyes—royal blue, loyal blue, his gaze solid and steady. His eyes angled down to a deep droop, sad but serious. Empathetic eyes. She found him stable and uncomplicated. She loved that his idea of a good time was sitting on the porch with a cold one listening to crickets. Her then-boyfriend's idea of a good time, from what she'd been hearing around town, was drinking and clubbing into the wee hours and exhibiting trashy dance moves that included grinding up on other women.

Jack listened intently while she talked incessantly—but how he made her laugh when she let him squeeze a word in. She ended things with her ex on the same day things became physical with Jack. And when she fell into bed with him, she also fell into a life with him.

Jack had loved Margie's laugh—how she threw her head back and cackled at full volume, full-force, her whole body shaking and convulsing; that even when the sound had tapered off, her shoulders still continued to tremor like an aftershock.

In the twelve years since they'd been married, she had realized that stable could also be construed as boring. And he had no doubt realized by now that her wild, uncontrollable giggle-fits were masking a woman with real needs. Needs he couldn't always fulfill.

Jack worked for himself in his one-man landscaping company, called Manscaping, registered just before the clever pun took on another meaning. Margie sometimes teased him about the irony of it, with his hairy torso, dark coarse curls poking out above the necklines of his shirts. Jack took it in stride, said he enjoyed working with his hands, being out in nature, and having the whole of the outdoors as his workspace, the ultimate contrast to his home office-laundry-weight room.

And he was a huge help with the kids, picking them up from school most days in his big beat up Manscaping van, its oversized lettering on both sides and roaring engine competing for attention in announcing its presence. A far cry from comfortable, she found riding in it jarring, unsettling, and she avoided it when possible. The shocks were so bad that it made her upper thighs jiggle and her breasts bounce; she often joked that she needed to wear a sports bra for a ride that rough. But the fact was, after a long day's work when it was filthy, she could hardly force herself to get into that vehicle. It was endlessly frustrating because Jack and the kids often took the van to the local Dairy Queen on Fridays for an after-school snack and then sometimes went straight to a movie. She preferred her sedan, and of course she could always meet them there, but after a long week she often chose a bubble bath and glass of wine instead.

On this particular Friday night she chose the latter. After all, Margie worked hard too, checking patients in at the local emergency room, and she was particularly knackered this evening. Yet she found her work satisfying. She considered it her calling, and put in long days without complaining, offering a kind word to the sick who surrounded her. She had a propensity for small talk and a smile that was contagious. The lighter the subject, the lengthier the conversation. The more afflicted the patient, the more animated her laughter, until her shoulders quivered and quaked. Many of her conversations ended with "well, c'est la vie," her catchall catchphrase that seemed to wrap up most of the chatter nicely. But even so, all that bullshitting and friendly banter took a lot of effort.

So she had soaked in the tub for almost two hours before settling onto the sofa. And that's how she found herself surfing Facebook alone, topping off her glass of wine and adding ice cubes as needed, easier now that she had brought in the entire bottle, as well as a big bowl of ice. She knew serving red wine cold was frowned upon in some circles, but this was Texas for god's sake, and even though it was winter, she was hot-natured—and besides, this was wine in a box, not a fine, aged Bordeaux.

She sulked, wondering if Jack and the kids were sharing a family-sized tub of popcorn. After all, she was part of the family, a key figure and an integral one: had she not birthed two of its members? Feeling left out, she contemplated where she could take them the following day in her sedan. The playground. The new rock-climbing wall in town. Screw it, she would drive them all the way to Disneyland! California, here we come…she imagined what a glorious road trip that would be.

The door flew open and high-pitched voices jolted her back to reality.

"How was it?" she asked. And then before waiting for them to answer: "I thought we'd go to Olive Garden for lunch tomorrow and then maybe a trip to the mall!"

"Breadsticks! Breadsticks!" they chanted in unison, running circles around the living room, Aimee shimmying her shoulders in a very grown-up way.

Jack leaned down to give her a quick kiss, but it landed on her left nostril when she looked up from the feed on her phone, which she had glanced back down at out of habit. Lately their timing seemed a bit off.

She was glad she hadn't taken a pill, one of her beloved benzos. She wanted to connect and catch up and needed to be focused. Yet even now as they chattered, she kept glancing sideways at the continual movement of the social media scrolling in her peripheral vision. So she set the phone on the coffee table face down.

"How was your day?" Jack asked her.

"Oh, it was pretty good, I guess. You know little Mitchell who lives down the street? His mom brought him in because he had a bad accident on his bike. His big toe got caught in the chain, and he was hollering and crying and carrying on—and then I could see why; his toe looked like a bloody pulp. I nearly lost my lunch signing him in—his toenail was ripped clean off!"

The family cringed in unison, the desired effect of any emergency room anecdote.

"Gross!" Oliver shouted, wound up because it was the weekend.

"Disgusting," Aimee added, lip curled.

"That's why I always tell you two to wear tennis shoes on your bikes and scooters. It was awful; it just looked so painful, bless his little heart… and his big bloody toe!" She tried to get a laugh from the kids. She got a giggle from Oliver, but he was the easy one.

"Sounds nasty," Jack said.

"Believe me, it was. But never mind…was the movie good?"

The kids talked over each other trying to describe what, frankly, sounded like a lame plotline, interrupting each other to add to the story. It was another superhero movie, and honestly, Margie wondered how many of those they could continue to make. She feigned interest, saying "uh-huh" in all the appropriate places, but she personally couldn't stand these action movies, and it was an animation to boot. Knowing how the high-pitched, over-exaggerated voices and silly jokes would have grated on her nerves, she looked at her empty wine glass and knew she had made the right decision. She was relieved to see she hadn't finished off the entire bottle and poured the rest for Jack.

And anyway, weren't they getting too old for kids' movies? Maybe not Oliver, at six, but surely Aimee was at ten years old. She preferred foreign films herself, *Amélie* being one of her favorites, and in all honestly, one of the few she'd had the patience to finish. As they began to describe extraneous details and argued over specifics, she was drawn to her phone, trying to pick it up so subtly that no one would notice.

Eventually they fell silent, sensing they'd lost their audience.

"How did the new job go, Jack?" she asked, realizing the room had grown quiet.

"Oh my God, the Martins' place is really over the top…fancy schmancy. It's in Wildwood Hills, so you can imagine. They have a fountain out front fit for a king, or a mobster—hell, maybe they are in the mob; you never see this kind of money around here. I had to go through the house to the backyard during the walk-through and it was dripping in gold…kind of showy, really. It looked like they were bleeding money."

"Must be nice," Margie said, but then regretted it. She'd meant it to be funny but it came out flat.

"Well, like I said, the house is gaudy in my opinion, but it's a big job for me. And the landscaping can stand to be improved—Margie will you put that damn phone down—and they have a budget to work with, for once, so I can actually design something cool."

"Well you're good at that."

"What?"

"Huh?"

"I didn't hear what you said."

"Oh, I said, *you're good at that.*"

"Yeah, well, I guess we'll see…are you really taking the kids to the mall tomorrow?"

She nodded.

"You know you're gonna be fighting crowds on a weekend—everybody and their dog will be there. Well, in any case, don't overdo it."

He turned and went upstairs and the kids were off playing in their room so that once again she had the house to herself. Which she really didn't mind at all.

She thought about their home, and the issue of taste, and how lucky she was to have a naturally refined aesthetic. Yes, she had grown up poor, but somehow she had always had an inherent flair for fashion and an upscale sense of style when it came to her house and herself. From furniture to fashion, from fries to kissing, she was especially taken by all things French, even inspiring her babies' names. She spelled Aimee exactly as they did in France, confusing the locals, and chose Oliver, which sounded so charming and seemed the perfect name for someone forced to wear berets as a toddler.

She would have preferred being called Marjorie, which was her given name and sounded sophisticated, like royalty, she thought. Resentful of her parents shortening it to Margie, a fatty's name when in fact she was not, she had made better choices for her own kids.

Regardless of having a hardy name from the heartland, when she saw the movie *Amélie*, Margie realized her looks could pass for Parisian: big eyes the color of rich caramel and full, pinkish lips. Not that she considered herself as pretty as Amélie herself—but she felt sure she was better looking than many of the supporting actors. Her skin tone was a bit lighter than some of the women she saw on the screen, but with a summer tan she would fit in perfectly on the streets of Paris, especially with her highly-developed sense of style, underappreciated in these parts.

Yet she knew her looks could also be considered all-American, the girl-next-door type: cute but not beautiful, a little button nose shared by half the South—cheerleaders and country bumpkins alike—perfectly shaped but in no way aristocratic, and full, rosy cheeks supported by strong bone structure. At forty, she was still attractive. Always had been, judging from the amount of male attention she'd received over the years, having had a string of serious boyfriends from the time she was fourteen.

Her hair was still voluminous and healthy, adapting and molding to any style from the Meg Ryan to the Jennifer Aniston to whatever was the latest trend. Born blonde, it had darkened to a mousy brown, but it held color incredibly well—absorbed it, radiated it—from rich reds to golden blondes to auburns. Her children had inherited the perfect combination of her thick hair and Jack's dark color, and she took pride in each family member's impeccably groomed head. Even poor Jack's, whose was balding rapidly, his already large forehead forever expanding. She instructed him to have the hair that was left cropped closer and closer to his scalp.

Margie didn't think she was being shallow, it was just that she took her looks seriously, because secretly she felt appearance was just as important as congeniality in her line of work. She wanted to look put-together to offer a subtle reminder to the saddest souls, those suffering the most in society, that they would eventually—hopefully—be well and healthy, and that they too could aspire to look fresh and attractive. She privately hoped her lively personality, light scent, lip liner and luminous hair might reinforce their will to live.

Nice hairstyles were important enough to be clipped out and taped to the bathroom mirror. Although at first she fought Pinterest, she finally broke down and created an account—after all, she invented it—and took it a step further, spewing out page after Pinterest page from the office printer at the hospital, registering patients when it was busy, registering items she wanted off the internet when it wasn't. She carried the images home in her briefcase, bought for this very purpose, to put on the appropriate wall. Cutouts of clothes were plastered on the outside of closets, while actual clothes were crammed to capacity inside. The kids, always immaculately dressed, had so many outfits that they overflowed into Jack's closet, eventually overtaking it completely. His items were moved to a rack in the laundry-office-weight room, which is where he spent more and more of his time.

With the closets overflowing, clothing littered the floors, especially in Aimee's princess-themed room, which was actually Oliver's room, too. When Oliver became too big for his crib, he moved in with her, and while Margie had big ideas for redecorating, she never got around to it, although plenty of pictures of dinosaurs and race car beds were taped to the side of his princess bunk. In truth both kids were quickly outgrowing all of the motifs.

When Margie and Jack fought she would let the kids sleep with her in the queen-sized bed, a comforting way to get back at Jack. So sometimes it was he who would find himself sleeping with the princesses in the Disney diorama, stuffed into a single bed lying underneath Ariel, whose larger-than-life image covered the comforter.

However, she and Jack usually shared a bed, and it was calling to her now, the wine making her sleepy. Or maybe it was the pre-sleep nightly pill that was beckoning, suggesting she extend the buzz she was feeling. She looked in on the kids who had fallen asleep at odd angles, turned out their lamp and headed upstairs, where Jack was still watching YouTube tutorials in his office. She kissed his forehead and told him she was turning in. Which she did, after taking a sleeping pill.

She was glad she would be able to sleep in a bit in the morning. And she needed her beauty sleep. How she wished the pill would kick in; just thinking about her meticulous weekday routine that started at five o'clock in the morning exhausted her. Each morning Margie jumped directly into the shower, scrubbing herself hard with a loofah, cursing the fact that she couldn't have her caffeine because she couldn't stand Folgers and they still hadn't bought the Italian cappuccino maker that she desperately needed. She always lingered under the hot water, washed and conditioned her crowning glory, and shaved her armpits and legs, never skipping a day. Unable to tolerate stubble, she only wished Jack had the same level of hygiene. She dried thoroughly, spastically, with a towel, before squatting in the bow-legged position she assumed to blow-dry her landing strip of pubic hair. Taught as a teenager that this prevented yeast infections, she had done so ever since.

All this before fixing her hair and applying makeup, putting cereal on the table, and then tending to the children just as closely, putting high-end products in Oliver's hair and sculpting Aimee's into tight pigtails. Where oh where does the time go, she wondered aloud almost every morning.

So she relished her weekends, reveling in the lightness she was feeling right now as all those stressful thoughts from the week dissipated, a weight lifting off her shoulders until she was lifted along with it, as the tight ball of tension morphed into an Ambien-induced cloud upon which she now floated.

The alcohol and drug cocktail allowed her to sleep, and deeply, until nine the next morning. But once she had showered, bathed the children, picked out an outfit for herself and her son, found shoes for Oliver and a headband for Aimee, it was suddenly mid-afternoon and they were running late. Aimee was of course old enough to choose her own clothes, but this was one of the things that delayed them as she was encouraged and then forced to change before reaching optimum color-coordination. In order to make it before they stopped serving lunch, Margie had to drive rather recklessly, flying down the four-lane highway to a nearby suburb, the "Children On Board" sign suction-cupped to the back window flapping wildly against the glass. By the time they finished their pasta and splurged on dessert, the sun was setting.

There are simply not enough hours in the day, thought Margie. She had originally planned to go to the Galleria downtown, the high-end three-story mall offering dramatic views of the oval ice-skating rink in the center lit by glass skylights high overhead. She felt it would be a good family activity for winter, and had envisioned them all skating together hand in hand when they finished shopping. Luckily she hadn't mentioned it because there was no time for that now with afternoon traffic, so she settled on a more local, if run-down, mall, which only required driving through several adjoining parking lots.

Time and money were the two things Margie never seemed to have enough of. But she did the best she could, and pulled out two crisp five-dollar bills for each of them to spend in the arcade, or however they liked.

"Thanks, Mom!" Oliver said.

"Awesome," Aimee added.

"You two stick together and let's meet back right here in one hour at this dried-up fountain. Okay?" Kids were so easily amused, she thought.

This mall was built in the eighties and still seemed to house some of its original occupants: Spencer's Gifts, 5-7-9, Bakers Shoes, Wicks 'N Sticks, The Foot Locker—franchises she thought had gone out of business years ago. She headed for Dillard's, inarguably the nicest department store in the decrepit shopping center.

She perused the purses, spotting a Coach handbag she had taped up on her nightstand. She noticed some Diesel jeans that she had clipped out of *Lucky* magazine just last month and was tempted to try them on, but instead went to the children's section; she felt less guilty when she overspent on them. She found a few matchy-matchy outfits that she just *had* to have, asking the saleswoman if she could hold them for an hour. This was a technique she had taught herself, to take a pause, to circle the store a few times or shop elsewhere and see if she still wanted—no, *needed*—the items. The answer was usually yes.

As she made her way to the main aisle, a display caught her eye. Upon approaching, she noticed a woman with a bouffant hairdo standing behind a table topped with pretty packages. The product being pushed was bubble bath, called Luxembourg Gardens—and came from France. The aroma was divine: jasmine and sage and other rich fragrances that smelled just how she imagined the heavenly scent of the streets of Paris. Her excitement grew when she noticed a jar of tiny pencils next to a small notepad on which you could enter to win a raffle—an all-expense paid trip for two to Paris—with each purchase.

At ten dollars per bottle the price was right. She thought three would be a good number, one for her and each of the kids. Then she realized five would be better: she could give them to her mother and mother-in-law. Margie thought about Jack in the spa tub, bubbles in his hairy chest and she smiled to herself and picked up another box.

The possibility of going to France was making her hands sweat, her heart race, and to the saleslady's dismay, Margie placed her six boxes back with the others, adjusting them just so. She backed away from the table, avoiding eye contact, and stuttered that she would be back, probably.

She began to pace the perimeter of the store once again to clear her head. She pictured herself sitting in an outdoor cafe, nursing expensive wine and eating escargot. She'd always wanted to visit the Louvre and see the *Mona Lisa*. The woman wasn't attractive; she was very plain, butt-ugly in fact, and she thought about the makeover she would have given Mona if she'd had the chance—but that wasn't the point. She knew there must be something special about the painting and wanted to see it up close with her own two eyes.

And she would go to the top of the Eiffel Tower, just about the most beautiful structure she had ever seen. On TV not long ago she had watched a travel show and was amazed by its scale and fascinated by the fact that there were kiosks and gift shops in each of the four leg bases.

When she was younger she had longed to travel. She had big dreams that took place elsewhere, in places she had heard about from friends or seen in movies. For as long as she could remember, she had wanted to go to Paris. If not Paris, Prague, or Peru. The actual destination didn't matter so much, as long as it was anywhere but here. She had wanted a change of scenery, an adventure, an escape. Still did, as a matter of fact.

Being married with two children, she often worried that she had missed her window. Her kids were a great source of satisfaction and she found motherhood fulfilling—in the sense that she had very full days and their needs filled all of her time. Sadly the family ended up vacationing in Florida year after year, while there were so many other places she yearned to see: Cabo, Bali, Mali, Milan, places she knew the names of even if she couldn't necessarily locate them on a map.

She had tried to save up for exotic vacations, unsuccessfully, wondering how other people always managed to have money for expensive trips. Her problem, which she felt could also be considered a skill, was that she knew a bargain when she saw it. She wasn't one to pass up a Victoria's Secret sale—four pairs of panties for thirty dollars rather than thirty-five dollars, and the fact that she needed twelve pairs only added to the savings, plus a couple of cute nighties (for around the house), as well as sexy lingerie (for Jack). At the cash register the totals always surprised her. But she had never been good at math, being a much more visual person, and well, she appreciated the finer things in life, which was just another reason she needed to go to Europe!

She would not make that mistake today, and decided then and there she would buy no other items, not the clothes for the kids and certainly nothing for herself, instead focusing on the matter at hand: directing her energy and money toward increasing her chances. She lost count of the times she had circled the store, but in terms of the product, ten wouldn't necessarily be too many, in fact ten wasn't nearly enough when it came to the odds of winning; she was sure this was a national campaign. Twenty chances would be better and thirty even better, and since she could give them as birthday gifts she would actually be saving money for months—maybe even years—to come. Yes, thirty would do. She circled back to the table, and very matter-of-factly, very calmly, spoke to the saleswoman, then systematically filled out the thirty forms.

"Oh, my! You are my best customer by far today, darlin'," the woman beamed beneath her helmet of hair. Three hundred dollars, plus tax. Her tired eyes lit up; she obviously worked off of commission. Margie collected the children and they all three were overloaded with boxes to carry out to the car and put into the trunk. She told them not to tell their father, because these were going to be given as special gifts—and one would be for him!

Upon arriving home, she snuck the boxes into the spare storage room. Jack was surprised when she came back empty-handed, looked relieved. Later that evening she googled Luxembourg Gardens, keeping the screen out of Jack's view. She found the grounds breathtaking. Paths rimmed in well-manicured wildflowers exploded with color. It was full of marble fountains—much nicer than the moldy, crumbling concrete structure at the mall!—and elaborate European sculptures, the likes of which you would never see in America. The French appreciated art and beauty. The contoured shrubs and topiaries certainly would have impressed Jack if she'd dared show him. But instead she felt a little guilty, closed her laptop, put the whole event out of her mind, and headed to bed.

When Jack turned in soon after, throwing an arm around her midsection in a semi-spoon and giving her a loving squeeze, the guilt wouldn't subside and was in fact compounded by more guilt as she lay there waiting impatiently for him to fall asleep. She then slowly got out of bed, careful not to wake him, closed the bathroom door, gently opened the cabinet so it didn't creak, and popped not one but two pills.

Again she began to question whether her usage had gotten worse, whether the cravings had always been this strong, and whether the amount required to serve their purpose—eradicate negative thoughts in order to allow her to sleep—was increasing. Now and then she took two pills when she needed them to kick in quickly, and she reassured herself that she had done so when necessary for years. So in that sense, it wasn't getting worse; it had always been that bad, which she considered good. In fact now she began to feel good all over, peaceful, blissful and she easily transitioned into pleasant dreams of Paris.

FEBRUARY

Winter dragged on and Margie went about her routine. Even though she was warm-natured, Margie despised cold weather because she would often sweat in her house only to step outside to be affronted by a gust of frigid air. And yet she always felt shocked by it, experiencing each winter as if it was her first. Even just walking from the house to the car, from the car to the office, her hands would immediately seize up, too cold to turn the key. Although these blasts were cold, they were quick, and probably because of that she never bothered to bundle up properly. So she considered temperatures below fifty freezing, and below freezing god-awful. In the depth of winter she couldn't even fathom what the warmth of spring felt like, hard as she tried to imagine it.

So she spent a lot of time indoors. Her Pinterest printouts piled up, as did the projects around the house. She busied herself by renovating the playroom—mentally not physically—which meant first getting rid of a few extraneous items: a mounted buck head with a lazy eye and a crushed ear, a stuffed armadillo with a Coors Light can propped up in its little rat-like hands, and a mythical creature known as a jackalope, created when deer horns are grafted onto a rabbit's head. This particular jackalope looked even more sinister with its wandering eye following Margie around the room.

Taxidermy was a hobby Jack had picked up in his early twenties before he started yard work. He had said it was a creative outlet, that he had enjoyed preserving nature, breathing new life into the bodies. Had said once that getting the eyes just right was the hardest part. Apparently, thought Margie. These were the only relics he had left, and she knew purging the creepy critters would be a challenging task.

Then again, Margie wondered if Jack would even notice if she disposed of them on the sly. He didn't really concern himself with interior design and made little effort to help out around the house. Lately the only way she knew he lived there was the seemingly infinite amount of empty Diet Coke cans he left around like a trail of breadcrumbs for her to pick up. In fact, Jack had spent much of the last couple of months hiding out in his laundry-office-weight room watching YouTube videos on gardening and weightlifting, while slouched down in his chair in the airless office.

Any domestic contributions he made were sporadic. Manic. If she asked him to help clean the kitchen, he would not do the dishes but instead mop every inch of the floor, then focus on the spice rack, dismounting it from the wall, scrubbing the racks and then each bottle thoroughly, almost violently. Unhappy with the results, he might then build a new spice rack entirely (after watching several videos), spending hours or days on the project. When he was finished certain areas would gleam, but dirty dishes would still be overflowing in the sink. She would stub her toe on the power tools he'd left lying around. Exhausted, feeling that he'd gone above and beyond the call of duty, he'd lounge around lazily for weeks afterward. Jack was in one of these lethargic stages now and she knew broaching the subject of selling his precious menagerie would rouse him.

"Jack," she said, interrupting a reclusive-looking, middle-aged man on the screen speaking in a monotone voice from a dingy basement. Jack didn't take his eyes off the instructional video.

"*Jack!*" she shouted. "Can you turn that thing off for a minute? I can't hear myself *think*! I'm redecorating the playroom...I want to hang lots of different-sized mirrors on the wall by the stairs. It is the cutest thing"—she handed him a clipping—"and it will make the room look way, *way* bigger. So we need to get rid of those animal heads. I mean, really, they're just hanging there, sort of decaying as we speak. Maybe we could sell them or something."

"Are you *shitting* me? No way! This is nature, Margie, God's fucking creation, stuffed with my own two hands. And you want to replace it with some crap you're gonna buy at the *mall*? I don't think so. You can't put a price tag on that kind of craftsmanship!"

"Well, yes you can, apparently. I found tons of them on eBay starting at fifty dollars and some going for as much as two hundred and fifty!"

He looked back at the monitor and went silent, indicating that the conversation was over.

She dropped the subject, not having the energy to argue, and then dropped the playroom project altogether, blaming Jack. "Well, c'est la vie," she mumbled to herself.

Instead she turned her thoughts to Paris, her fantasies keeping her occupied. At work her days were spent searching travel sites and discovering Top Ten Things to See and Do. Her browser was full of all things Parisian and she was learning, studying too, not only looking at photos of the Notre Dame but reading about the architecture, about its flying buttresses. She definitely wanted to take a river cruise down the Seine, to drink a glass of wine along its banks. She looked again at the *Mona Lisa* and other paintings she would see at the Louvre, and then downloaded an app to learn how to say the word Louvre properly, along with other important French phrases. Even though she kept the volume down, "s'il vous plait" would float out into the waiting room now and then, as she would repeat it, trying to curb her slight Southern drawl: see-view-play.

After work she busied herself with the kids, who were hauled around town, shuffled from the Manscaping van to the sedan, from after-school activities to soccer practice to birthday parties. Occasionally the four of them would find themselves in one place for a pizza night or a movie at home, after work but before Margie's nightly routine, almost as involved as the morning routine but in reverse, taking off layers of makeup and applying various ointments and anti-wrinkle, age-defying creams.

Whether she willed it to happen or global warming was responsible, warm weather arrived early, in late February, and with it, signs of life from Jack. One particularly nice evening, Margie emerged from the bathroom after applying a facial mask to find Jack in the garage digging out the antique churn. In town earlier he had secretly bought the ingredients to make homemade ice cream, a kind of tradition in their family on the first warm day. The pleasant weather snuck up on them on the heels of a rainy week culminating in an intense electrical storm. The kids watched in anticipation as Jack churned the cream vigorously, stopping only to add rock salt and sugar. Margie, too, felt charged with energy, the heat and post-storm static in the air streaming through her like a current, further exaggerating the intense expression on her whited-out face— with only her encircled eyes bulging out—and her usually perfect hair frizzing up.

"You look like a scary bird, Mommy, like a mean owl!" Oliver said.

"Hoo, hoo, who wants some ice cream," Margie teased in a haunting voice, sneaking up behind Aimee and then chasing Oliver around.

"I scream, you scream, we all scream for ice cream!" Aimee shouted, a family joke recycled annually that the children never seemed to tire of.

They laughed in between heaping spoonfuls. Even though she was on a strict diet Margie helped herself to a generous portion; she couldn't resist the taste and texture of freshly churned ice cream.

Margie appreciated these small gestures from Jack. Thinking about it lying in bed that night, she was glad Jack was satisfied with the little things in life. She, however, wanted big things. Had big dreams. In her mind it came down to having ambition. And the next big thing she needed was ambitious indeed: identical new iPads for the children with colorful designer cases she had pinned. She would let them choose the colors to assert their individuality and allow them self-expression, which was why she didn't want them to have to share.

She'd had to share everything with her brother Bobby—and personal things that weren't meant to be shared like sweaters and stuffed animals—including well-worn clothing and a few toys that arrived in boxes from the church a couple of times a year, some of which were already damaged. Like 1000-piece puzzles, a few pieces always missing, making the process extra challenging and the end ultra frustrating, never allowing them the sense of completion that is the whole point of puzzles. Or the Raggedy Ann doll that was raggedy indeed. Like the gorgeous rabbit-hair jacket Margie received in fifth grade. Although she'd loved it, she'd had to leave it hanging open all winter because the zipper was broken. Margie wondered if the church realized there was a *reason* deacons' wives were giving this stuff away, and it wasn't always the goodness of their hearts.

Yet going through the boxes, they would dig in as if it was Christmas morning, grabbing things from each other like pigeons fighting for a crumb. That's when their mother told them to share, as if it was a godly pursuit and not just because they were hard up. She remembered sharing Snuggle-Bear, and taking turns sleeping with the stuffed bear, whom Bobby had named Bernard, creating an identity crisis for everyone involved. And sharing clothes didn't help the matter. Although she was a year older, he was a bit bigger, and pudgy, so he'd handed down hand-me-down clothes to her. She'd had to wear his sloppy seconds, which were actually thirds, or maybe even fourths, including boys' shirts and jackets. And that is how she learned, by being teased at school, that buttons on boys' shirts were on the other side. So for those reasons, among others, Aimee and Oliver would not be sharing an iPad.

The next morning when she brought it up, Jack was against the idea. "Do you have any idea how much those ridiculous things cost? Besides, they're way too young to have their own hand-held devices."

"But how can someone be too young to stream cartoons and movies?" Margie argued. "It makes no sense! At the hospital I see young children, toddlers, fully capable of using iPads, looking thoroughly absorbed, and I don't want Aimee and Oliver to fall behind the curve."

She herself loved being online and knew firsthand how entertaining it could be, spending hours a day posting and checking statuses on social media. Jack argued that they should wait until next Christmas, that it was too extravagant a gift to buy for no reason. But next Christmas was ten months away, and there was no way she could wait that long; Margie had convinced herself they needed them now.

Lately she had been taking the children's boredom as a personal affront. They often stared up at her with big needy eyes while she was updating Facebook—well it nearly broke her heart!

This was something they could all do together, sitting on the sofa, clicking away. And didn't Jack say she should spend more quality time with the kids? Sometimes she felt motherhood didn't come naturally to her, that she was missing certain tools, and these two tools would certainly help her out.

She didn't exactly need his approval on the purchase, and really didn't have to tell him at all. When she had gone back to work after Aimee was born she had opened up her own checking account after discussing it with Jack, into which she would put a certain agreed-upon amount aside for "me money." But when she shopped for the children, the "me money" became "we money," so she needed more and more of it.

At first she used the debit card linked to the account. But she soon outgrew it, her compulsive purchases exceeding the limits of available funds. Between the new duvet cover and matching pillows, the silver rowboat-shaped salad bowl with wooden oar serving utensils, the kaleidoscope necklace for Aimee, the microscope for Oliver, and so on and so forth, the demand simply surpassed the supply. The bank began to contact her by mail and follow-up phone calls to see if she would like to upgrade to a credit card associated with the account and she said yes, flattered to have been chosen. And when they kept increasing her credit line, she also took that as a compliment.

Margie never told Jack about the upgrade, since the credit card was tied to her own private account, and therefore really none of his concern. Jack sometimes questioned where the money was coming from, or at least he used to. Other times he seemed to play dumb. But then again, she constantly fed him little fibs, omissions, and exaggerations—that would soon evolve into flat out lies.

She began to rack up reward points, which she was thrilled about, along with debt, which she was less than thrilled about, but tried not to dwell on. The deeper the hole she dug and the more impossible it became to pay off, the more she spent. After all, what's more impossible than the already impossible?

One evening, she sat with Aimee and Oliver after dinner, one on each side of her with their orange and green iPad covers, busy retouching a recent photo to upload to Facebook. Using Photoshop, a program she learned from a friend for this very purpose, she altered reality in virtually every picture in this virtual reality. Beyond doctoring the photos, she promoted herself to plastic surgeon, removing her slight double chin, erasing crow's feet, and performing instant Botox. With the clone tool she could wipe away her forehead wrinkles with one fell swoop, and finally, implement liposuction all over, a time-consuming operation but well worth it, removing ten to fifteen pounds.

As far as updates and activities, she was truthful, posting action-packed pictures with her adorable children and occasionally Jack. Sure, sometimes she put the children into poses, creating a scene that wasn't really happening—but would have been funny if it was! She'd always had an active imagination so she took creative liberties, not unlike a movie director, she supposed.

And she was a loyal Facebook friend, always supporting her friends and relatives, preferring positive posts rather than bitching and moaning, ranting and raving, pet peeves, politics or prayer requests.

After another successful procedure, she clicked Post, waiting eagerly for the likes to pour in. Meanwhile she read her feed, seeing what the rest of the world was up to this evening. There were birthday parties, anniversaries, people eating out, planting gardens, running marathons—everyone's life looked so damn great. And maybe hers looked great to other people too, but *was* it, was it *really*? She was content at the moment at least, with Aimee and Oliver by her side generating a communal warm spot on the couch. They busied themselves with games. Educational, she hoped.

She did a double-take as she scrolled down, the computer refreshing rapidly, struggling to keep up with her. Was that *Stephen Singleton*? She stopped mid-feed and scrolled in reverse, passing the picture again, then moved forward more slowly, searching intently. Yes, it most certainly was. Tagged by a classmate from high school, he had been a friend with whom she'd had a close, flirtatious relationship. He was still a major hottie, unlike most of the middle-aged men her age that popped up on her feed with massive beer guts hanging over their Wranglers.

She clicked on his profile, but being that they weren't "friends,"—not yet anyway—she didn't have access to many photos. She studied the available images diligently, analyzing the angles, zooming in, searching for full body shots. He still had that devilish grin. Good Lord, those dimples! That cowboy hat! She felt flushed as she zoomed in closer and closer on his aquamarine eyes, as clear and bright as pictures she'd seen of the Caribbean Sea. Elfin, laughing eyes that when directed on her, she remembered, made her feel extraordinary. In high school he had been the perfect mix, a bit of a player, but a "sensitive asshole," pretending to be arrogant and removed on the outside so that when he finally did give you full his attention, even as a friend, it made you melt a little bit on the inside.

Thinking back, she was surprised that they had never hooked up in high school or when they were both home from college or hanging out in Dallas; it wasn't as if she'd never had the chance. She had spent two semesters at University of North Texas in Denton before transferring to a community college downtown, and for many years he had attended a nearby community college, though she didn't think he'd graduated. Then again, neither had she.

He had hit on her at house parties but she had chosen the friend route, probably afraid of his reputation. She remembered the rush of stealing street signs with him her freshman year of high school in the dead of night—he was a couple of years older and had just gotten his driver's license and picked her up after she snuck out of the house. She'd savored the simple thrill of driving around all night long, traveling familiar roads made mysterious in the blanket of night while warm winds poured in open windows ratting up her permed hair, hot gusts of air trying furiously to penetrate her wall of bangs. She had stood guard, drinking wine coolers in the back of his truck, his trusted accomplice in vandalizing the neighborhood.

Another time she ran into him totally randomly in South Padre on spring break, and they partied together the rest of the week, doing ten-cent shots in Mexican bars wearing matching panchos, stumbling back across the border drunk each night. Why, oh why hadn't she slept with him when she'd had the chance? She always wondered what he'd be like in bed, and never more so than now.

"What *is* that, Momma?" Aimee asked, looking at the giant eyeball staring back at her.

"Oh, it's no one. I mean, nothing. Just a guy I used to know."

Oliver looked over, getting a good look at Stephen Singleton as Margie was zooming out, trying to close the window, her finger having a spasm on the button.

That peaked his interest even more. "Who was that man in the hat, Mommy?"

She was trying to decide how to answer when Aimee started back in. "I want to see again. *Show* me, Mom. Go back!" she demanded.

The kids seemed to sense Margie's frenetic energy, with Oliver running around the couch in circles, chanting, creating a silly song: "Show *me*! Show *me*! I wanna *see* that man in the *hat*!" Aimee joined in, even though she was entirely too old for that kind of behavior.

Oh, God. They wouldn't let it go. What on earth had gotten into them? She answered that it was an old friend and it was time for bed.

As she tucked them in she couldn't get Stephen Singleton out of her mind. He went by his full name the way ultra-popular kids did—not just any Stephen but *Stephen Singleton*. You had to say both names so everyone knew *which* Stephen you were talking about. He was Stevie once she got to know him better. She wondered if he now went by Stephen or Steve and what he did. Finance maybe? A lawyer? He hadn't exactly been an honor roll student, so maybe car salesman or restaurant manager would be a better guess.

With the kids in their beds and Jack still upstairs, Margie sat on the sofa and sneaked another peek, sending a friend request before she could stop herself. She had been weighing the pros and cons for the last couple hours as she went through her nightly skincare routine. He had been a platonic friend, and what was the harm in reconnecting? In fact, it would insinuate something if she purposely *avoided* befriending him.

Flipping through a magazine, Margie checked Facebook every few minutes, her fingers activating the screen of their own accord before her brain even registered the action. She was an excellent typist and knew her keyboard by touch, barely glancing away from the article she was perusing. Finally, a tiny red notification appeared on the screen in her peripheral vision, and yes, he had accepted! That very evening! She was disappointed that there was no private message, and was soon lost in thought analyzing what that could mean as she pored over his profile.

"Do you want some ice cream?" Jack startled her, staring at her from the kitchen, holding the freezer door ajar.

Margie jumped, pulling a muscle in her neck while clutching the items in her lap, but she didn't miss a beat. "Homemade?"

"No."

"Then no thanks."

She gave him a quick smile and got back to her magazine, underneath which was her laptop, generating so much heat she thought it might burn through her stretch pants as she dug deeper into Stevie's feed.

Now that they were "friends" she had access to more photos and saw someone who might or might not be his wife, and a couple of kids, much older than her own. She saw that he lived in Charleston, South Carolina. The fact that he was so far from home indicated a certain amount of success in itself. She had never been there but loved the way it rolled off the tongue. She said it aloud softly with a lilt, the syllables as smooth as butter.

She read a month's worth of posts. In no way was she stalking him, she told herself, she was simply and suddenly dying to know what he had been up to the last twenty years. With no mention of a wife and no cheesy date night posts, it looked like he could be divorced. The mystery woman could have easily been an office buddy or a cousin. If he was married they clearly led completely separate lives, and if it was a loveless marriage that was practically the same as being single. She scolded herself for even dignifying that line of thinking! Then again, of course she was curious about an old friend; she would be coldhearted not to be. Before bed, she sent a message to his inbox: *"Long time no see! How the hell are you?"*

That night she made passionate love to Jack, taking him by surprise. She hadn't planned on it herself. Always hygiene conscious, she usually washed her nether regions with a washcloth and sprinkled the area with baby powder before lovemaking, but this session was spontaneous, raw—and dirty—in a good way.

Her exhaustion should have sent her right to sleep, but lying there, the afterglow lingered. Her thoughts kept drifting back to Stevie, or perhaps they had never left him. Lately, she had been having more trouble sleeping than ever, an avalanche of thoughts rushing through her head. Her mind had a mind of its own, and she seemed to have less and less control over it. What's worse, there were other things she was losing control over: her spending, her kids, her time.

If she couldn't control her waking hours she would at least control her sleeping hours, which was the excuse Margie fed herself for resorting to some sort of sleeping pill almost every night, more and more consistently, and she worried again that the meds were becoming less effective. It really was an awful cycle, because analyzing *why* she needed to take the drugs, what was the driving force or motivation, was so exhausting and nerve-wracking—there were so many reasons—that it was the very thing that made her reach for the meds, which caused her to question if she had a mild addiction, which required her to reassure herself that she did not. Once they kicked in she felt even more sure that she was okay, and the high would allow her to relax and to sleep, until the next night when she felt doubly guilty, until it created an endless spiral of angst, which was part of the problem, as she was well aware.

And she should know. In the hospital she had seen real addicts, real junkies, but she had also seen many patients treated effectively. Self-educated on the subject, she had discovered the difference between benzodiazepines and non-benzodiazepines just by looking at the hospital patients' charts and judging each individual's anxiety levels and mental problems as they sat in the waiting room. You don't have to have a medical degree to observe someone walk in a complete nut job and walk out a calm, functioning member of society. And she learned by listening. Prescription drugs were discussed around the water coolers at full volume in regards to their effects on patients, as gossip when it came to the doctors' and nurses' use, and in whispers when it came to personal use. And the meds were easy enough to get ahold of in the break room in the context of one stressed out mother to another.

Other than alcohol, Margie had never done drugs of any kind when she was young, so she was in her experimental phase. And she had been for quite some time, if she was being honest. She had tried the hard stuff, opiates: three Oxycontin placed in her hand by a co-worker at a happy hour years ago. Curious what all the buzz was about, she popped one on a Saturday morning, another on Sunday and the last one on the following weekend, realizing she had best never take them again as it was the most intense peace she had ever felt, like being suspended in a dream inside a dream. It was as warm and welcoming as the womb and brought back the fuzzy memory of actually being in her mother's cavity, gently suspended and perfectly centered within the universe. Throughout those three days she was in a beautiful daze, in another world, one she liked much better, finding a euphoria and joy she instantly loved more than her own family. So she switched to benzos, which she knew were less addictive and thus seemed safer.

She was currently rotating between Xanax, Ambien and Valium, gauging their effectiveness not only in treating insomnia but also their capability to blot out bad thoughts, eradicate awful memories, and obliterate future worries. She analyzed the subtle highs, the weightlessness versus heaviness, some sending her hovering slightly above her pillow as free as the air she breathed while others sank her, sucked her into a dark place, if not quite as intense as the womb, like a rocking bassinet covered in warm blankets. That night she chose a Xanax, which made her melt rather than float, before swaying her to sleep.

The next morning she felt groggy even after her shower and made a mental note that two milligrams might be a hair on the high side. Before leaving the house she checked her Facebook feed. Instead of the one line she expected, she was pleasantly surprised to get a long-winded two paragraphs from Stevie, lengthy enough for him to have put some thought into it but not long enough to appear psychopathic.

He started the email with "Hey Large Marge," a nickname that stuck from high school as a joke when she was stick thin. She cringed, wishing she were ten pounds thinner now, or twenty-five to match her high school self.

He recalled a couple of their college memories, and explained how he'd ended up in Charleston. After falling in love with the town while on vacation five years ago, he'd applied for a job and up and moved there. A beach bum at heart, he enjoyed living on the coast. He managed to reveal certain things about himself while hiding others; although he said he enjoyed spending time with his kids, who were both in high school, there was no mention of a wife, a divorce, or a separation. It was friendly, funny in parts, and grammatically correct. He ended the message with the line: *"Hope life has treated you well."*

As she drove the kids to school she repeated the line in her head again and again. Even though it was a simple wish, a polite closing and not at all unique, it seemed like the most thoughtful, genuine thing anyone had ever said to her. In fact she wondered if anyone else really cared how life had treated her—until now no one had thought to ask. And what's worse, she realized she didn't know the answer. She was happy in some ways, but had it really treated her, well, *well*?

It was hard to say. Life had actually treated her badly at times, and up until now it had been average at best.

She thought about it harder. How had it treated her, really and truly? She had gotten not one but two traffic tickets this month, the car was making a strange sound and needed to go to the shop, and she was broke—no, worse—in debt. She had only travelled to seven states in her whole life, had never left the country, and did not have a passport. Her parents were nutjobs, her kids seemed to be rebelling, and her husband was lazy and spent too much time watching sports and YouTube videos.

On the other hand, she had a roof over her head and a family who loved her, and whom she loved deeply, most of the time.

Now she had the challenge of responding to him with a private message of equal length, depth, humor, and quality. Without oversharing. She worked on the rough draft at work and fine-tuned it that evening before dinner, changing her mind about the wholesome meal she was going to prepare and pulling out frozen dinners instead. The children often complained about her cooking anyway and even Jack preferred junk food, so what did it matter? While the kids worked on their homework she worked on hers, brow furrowed, careful to keep her screen at an angle just out of view. She reread her final draft, torn over whether to call him Steve, Stephen or Stevie. He had signed off with Steve but that just didn't sound right to her.

Hey Stevie,

So good to hear from you! Your life in Charleston sounds lovely; I've always wanted to live near the beach. I'm still landlocked here in Prairie Mound. Ha ha! I work here at the local hospital, checking patients in at the emergency room. I suppose life has treated me pretty well, overall. Thanks for asking! I have a ten-year-old daughter, Aimee, and a son Oliver, six. They're sweet kids, my pride and joy.

She didn't feel the need to mention Jack or that she was married, since he hadn't divulged. But her husband was listed on her Facebook page, while no one was listed on his.

I was remembering all the adventures we had in high school driving around in your old pickup truck—we were quite the little hellions! Those were the days. I have thought of you often over the years. I'm so glad we reconnected!

She pushed Send just before bed, the word "often" causing her to toss and turn with anxiety. Was that too much? Was it even true? She had thought of him from time to time but wasn't sure exactly how often qualified as often. In any case, she felt the phrase had a nice ring to it. But she wished she could shut down the frantic feed that kept scrolling through her head! After trying to drift off on her own for an hour, she pondered upon which pill to pop, settling on a strong dose of Valium.

Although it would take longer to kick in than Xanax or Ambien—and the waiting made her more anxious—she knew it would have a more powerful and long-lasting effect, giving her a lightheaded calmness, then sending her soaring while suppressing her raging emotions, and finally dropping her into a dreamless sleep, a near comatose state of being.

MARCH

By the time the weekend arrived, Margie had crash-landed. Five days had passed and she hadn't heard back from Stevie. Ten weeks had passed and she hadn't received word from the Luxembourg Gardens company in regard to the Paris trip, which was worrying. She made a mental note to take the initiative and call the manufacturer from work on Monday to find out the status of the drawing. Still debating the issue of whether life had treated her well, she decided it had not. She had never been lucky, never won anything, not so much as a school raffle, even though she had participated in plenty.

She was beginning to wonder whether she was having a series of bad days or if she was depressed. And whether she was truly depressed, or merely disappointed. She often contemplated how one contemplates such things.

Sometimes when she had these down days, she was sure she fell deeper than other people did. Small frustrations, like not winning something and therefore not getting what she felt she deserved, and little slights, like getting passed over for a promotion or even getting cut off in traffic, filled her with an overwhelming sense of rage at the unfairness of it all. Minor humiliations, like when Jack rolled his eyes or raised his voice at her, seemed magnified by her original humiliation. Everyday aggressions harkened back to something darker, always stemming from and leading to the root of her original anger: being the child of an alcoholic father. She felt it like a ripple effect, but also a reverse ripple, funneling forever downward. She could hardly get her head around it; she certainly couldn't verbalize it. For her, even self-awareness seemed just out of reach, like so many things.

But she was all too aware that growing up she had been full of fear and hurt, a hurt so vast, so expansive, that she'd had to compact it down tight, to stuff it and stomp it to the bottom of her being. Which left a lot of empty space. She imagined her core like a deep well, that ironically couldn't be filled, a bottomless pit swallowing up all that she put there, took in, consumed. Yet it somehow remained hollow. That's why she tried not to let herself get dragged down by these dark thoughts, lest she get sucked into that vacuum and free fall into the abyss.

Instead, she tried to be a positive, upbeat person. To put on a smile, push through each day, as she had done since she was a young girl. The one thing Marjorie Moore knew for sure was that she wanted more. More excitement. More passion. More adventure.

C'est la vie, she thought, and forced herself to think of something else. She shifted her focus to the weekend plans.

Sunday the whole family had been invited to a barbeque at their neighbors' house. Katie and her family had moved to the neighborhood a year ago from Dallas proper, where she had worked at a top advertising agency. They had chosen Prairie Mound in search of more space and a slower pace of life. Be careful what you wish for, thought Margie. Her husband Brett was an appraiser and he and Jack had hit it off quite well, which was unusual with Jack's introverted, anti-social tendencies. She enjoyed spending time with Katie, who was a more creative, artsy type than most of the conservative, church-going, minivan-driving, helicopter moms waddling around in their mom jeans, discussing their family's dietary needs in-depth or offering diatribes on their disciplinary philosophies. Margie wasn't that kind of a mom; she just did what came naturally. And when it didn't come naturally, she improvised.

Katie and Brett's house was just down the block and had an identical floor plan to their own, but rather than the McMansion it was, their house felt airy and light, like a quirky but comfortable art gallery, with friends' oil paintings and large-scale advertising prints on the walls, all nicely framed, and artifacts and handicrafts from Arizona—where they were originally from—scattered thoughtfully throughout. Margie loved the look of it and tried to think how to incorporate some of the ambience into her own home without directly copying Katie's ideas.

Her children were close in age but in reverse, boy and then girl, which actually worked out well. Lately Margie worried that her kids were in role reversal. Oliver was the sensitive, feminine one, while Aimee was pure tomboy, adventurous with no fear, suddenly hating dresses to Margie's dismay. At least she could still dress Oliver like a little doll, with his newfound love of bow ties and suspenders.

On Sunday afternoon, she dressed him like a young Kennedy in one-piece coveralls with bloomer-like shorts. She wondered if he was getting too old for this as he was no longer a toddler, but since he was petite he still looked the part—with chubby cheeks on both ends, the tight bloomers accentuating this fact. Upon arrival the older set took to climbing trees and the younger set played house with stuffed animals, Oliver begging too loudly to be the mom.

The women greeted each other in the usual female fashion.

"You look *great*, Margie; *love* your sundress."

Margie savored the compliment as she had struggled with what to wear, hoping it wasn't too summery and that the weather wouldn't dip when the sun went down, but responded with the necessary self-deprecation.

"Well thanks, but I'm a *mess*...no, *you* look great. Your skin looks so healthy—and I *love* what you've done to your hair." She did look fresh and attractive as always, her dark hair swept into a loose topknot rather than her usual no-nonsense ponytail. It looked easy-breezy, yet each strand seemed perfectly placed, even the wispy tendrils that escaped the rubber band.

Brett and Jack discussed seemingly inexhaustible man-topics: their latest DIY projects, real estate, home values, and motorcycles. As she listened to them drone on from across the yard, Margie asked Katie in a mock whisper: "Is it still considered mansplaining when they do it to each other?"

"No, I don't think so, because they use a less condescending tone... but it's equally as tiresome!" They giggled, and then escaped into the kitchen to mix up more margaritas.

The tequila from the first one was creating a powerful urge within Margie to spill all about the Stephen Singleton situation, but being that it wasn't yet a situation, just the beginnings of a flirtation—and *was* he flirting?!—she stopped herself. With all of the family fun it didn't seem appropriate, and besides, Katie's friendship was relatively new. They were just now reaching the stage of complaining about their husbands, a necessary precursor.

Katie, however, did begin to open up, sharing her frustrations about the adjustment to living in the suburbs, having trouble meeting interesting people, and finding Prairie Mound lackluster. Even the name didn't make sense.

"How can a prairie also be a mound? It's an oxymoron!" she chuckled. Margie laughed too, unsure of the word's exact definition but understanding the context entirely. "It's nothing more than farmland and flat fields with the occasional subdivision. And all the moms meet at Starbucks—I mean for god's sake it's a drive through. And it's so small inside that the whole place smells like car exhaust! I just can't stand it in there; makes me woozy. Yes, the schools are good and safe, but where is the stimulation? It's all so terribly sterile."

"Welcome to Starbucks," Margie said. "Would you like to try our new a car-puccino? How about a mocha gas fumé? Or better yet why not just make your coffee at home and then go to the garage, turn on the car and suck on the tailpipe—and save yourself a trip!" Margie let out an infectious belly laugh.

Katie cracked up too, and then continued. "The problem is that these towns—if you can call them that—have no history, no character, no culture."

"Tell me something I don't know!" She loved that Katie was cultured enough to notice.

Katie explained that she was having difficulty sleeping, because of the change of environment, she guessed, and that the lack of things to do during the day made her mind overactive at night.

Margie, always eager to help—and in this case connect—said she could get pills at the hospital, explaining her own sleep issues and the success she had had with medication. Katie was hesitant at first, but came around after some convincing, adding that of course she would pay her for them, for her trouble.

Finally they joined the others. After dessert and a long and lively game of charades on the porch, the whole family chattered away on the short walk home, getting to bed quite late for a school night.

The next morning Margie brought a bottle of bubble bath in with her to work, wanting to use the information on the package to call the manufacturer. Since they'd been sitting for a while, she opened the bottle and took a quick whiff to see if the scent was still strong, and found it extremely potent indeed. Afterwards she was going to give it to her boss, as a surprise gift-for-no-reason, but began to question her decision as commentary drifted in from the waiting room.

"What's that funky smell?" someone asked.

"I don't know but that shit smells *nasty*," someone answered.

After a series of phone calls and transfers, she finally got connected to a woman in marketing, who told her matter-of-factly that the winner had been announced weeks ago. "I'm sorry to inform you," the woman started out, her British accent making her politeness sound condescending. Margie received the news like a blow to the gut. The lady could have at least been friendly. Her usually impeccable phone manners failing, Margie let her have it: "Well, I hate to be the one to inform *you*," she replied in her most refined voice, enunciating every syllable, "that this product *reeks*. Literally. It smelled good when I bought it, but it's not aging well. I bought thirty of these bottles and they are stinking up my entire house like *rotting meat*."

"*Thirty* bottles?" the woman interrupted.

"Yes, *thirty*…" The woman seemed to be missing the point. "And it seriously smells like *death warmed over*. So sadly, I regret to inform you that you have just lost a very good customer."

Her hopes dashed, once again. Always just out of reach. She would have to find another way to get there. Meanwhile she tried to distract herself by checking Facebook. Nothing of interest. Depressing *and* disappointing.

So she moved to her next item of business, securing meds for her friend. She wanted to start Katie out on Valium, which she found as of late to be the most flowery of the highs. Less addictive than Percocet and the like, it still obliterated anxiety entirely. It was impossible for Margie to worry while on it, because when bad thoughts entered her mind they no longer seemed worrisome, just extenuating circumstances that were in no way associated with her feelings. Another pleasant side effect was a surge of self-confidence. When she took it at night and got up to use the bathroom, the reflection staring back at her looked pretty, like an angel, and thought angel thoughts. Everything radiated warmth. Even her toothbrush looked like a fuzzy-headed friend, loyal and loving. The glowing white tiles were perfectly positioned, beautifully spaced, and she would stare at their intricate patterns, which would morph into different but equally entrancing arrangements.

Margie had taken meds at her job on a few occasions, on exceptionally mundane days, so that even moving a paperclip felt like a rewarding experience. Even looking at a paperclip—tightly twisted wire, a utilitarian piece of art—was entertaining. But she did so rarely; she had standards after all. Craving a pill now, she fought the urge and snapped out of her daze, redirecting her mind back to the issue at hand.

In terms of payment, Katie had a good job, freelancing for the same agency she used to work for downtown. She wondered how much Katie made per hour; it was probably three or four times what she herself made at the hospital. Easily five times as much. Besides, she wasn't a dispensary or a government-funded free clinic. And she knew that it would make Katie feel better; she personally hated being indebted to a friend. In fact she hated being indebted at all, and yet she was, deeply, on a grand scale—and knew firsthand that it was an awful feeling. She wouldn't wish that on her worst enemy. Katie had said "for her trouble," and after all, she would have to ask a doctor for a prescription. She hesitated to give away her own personal stockpile of Valium at home, should she need it, and she knew she would.

Fortunately, when she walked into the break room Dr. Ford was pouring himself a cup of coffee. On such good terms, she called him by his first name, John. He was on friendly terms with her too, to say the least. He had hit on her at the company Christmas party a few years ago while sipping on his third martini. She wasn't sure he had technically hit on her but he had certainly been too forward, leaning in too close, asking if she was happily married, ogling her cleavage, a perverted twinkle in his glazed eyes when he finally looked up. She had felt uncomfortable but somewhat flattered; he was a successful doctor after all, and in any case, it served her well now. She asked about his children, said she hated to bother him, she knew he was busy, but would it be possible to get a prescription for Valium, explaining that she was actually still having trouble sleeping, and having quite a bit of anxiety, and that she didn't know why, except for the fact that Jack's work had been slow and Oliver was having trouble in school. He agreed so eagerly that Margie smirked to herself as she walked away, thinking it was almost too easy.

In between patients she checked Facebook again. She saw a red inbox notice, and to her delight it was from Stevie.

Great to hear back from you! Sorry it took a while to write you back. I was out of town this weekend at a family obligation. I'm glad you're doing so well. Sometimes I miss our old stomping grounds down in Texas. My parents are still there but I don't make it back as often as I should. My dad is really getting up there, and he suffers from Alzheimer's, so it's hard on all of us, especially my mom. Are you in touch with any of the old gang? Your kids are really precious, and you look great—you haven't changed a bit! What do you do for fun these days? I assume you're not still sneaking out at night, drinking Strawberry Hill and cow tipping? Lol. As for me, I'm hanging in there. Sometimes your life isn't what you expected. And then sometimes the unexpected happens. Followed by a winking smiley face as a sign off.

A philosopher, she thought. Were winks *always* sexual or just sometimes? She couldn't say, but began to sweat profusely, springing a leak under each armpit, two dark pools spreading out on opposite sides of her chiffon blouse like inkblots.

Once again he'd managed to keep certain things about himself vague and mysterious, like the family obligation, while making other parts feel personal, sharing something very private about his parents, while being thoughtful, complimenting the kids, and *her*, saying she hadn't changed a bit! It was an effective combination.

She was digesting the email, lingering on each line, then rereading the entire chain again from the beginning to put everything in context, when a "bling" sound made her jump. It was an instant message chat notice. It was *him*! She wasn't ready for this now, Good Lord, not here in the waiting room. Someone could walk in, and what would she do? More importantly, what would she say to Stevie? She was good at flirting in high school, but she'd used her resources: her eyes, her smile, her hair. Now she would have to rely on words and one-liners, shot out as fast as her fingers could flutter, and unfortunately she typed at a much quicker rate than she thought at. She was the kind of person who always came up with a funny or biting comeback hours or even days later. She would then share it with Jack, what she should have said, what she could have said, laughing wickedly. She panicked.

Yet she clicked on the message.

"Hey Large Marge—I see you're online… Happy Monday."

She made a mental note to look into changing her settings so he couldn't tell when she was online.

"Just another manic one. j.k. It's kinda slow around here. I'm at work."

"Me too." While she was thinking of a response he blasted her again.

"So you work at a hospital? Checking people in? That must keep things interesting. I'll bet you see some real characters."

She typed fast before he fired off another line and she fell behind.

"You have no idea! Well, it gets a little slow in this one-horse town. Sometimes I wish there was more action but that's awful to say, especially in the ER."

More action? She cringed. Almost everything sounded leading when broken down to five and ten word soundbites. She didn't like these mini-sentences and micro-thoughts. But she supposed it did force one to get to the essence of things.

"Shit. There's my boss. Gotta run. Chat later?"

"Sure." She finally responded after a stunned silence—did he mean later *that night?*—and he was gone.

Well, that was rather painless, she thought. But her pulse was pounding.

She always used the time on the drive home to unwind. Sometimes she would turn the station to eighties or nineties tunes and sing at the top of her lungs. But today she was lost in Stevie's virtual world, rereading lines from the email on her internal processor. *Sometimes your life isn't what you expected. And then sometimes the unexpected happens.* Was he talking about himself, his divorce, and his move to Charleston…or was he talking about *her*? Her life certainly wasn't what she'd expected, and truthfully she worried she hadn't really lived up to her potential—but how did *he* know that? Or was he talking about her and him, *them*, and about her befriending him on Facebook? It was so vague and mysterious yet so tauntingly romantic.

Yes, this was unexpected, as he said. And she realized now that things could escalate quickly. As spontaneous things do! She liked the buzz it gave her, as strong and pleasant as her pills. She liked having possibilities. She fantasized about what his life was like, what it would be like to have a little excitement in hers. Losing out on Paris, maybe this was her chance for a different kind of adventure. It did cross her mind that she loved Jack and was relatively happily married, but it was all happening so suddenly that she hardly had a chance to dwell on it. And the last thing she wanted to do was overanalyze it. Actions were already put into motion and never did she question where the flirtation could lead, what would unfold, or what the impact might be.

When she walked in through the front door Jack and the kids were making homemade pizza. Oliver was dressed in her apron—and her heels—watching Aimee who was chopping onions intensely, fiercely, learned from watching her father. How she looked like Jack, her hair pulled back exposing a bulbous forehead, with oceanic eyes focused on the job at hand. She had Jack's angled eyes, but while his drooped from age and fatigue, hers big and round and curious, giving her an otherworldly look, like an adorable alien.

Oliver was the spitting image of Margie, inheriting what she considered her best features, with his irresistible button nose, full cheeks just aching to be pinched, and cherub lips that broke into a wide smile at the slightest prompting. Sometimes she found him so scrumptious she was tempted to take a bite of his cheeks, as soft and pillowy as freshly buttered biscuits. Dark eyebrows, from Jack, framed his face, amplifying his intensity. He was her sensitive, thoughtful child, and while she held back from suffocating him with affection, she tried to encourage his sweet nature.

"Momma, I've been helping Daddy and Aimee. I'm wearing your

shoes so I can see over the counter top."

"That's nice, Oliver," she said. But the catwalk circle he took around the dining room begged to differ.

It was a heartening scene, comforting after a long day. It would have been even better had they all been sitting on mid-century modern stools around a kitchen island with pendant lights, none of which they had yet, but the soft light from the exposed bulb and preheated oven created a warm glow nonetheless. Feeling guilty, she changed her mind and hoped Stevie didn't plan on chatting that night—if that was indeed what he intended.

Before tucking the kids into bed she read to them on the bottom bunk, one snuggled up on each side, wanting to spend a little quality time with them after they had prepared such a lovely meal. They chose *The Adventures of Paddington Bear*. Margie put on a thick if sometimes inaccurate English accent for all of the characters' dialogue, some in low tones and others frighteningly high, until Oliver fell asleep and Aimee's eyelids grew heavy. When she emerged from their bedroom, Jack was in the living room watching a basketball game and she sat down next to him with her laptop. He told her about a crazy new client and she told him about a crazy old patient.

"You know, with summer just around the corner maybe we should think about putting some money aside for a trip to Florida. It'd be nice to have some beach time with the kids," Jack mused.

She knew he meant well, but *Florida?! Again?* Putting money aside, yes, she thought, remembering to look up street prices for the pharmaceuticals, but Florida, no freaking way. She couldn't get inspired by that same strip of coastline she had already seen time and time again. But Jack acted as if it was the only place on earth, so stuck in his routines. She would rather save for something else—exactly what she didn't know.

"Yeah, maybe," she said, giving his thigh a quick squeeze, not in the mood for an argument.

She tilted her screen and googled her meds, easily finding the street prices, which surprised her. Fifteen dollars for Valium or Xanax—for just one pill! Twenty dollars for Oxys and Percs, which she could also get her hands on, not that she would encourage their use. She got along well with all of the doctors and they had written prescriptions for her many times: for antibiotics when the kids were sick, for an aching back after a long day, even performing minor surgeries like mole removals for free and providing shots of Botox now and then, saving her the trouble of retouching her Facebook photos, temporarily at least. They scribbled out remedies in their chicken scratch for everyone on staff, and more readily for the people they liked.

Yes, she would charge Katie. And then maybe even expand her network.

She thought of her friend Candace, and how stressed-out she always was, her negative energy and non-stop talking annoying everyone within earshot. She could use a Xanax or two whether she knew it or not. She thought about Stephanie and how haggard she looked the last time she saw her, and with four kids it was no wonder. She needed something to take the edge off. She remembered Janet and her recent divorce, Joan and her health issues, Allison recently losing her job, Karen and her constant mid-life crisis. The list went on and on, Margie conjuring up a menagerie of friends, and all with major issues!

Each and every person on the list could benefit from meds in one way or another. After all, life wasn't easy, and she had the means to help make it more bearable. It was a win-win situation; she would be helping them out, while helping herself solve her monetary problems. With the atrocious state of healthcare, which she knew all too well, she would do the dirty work, saving them the trouble of getting referrals, expensive co-pays, having to go to the doctor and fake illnesses. She would be providing a service, and people get paid for performing services all the time. She would reconnect with the women, plan a girls' night out.

Lying in bed that night she pondered what she could use the money for. Obviously paying off her debt would be her main priority, but there might be some left over for other luxuries if she planned wisely. She was an ambitious person and she had dreams, if somewhat undefined, and she believed this might make them all come true, as she swallowed a pill herself, and drifted up, up and away.

APRIL

After catching up on the inpatients' paperwork at the hospital the following day, she was starting her group email about the girls' night out when she was interrupted by a bling—Stevie again. She jumped and glanced around. The waiting room was dead slow, just a couple of unsavory characters that came in again and again for every little sniffle, taking advantage of the system. In fact they came in so often they'd acquired nicknames: Big Bertha, an obese woman from the nearby housing projects, and Dirty Hairy, not named after the Clint Eastwood character her parents had loved to watch, but simply because he was dirty and hairy, a disheveled old man with a black beard and ample back hair who she often spotted around town pushing a grocery cart down the side of the road shirtless. Yet she knew deep down they were mostly just lonely and would lend them an ear when she checked them in on slow days, patiently listening and nodding. She could deal with them and Stevie too. She smiled, interpreting him reaching out to her again so soon as a very good sign.

"*Hi! Sorry about yesterday,*" he said. "*That was kind of a quickie. Ha ha. How are you?*"

"*No problem. I'm good!*" she said. "*It's a little hard for me to chat while working. But I'll give it a try! I've just got a couple of deadbeats in here so I'm good to go until a real emergency comes in. How are you doing?*"

"*Better now!*"

Oh! She was quite sure that was a direct flirtation. "*Are you at work? What is it you do? I couldn't tell from Facebook but the company name sounds important.*"

"*Sales.*"

"*You're probably good at that! I'll bet you could sell ice to an Eskimo!*" She scolded herself for using too many exclamation points.

"LOL. I'd rather be surfing right now. It's a gorgeous day out here. I taught myself to surf after moving up here and it was the best decision I ever made."

"Oh cool, well you always were sporty...that explains the T-shirts and surf shorts I saw on Facebook. Looks like you're always dressed for the beach, you lucky dog!"

Dang it, she realized she used another exclamation mark before she could stop herself.

"Yeah, I go as much as I can. I'm only about three miles away from it, living in a log cabin in the woods."

"Sounds lovely, you should send me a picture of it." she wrote. Then boldly, "Do you live by yourself?"

She instantly regretted it, feeling she'd been too transparent.

"Got separated about a year ago. It's just me and I have the kids every other weekend."

She was thinking of what to say when another blurb appeared.

"But I want to know more about you, about your life," he wrote. "Are you still as fun-loving and adventurous as you were in high school? It seemed like you were always laughing; I remember how your shoulders would shake like you were having a convulsion!"

"Well, yes, that still happens when I laugh hard—I can't control it—but I suppose I laugh a little less often. I mean life gets a little more serious. But I'm still the same old me!"

"Well that's good to hear...you shouldn't change a thing."

"Aw, you're sweet."

They chatted for almost an hour when a patient came in and she had to go rather abruptly.

But even after she said goodbye, two more blurbs popped up from him:

"Margie, I really am glad we reconnected."

"It's so nice to see your face and you really do look amazing."

Amazing? It was kind of amazing. She knew it was mostly innocent banter, but wondered if he was just being nice, joking around or if it really could be possible that he was actually interested in her.

Her days at the hospital were becoming increasingly filled with personal matters, which at least made the monotonous minutes tick by more quickly. She had chatted with Stevie a couple of more times, and she had painstakingly composed the email about the girls' night out, struggling with the wording, questioning whether she should go through with it. Instead of pushing Send, she saved the draft and focused on her meeting with Katie later that day. With both women working and caring for kids, and therefore hardly a moment for themselves, over a week had passed before Marjorie and Katie had a chance to get together.

She walked briskly down the long central corridor to the hospital's run-down but effective pharmacy. It looked ancient, with some dusty vials and beakers on the counters that she hoped were just for decoration, though she didn't know for sure. But she actually liked seeing and chatting with the pharmacist, Ed, an old-timer who had been at the hospital since she started thirteen years ago. However, since she was running late she didn't make much small talk. She thanked him and shoved the prescription in her purse, then raced out the door in order to make her five o'clock appointment.

They agreed to meet at the Starbucks, or Carbucks, as they now called it. Unable to think of anywhere with more ambiance—because there was nowhere in Prairie Mound—they decided next time they would drive to downtown Dallas and have a nice lunch, but for now the toxic coffee shop would have to do. The smell of idling motors, burnt fuel and bitter coffee filled her nostrils as she waited for her friend—and first client. She kept telling herself it was an innocent outing, nothing more than a mommy meet-up. But checking her phone fanatically, she was as fidgety as any felon or hard-core dealer.

Margie was calmed by the sight of Katie and the easy conversation that followed; they gabbed about their children, their husbands. She carried on about Jack wanting to go to Florida yet again, and how regimented—and downright boring—he was. Katie complained about Brett's obsessions with his hobbies, music and motorcycles, at the expense of spending time with his children. Margie mentioned Jack's how-to video fixation; turns out Brett was also a fan of tutorials.

"Aren't there certain things men should just know how to do? What happened to primal instincts or just plain common sense? The male species has evolved for millions of years before the internet, and now they think they have to consult it before hammering in a nail, before fixing a leak, probably before taking a proper shit, I mean, *really*!" Margie laughed until her entire torso ricocheted.

"And Brett surfs around on eBay morning, noon and night. I think his true hobby is buying equipment for his hobbies. He spends much more time online shopping than on the actual activities themselves. When we have a mortgage to pay and two kids to support!"

That struck a little too close to home for Margie, and she tried to steer the subject back to common ground.

"I know what you mean. The other day Jack was watching tutorials on working out, something he knows good and well how to do, with his hand stuffed in the front of his pants like Al Bundy, looking like a total slob, surrounded by sets of actual dumbbells just sitting there collecting dust!"

When Margie finally glanced at her watch, two hours had passed. She quieted her voice and said that—oh!—she had the Valium with her. She explained that while she personally would *give* them away if she could, if she had an endless supply, how each time she had to ask a favor from a doctor, and how she supposed she could get in quite a bit of trouble if she got caught, and so she felt she would have to ask for around twenty dollars for each pill. She had rounded up.

Katie looked a little taken aback but attempted to disguise her surprise by digging around deep in her purse for her wallet, finally pulling out a stack of twenties from the bowels of her bag. She asked Margie if she felt ten Valiums would be enough to start with. Margie said she thought that twenty was a good number.

"After all, they come highly recommended," she said with a wink. "Satisfaction, guaranteed!"

Always short of cash, that was the most money she'd held in her hands in quite some time—and the easiest she'd ever come by.

Speeding into the short driveway too quickly, she lurched to a stop and walked through the empty house to discover Jack and the kids in the backyard, Jack hacking away at a patch of barren soil with a shovel.

"Mommy, mommy, we're building a turtle pond!" Oliver said, dancing in circles, toes as pointed as a prima ballerina's. Aimee was involved too, searching the perimeter of the fence for small rocks to decorate its edges. Margie hated that the houses were too close together in this subdivision but at least the lots were deep. Like the interior of the house, the yard was also unfinished. The grass was blotchy, mostly covering the center directly behind the house but never spreading or taking root in certain spots, becoming more rugged as it extended back. Mr. Manscaper had never gotten around to his own backyard, pun intended. Although he considered all of the great outdoors—in this community at least—his canvas, he was less proactive about household projects until prompted repeatedly. And yet here he was digging a hole in one of the driest spots to the left of the back porch.

Now that it was April and business had picked up and he was spending more time in the sunshine, Jack was rejuvenated, looking tan and healthy. Almost virile. Even his hair seemed to be sprouting on his head in places Margie was sure had been bald for years. She made a mental note to remind him he needed a tighter trim. Watching him work had always stirred something deep inside her; she did love seeing him in his element. She felt a tad guilty about her prior conversation with Katie, as well as the instant chats with Stevie—now there had been four. Jack was a good man. A simple man.

And he was proud of that fact, which sometimes bewildered Margie. Said all he needed was fresh air to breathe, hard work and exercise, things to build, greenery to groom, projects to complete, a sense of accomplishment. Honestly, he was so easily satisfied, whether with a warm hearty meal, a good night's sleep, or the sound of the children's laughter. Must be nice, Margie thought.

So she felt this turtle pond would be a good project for him—and the kids of course. And maybe she could come up with a clever way to get involved. She wasn't very handy and didn't have a green thumb. Yet when it came to operating power tools and the like, she was all thumbs, clumsy, a hazard. Totally ill-equipped for these kinds of projects, she was sure she would only get in the way.

Jack, on the other hand, needed to create and took pride in it, whether that was designing a glorious garden walkway, preening perfectly shaped shrubs, or even building a smelly septic tank. He told her he liked having his hands in the soil. He told others, when asked what church they attended—a common question in these parts—that nature was his religion, that he found it transformative. At this moment she agreed with him, as the last rays of the golden hour shot sideways across the grass, warming her face and shoulders. She sat in a lawn chair and watched them work, each mirrored by a long, distorted shadow. Now the sun bore into the same spot between her shoulder blades and she shifted, breaking the seal of sweat that fused her to her seat. They all looked so contented. Should she grab a hoe and help Jack, help Aimee search for smooth stones, or entertain Oliver who was spinning in circles and then falling into the grass repeatedly? But unfortunately she was hot and tired, and after a long day at work she simply couldn't muster the strength.

Unlike what she'd told the good doctor the week prior, Jack was busy at work. Having a better spring than usual, he was manhandling land all over town. His reach now extended to nearby suburbs and he was racking up miles in the Manscaping van. Over dinner, he told Margie that he was considering hiring an assistant and had met a good candidate through a mutual friend.

"Nice young guy," he said while wolfing down leftovers. "I think kids call 'em hipsters, you know, scraggly but not bad looking. His name's Auden, for god's sake. He's passing through from the Northeast, comes from Oregon. I'll bet he drinks artisanal coffee and eats a lot of goddamned kale." They laughed heartily. "But seemed like he could do the job, kind of a mountain man. He's interested in staying for the summer."

"He probably eats quinoa and rides a bike everywhere and carries all his clothes in a filthy backpack…and wears his flowing hair in a man-bun," she added, pronouncing quinoa the way it looked, drawing it out into three syllables, as she had never heard it pronounced out loud. "Does he have a beard?"

Jack chuckled. "*Oh* yeah, damn thing's down to about here."

"Well then he's a *total* hipster." She told Jack he should hire him, privately wondering what in the world a hipster was doing in Prairie Mound.

Later that night, kids asleep, Margie was binge-watching a new series while retouching a recent selfie that she wanted to post upon Stevie's request. She had a new haircut and color, lighter for the summer months, more golden than before. The cut was sleek and chic, falling just below the chin and slightly longer on one side, its asymmetry giving it an urban edge, she thought. She considered the photo flattering. But it would be even more so in a few minutes. Taking multi-tasking to a new level, lately she found that if she couldn't focus on multiple things, she had trouble concentrating on any one thing. With her laptop on her thigh, cell phone within inches, and two tablets that the kids had already grown tired of directly in front of her on the coffee table—a coffee table she wanted to replace—there was no shortage of devices in the house. She shot back the few texts that buzzed in while "liking" this and that on Facebook, while working on the photo, while watching her show.

An instant chat dialogue box popped up. It was Stevie. She had grown accustomed to the medium and more comfortable with him, as comfortable she guessed as she would be on any fifth date. Not that she considered these chats "dates"—that would be weird—but she supposed someone could make the comparison. She found that you could read a person's humor, depth, and interests as easily online as in real life, which also required real-time replies. She realized it was just as easy to blurt out something stupid on the phone, which put her mind at ease somehow. Both interactions had the exciting urgency of the awaited responses, and in fact typing allowed for a fraction more time to think. When he had used "brb" the first time she searched it in a side window to see that it meant "be right back" and now she used it often—even when she hadn't gone anywhere, but needed to buy some time. The newness of the whole experience made her feel young, almost millennial.

"*Hey you,*" the dialogue box read.

"*Hey you back,*" she said. "*Had a nice evening with the kids outside.*" He now knew she was married but she didn't mention it much in their chats. It didn't seem appropriate with his separation and for other obvious reasons. "*I just love these Texas summer nights. You've gotta miss those.*" she typed. Duh, she realized it wasn't officially summer yet.

"*The nights here in the Carolinas are pretty great too.*"

"*Do they have crickets and cicadas there?*"

"*Yep, I hear their chirping loud and clear. They're singing quite a tune tonight.*" he said. His country cottage sounded divine.

She wondered if they had crickets in Paris. Well, not in the city center but in the countryside. In the Riviera or wherever. Or in wine country. Provence and Marseille she'd heard of, and Bordeaux of course.

"*Did I tell you I almost won a trip to Paris?*"

She told him the whole story, how she'd gotten carried away, how silly and irresponsible she'd been. How she'd hidden the boxes but couldn't eradicate the horrible scent.

"*I'd take you to Paris in a heartbeat,*" he blurted back. It wasn't even what he said so much as the speed in which he typed it, blasting it off with no hesitation whatsoever. She got chills all over and then became immediately damp.

"*brb*" she typed, paralyzed. *Yeah, right! I wish! You're crazy!* were some of the replies that came to mind but she really had to think this one through. She felt someone's presence and realized Oliver had come in, and was standing beside her looking over her shoulder. For once she was thankful he was still not reading well, one of the slowest in his class.

"Mommy, can I have a glass of milk?" he asked.

"*My son woke up and I have to get him a glass of milk,*" she typed. And again: "*brb.*"

"Here you go," she said, ruffling his hair. "Good night, sweetie."

To her dismay he followed her back to the sofa and sat down beside her.

"Go drink that at the table, sweetheart," she said. With him so near she couldn't concentrate.

"*That sounds nice,*" she finally typed. As a hypothetical, of course.

To distract from the intensity she began to type a nervous one-sided discourse about Paris, a monologue really: what she'd read about it, what she wanted to see, and then to change the subject somewhat she began listing other places she wanted to go: Rome, Barcelona, Brazil, Rio, Aruba, Jamaica, frantically typing any exotic-sounding location that came to mind. He jumped in too, mentioning places he wanted to visit: the Grand Canyon, Utah, Mexico, so that she hoped now they were just having a general conversation about places on their individual bucket lists.

The conversation had finally begun to flow more naturally, and as usual, time flew. When she looked at the clock an hour had passed, so she said goodbye and prepared for bed. Jack was already sleeping.

When her head hit the pillow she was exhausted, but rather than wind down, her mind sped up, wandering wildly. As always, one train of thought would lead to another, taking her on the most surreal journeys. For example, she was now thinking about running through green pastures in Arkansas with her cousins at the age of nine, chasing rabbits, then standing on bales of hay like kings of their castles. She wondered whether she had ever felt so free and alive since then. She had a flash of memory: catching fireflies at night that same summer, collecting them in jars, spreading their glowing guts on their forearms and under their eyes like banshees. She felt bad killing them, she remembered, but it was so incredible how their light glowed for hours after, and during that time she felt she shared their magical powers.

How she loved those summers, sharing a small A-frame house with her five cousins, the girls sleeping in one room and boys in the other. They spent most of the time outdoors anyway, as her aunt and uncle owned acres and acres of farmland. Their parental style was laid back, to say the least, and the kids were allowed to roam free in the rolling meadows. The boys built campfires and forts and the girls decorated an abandoned barn with found objects, creating a comfortable clubhouse, where they collected and cared for a fresh batch of baby chicks. The boys would put firecrackers in cow patties and they would all gather round to watch them explode, the evening's entertainment.

They made mountains of peanut butter sandwiches, she remembered, with homemade jam or fresh honey, leaving a sticky mess in the kitchen. They snacked in-between times on wild blackberries and sweet honeysuckle. And the best part was her father wasn't there to embarrass her. He liked to tease her when he was drunk—torment her really; he gave her too much attention. Attention she would have relished had he been sober, but when he was wasted she wished he would just leave her alone.

Not allowed to wander the trailer park at home, and not wanting to, she often tried to escape into a good book.

"Get your nose out of that *goddamned book*!" she remembered him yelling once, his tone scaring her, making her heart jump out of her chest. "Get off your *precious little ass* and help your mother." He never cursed except when he was drinking; it wasn't allowed in their household. But he broke a lot of rules when he was drunk. Exceptions were made for him, a form of enabling, she later learned. She cringed, shifting in bed.

Why, oh why, did these dark thoughts insist on popping into her head, disrupting such a pleasant, vivid scene? She wished she could control them, and for years she'd been trying to eliminate them entirely. But they persisted, often when she least expected it. Always at the most inopportune moments. Well she was half-awake now, and she steered her thoughts in a different direction, backtracking to the original thought pattern and retracing the links, like following the fragile thread of a winding spider web.

She strained her brain to recall what she had been thinking of directly before, before her dad, before the bunnies. Chipmunks had led to the rabbits, Chipmunk Cheeks being her nickname in sixth grade. It was another unsettling memory, unfortunately, referring to her prominent overbite and full childlike cheeks, topping off her prepubescent body with a buck-toothed baby face—when she had been so eager to grow up. Its originator, Mike McMannus, had taunted her at a home football game in the ramshackle stands. Others had joined in. Her parents could not afford braces for her or her brother, and it was a miracle that her face had grown into, or around, her teeth, and her cheeks had hollowed somewhat to reveal fine bone structure underneath. An instant before that she was worrying over whether Aimee would need braces and how much that would cost, after thinking she needed to go to the dentist for a cleaning herself.

With more concentrated thought rather than a random stream of consciousness—she was suddenly fully awake—she realized if she was to afford braces for Aimee, or anything else they needed as a family, anything *she* needed, any sense of the freedom she tasted as a child foraging in the fields, any of the travels she was discussing with Stevie, she would have to extend her drug distribution network. She was so painfully wide-awake now that she grabbed a Valium from her nightstand drawer, swallowing it with a gulp.

Another option, she realized as the calming effect of the medication kicked in, was to come clean to Jack and ask him for help now that his business was doing well. For a split second it seemed a viable option and she thought about putting the problem in his strong capable hands. But the amount—he would die, it would suffocate him. She didn't have the heart to do that to him, and feeling a false sense of empowerment from the meds, decided she would have to take control of the situation herself.

MAY

Brow furrowed in concentration and nose inches from her screen, at work the next day Margie finally pushed Send on the email she'd been carefully constructing and then continually editing for weeks, inviting twelve of her most anxiety-ridden friends for a girls' night out a week from Saturday at Chuy's, a popular Mexican restaurant downtown. It was tricky, because she hadn't seen them in a while, which she blamed on being stuck in a 'burb of a 'burb. She apologized for being out of touch and stole a line from Stevie: *I hope life's been treating you well.* If they, too, thought maybe it had not, it might make them more receptive to the meds.

It was an exciting day as the ladies' responses trickled in, first one, then two, coming to a total of seven who could make it. Not bad. She herself hadn't been to Chuy's in years, a festive bar and restaurant in a trendy, upscale neighborhood. She hoped it was still as popular as it had been when she'd lived nearby in her twenties, in a huge apartment complex on Greenville Avenue, as impersonal and nondescript as they come. But no matter—she remembered the fantastic restaurants, boutiques and bar hopping, in the few walkable blocks in Dallas at a time when anything had seemed possible.

She had transferred from the University of North Texas to a community college downtown because of a family issue. After her first year of college her father had lost his job and could no longer help pay for her education. At first she was devastated. But although she had enjoyed being at the university, in truth she had never felt she fit in completely; the students there seemed so worldly, so smart and sophisticated. In downtown Dallas she felt like she was in her element, like she had finally come into her own.

She was working full time as a waitress while taking a course or two at a time, all she could afford, toward getting her nursing degree. She had liked the idea of healing and helping people—until she got grossed out by the whole profession, nothing more than glorified yet underpaid chamber maids cleaning up vomit and changing adult diapers. So she quit school entirely and got a job at Parkland Hospital, in an inner-city emergency room. She liked the rush of checking people in at the action-packed waiting room. She was a first responder of sorts, her fresh face and calming tone counteracting the trauma. Her wide smile, friendly manner and mild flirtation seemed to make the patients feel better. "Where did you get that haircut?" she would ask a patient with a gushing head wound, focusing on the voluminous unmatted side. "I love that shade of lipstick on you," she would say to a prostitute who had overdosed and had it smeared all over her face. Sarcasm wasn't in her nature. She had a strong stomach and an excellent bedside manner, or deskside, as it turned out.

It wasn't her life's dream. What her life's dream was wasn't clear, just a notion based on a vague feeling. A dreamer's dream, unfounded and undefined. Yet her future seemed full of opportunity the way it does regardless of actual circumstances when one is twenty-three years young. Growing up with her strict, religious parents, she couldn't wait to fly from the nest at the age of eighteen, and since the age of nineteen she had been totally self-sufficient. When she finally had her own apartment with no roommates in her early twenties, she experienced true independence, her evenings full of dinner parties, dating, and dancing to her heart's content.

But it was short-lived. A series of boyfriends pulled her further and further away from downtown, first to Addison, then back to her hometown, then beyond.

She was ecstatic when Saturday finally rolled around, changing clothes five times, spreading her spastic energy through the house. The kids were hyper, hovering around, asking her repeatedly to bring them something, a surprise. Jack was in full support thinking it would do her good to see old friends and get out of the house, and agreed to watch the children without any convincing. She wanted to look regal and refined, but every outfit fit for a night out verged on raunchy, inevitable when you're ten pounds larger than the clothes you own. The upside to her too-tight little black dress was that it enhanced her cleavage, and with her jewelry, accessories, and perfect hair, she did look attractive, if not as elegant as she aspired for.

She invited Katie too; they would drive down together. She genuinely enjoyed her company and felt introducing her self-possessed, well-spoken new friend to her old ones would add to the overall dynamic. Yet her ulterior motive was crucial to the plan. She would wait until they were all on their second or third round of drinks, buzzed and tipsy like the lightweight wives and mothers they were, then she would casually ask Katie how she was enjoying the meds. It wasn't a secret after all; Katie had never said not to tell anyone. The conversation would continue down that route, flowing freely, and the door would be opened and she would answer, yes, I can get more, sure, but of course!

Margie and Katie arrived at the restaurant right on time. Two of the women were already there and the remainder trickled in in a timely fashion, so that they could all be seated at a large round table. Chuy's was well-known for its strong twenty-ounce margaritas and everyone indulged when the drink orders were taken. Introductions were necessary since not all of the women knew each other, creating that inevitable awkward social tension that occurs when bringing a few friend circles together. But like the colored circles of a Venn diagram, she hoped they would find things in common that would overlap in the center, creating a new hue that would bind them together as a new group. And she secretly anticipated the use of medications becoming another commonality in the center of the circles.

It seemed that the women were doing well, putting their best faces forward and framing their lives in the most flattering light. They complimented one another and expressed interest while making slightly self-effacing remarks.

"Katie is a graphic designer and creates the most clever campaigns," Margie said. "Meanwhile I'm still at the same hospital, surrounded by all of Prairie Mound's sick and wounded—the poor, sad lot."

"Well that's important, Margie," Katie countered. "I spend all my time designing marketing materials selling this, that, and the other, that people will look right past, or brochures that will promptly end up in the trash! Allison, what do you do?"

Knowing about Allison's career struggles, Margie wondered how she would answer. And she was curious too, since the last time they spoke Allison hadn't been able to find work after she had been laid off from her job in finance when the market had crashed.

"I'm an *entrepreneur* these days, believe it or not," she said to the group. "I was in finance but a couple of years ago I decided to start selling a high-end skin product on social media. It's a real miracle cream. I actually hated the corporate culture of working in banks and now my boss lets me take off any time I want!"

Polite laughter spread around the table.

"How are your adorable kids, Stephanie?" Allison asked. "How old are they now?"

"I have two teenagers! It makes me feel so *ancient*. They're a handful. They're good kids, but they do keep me on my toes. Katelyn, the youngest, is now seven—can you believe that Margie?—and she is a doll, the most thoughtful child, and smart too. She just won the second grade spelling bee at her school."

"Oh, that's such a great age," Janet chimed in. "What school does she go to? My Michelle is eight and she just got accepted in the Gifted and Talented program at Country Day. Since the divorce it's just the two of us. Well, my ex has her every other weekend, but I love having so much quality time with her. Even though the divorce was ugly, I guess I'm feeling kind of empowered lately. Girl power, you know?"

"Speaking of girl power, guess who just ran a half marathon earlier this year? *This* girl!" Joan added with a chuckle, pointing at herself with her two thumbs. "It nearly *killed* me, mind you, especially with my lupus, but I managed to finish."

Shit, thought Margie, the ladies seemed to have gotten their lives together as of late. This might be more difficult than she thought. Beyond that she feared the subject of taking meds might be too personal, too shameful for these suburban wives and soccer moms to discuss.

However the women were connecting, and by the second and third rounds of drinks, some sticking with margaritas and some switching to wine or beer when dinner arrived, the social lubricant kicked in and the interactions became a bit more genuine, honest, and therefore more revealing—to Margie's delight.

Candace was a talker, a ranter and a raver who often over-shared, which not only kept the conversation flowing, but shifted its tone. She shared a drawn-out story about how she had recently been dumped, and complained at length about how difficult it was to date as a single mom, how she couldn't understand what was wrong with her and why the few dates she did have never called back.

Your constant yacking, Margie thought to herself, and took control of the conversation before Candace began to dominate it entirely. "Married life is no walk in the park, either, I can assure you," she said. "My life is so exhausting sometimes I feel like I'm at the end of my rope."

Now the women grew animated, one-upping each other, not about how great their jobs and families were, but how challenging their lives were, who was most stressed, who was worse off.

"Now that they've *finally* diagnosed me with Lupus, after *two years* of expensive appointments and testing, I've been on the phone every damn day with my health insurance company, who are flat out refusing to pay for some of the services. The state of health care is a *mess* in this country. It's ridiculous!" Joan said.

"I hear that," Janet piped up. "My divorce settlement has been dragging out for a year and I've been fighting with my husband, *and* my lawyer, and the legal fees that have piled up, well it's *insane*. The whole process has turned into a shit show."

"To be honest, my bratty brood is putting such a strain on our marriage that I'm afraid *I'm* going to end up divorced—and soon—if things don't change," Stephanie now divulged. "Having four kids is just too much for me to handle sometimes. The oldest one is kind of out of control, skipping school, and smoking pot."

They all opened up about their problems, outdoing each other until they were all one unified hot mess. The groundwork was laid. The conversation hardly needed guidance and naturally led to advice, solutions, and thus, meds. Margie leaned in dramatically, drawing in the other women's heads like a magnet, and admitted in a hushed tone that she had found relief with prescription pills. Katie disclosed without prompting that she was sleeping better than ever on the Valium, and thanked Margie in front of everyone. One of the women conceded, in a soft, mousy voice, that she was already on antidepressants and by evening's end it was clear that another of the ladies drowned her problems in alcohol—might have even had a problem with it. But in the end no fewer than five friends were interested in trying prescription pills.

She recommended Ambien and Xanax, and the women seemed eager to give the pills a try. Only Joan suggested—then practically demanded—Oxycontin. She had used it before for pain and found it delightful, she said, or rather, effective. Margie was trying to avoid opiates not only because they were more addictive, but precisely because of that she knew they might be a little more challenging to get her hands on. But she agreed to try.

Margie had limited her drink intake to only one beer after the first margarita, which was part of her strategy, but volunteered to pick up the entire bill, which was not. On a natural high, she decided to treat everyone. Initially the total had stunned her, but she tried not to let her face show it, and quickly perused the bill, thinking it must have been a mistake, but with the women drinking like fish of course it added up, and she had to remind herself that the cocktails had helped her cause. Besides, the night had been a huge success, and she would be rolling in money soon enough. She struggled to figure out the tip, which brought the total to almost 400 dollars, but she knew it was money well spent. After lengthy, lingering goodbyes, the women made their way to the door. Suddenly remembering a surprise for the kids, Margie grabbed a handful of peppermints from a bowl near the exit and crammed them into her overstuffed purse.

But driving home she felt a little panicked. It was 400 dollars she didn't yet have. Perhaps to take her mind off of money, she told Katie about reconnecting with Stevie and the flirtation that followed, omitting the Paris part. Katie answered in the only way a well-meaning girlfriend can, first wanting the juicy details and in giddy, girlie support but then questioning and cautioning about where it could lead.

"I thought you were happily married. I mean Jack is just...just *great*. So laid back and good with the kids," she said, a bit too seriously for the tone of the evening, in Margie's opinion.

"Well, yeah, I know, but it's just that, it's like you know how some women do yoga or spin class, or go to the spa for 'me' time? Well, I never have time to spoil myself, to go get a massage or whatever, and I work so hard and do so much, so instant chatting is kind of like my 'me' time, where I can have a moment to myself, but with him."

"Hmm," she said. "Well...I guess it's harmless enough."

Margie didn't want to think about it anymore and put it out of her head, silently scheming on how she would acquire the necessary meds. It was no small amount. This would require favors from multiple doctors in different departments for multiple fake illnesses. Luckily she had been working there like, forever, and had just such a network. She prided herself on getting along with every single person at the hospital, no easy feat with the arrogant doctors, bitchy nurses and other crew of characters, but she was friends with everyone, and even knew all of the janitors by name. Little did she know that nurturing these relationships for years had all been part of a master plan.

The entire household slept in the following morning, a lazy Sunday, all rising on their own natural timeframe, stretching, wandering into the kitchen one by one. Everyone seemed to be in a good mood for their own private reasons. What the others' reasons were, Margie did not know. She made homemade pancakes rather than frozen ones and reported some of the highlights of her outing as she grappled with the batter, updating Jack on old friends he hadn't seen in ages and hardly knew, who had had another child, who had a new job, and of course, the juiciest morsel, who had gotten fat.

"Joan has really *ballooned out*. I hate to say it, but it's *true*. She was recently diagnosed with lupus, the poor thing, so maybe that's why, but for whatever reason, she has packed on the pounds…said she ran a half marathon recently but I really can't picture it; I mean what a visual, her literally *bouncing* around the course with all that blubber. Remember how tiny she used to be?"

"Now *who* is Joan again? Did I ever meet her?" Jack did his best to feign interest.

Baby turtles, she learned, were what the kids were excited about. Jack would allow the kids three turtles each, and if all went well they could fill the pond with water by the day's end. While Margie battled with the bacon, jumping back a few times when stung by the hot grease, Jack disappeared up to his office to watch instructional videos. He reported over breakfast that before the trip to the pet store, the pond would need to be treated with chemicals and sit for two days. The kids listed off potential turtle names over breakfast: Pokie, Shelly, Susie, Tuttles, Puddles.

"Some of these deformed pancakes kind of look like turtles," Margie said, pointing to the last pancake on Oliver's plate, with edges protruding with the last drops of batter. "See, look here, a head and smaller arms and legs."

"Aw, Mom, that's funny!" Oliver giggled. Then the three of them, thick as thieves these days, raced outside as soon as he swallowed the last bite.

A twinge of jealousy was followed by guilt-ridden relief at having the house all to herself. The thrill of everything that was happening sent Margie on a wild shopping spree from the comfort of her couch, thanks to her favorite online retailer. She had a membership to the site, receiving free delivery on every order, the value of which couldn't be underestimated living way out here in the boondocks. She carefully removed a few images from her kitchen wall, clippings that had been hanging around all too long, things she'd been meaning to buy for absolute ages, ordering not only the Italian cappuccino maker but a

French press coffee maker, as well as gourmet coffee. Sticking to the theme, she bought a new coffee table that would drastically improve the living room. Once the purchases were complete she wadded up the visuals dramatically and tossed them into the trashcan, feeling a huge sense of accomplishment.

She bought some things for the kids too, ripping some cut out images from their bedroom walls. A fancy jewelry box and cute floral overalls for Aimee, a magic kit for Oliver, complete with a top hat and wingtip shoes. She thought about buying something for Jack, but he never needed anything, self-sufficient as he was, and what's weirder, he never even *wanted* anything.

The totals would have surprised her, but being that some of the orders were from different companies, she didn't have an exact tally in her head, yet she felt quite sure that the total was, well, a *lot*. In the light of day, the intense anxiety about her debt from last week seemed a distant memory, the idea of telling Jack, ludicrous.

Just then Jack came in for a glass of water, startling her. She glanced at the screen in front of her as he neared, relieved that none of the thank-you-for-your-purchase pop-ups remained; her Facebook scroll was front and center and she enlarged the window. He told her he'd invited Auden over for dinner and wanted to throw some burgers on the grill. They'd been working together for a couple of weeks and things had been going well.

Hours before the time of his arrival, Margie found herself primping extra long and hard, over-plucking. Remembering that dominant, angled eyebrows were in now, from what she'd seen the young women wearing at the hospital—in some cases it was like the eyebrows were wearing the women—she filled in the over-plucked part with her darkest pencil.

She supposed she wanted to look good, youthful—after all, he wasn't the only hipster in town! Her thrown-together look was, in actuality, painfully purposeful. She scrunched her hair loosely and chose a well-worn T-shirt that she would normally never be caught dead in in public, but now seemed ironic, and skinny jeans. She fretted that her skinny jeans made her look anything but. Annoyed at another trend designed with only supermodels in mind, she stared in the mirror debating whether she looked fat or just curvaceous. She kept putting on higher and higher heels until she felt more proportional, and then pulled herself away to gel and then ruffle the children's hair, dressing them in colorful plaid and lumberjack boots.

"God, Margie, this is a casual thing, what the hell are you doing?"

"And don't we look casual?" Margie beamed.

When Auden arrived, he was exactly like Jack had described him, only more so. He was tall, must have been six foot two, lean and scrappy, and undeniably good-looking. Dark curly hair fell around his brown eyes from his obligatory man bun. His thick eyebrows were balanced by a warm smile that parted his massive beard and mustache with a flash of white, like a flash of light. She noticed one front tooth stuck just slightly farther out than the other, a welcome quirk that broke up perfection.

Well, she had to assume the bottom half of his face was as well-balanced as the top, since it was covered in the most burly beard she had ever laid eyes on. When he wasn't smiling his mouth disappeared completely into a thicket of coarse curly hair, a hedge of hair, wild and wiry. She decided it was more like a forest, half-expecting to see a squirrel poke its head out or a miniature deer run through the tangle. Like Moses, before he'd gone gray, like the rugged John the Baptist wandering the wilderness, or like Jesus himself, hanging on the cross.

He seemed utterly relaxed and radiated a quiet strength, his biceps and calf muscles flexing when he made the smallest of movements, whether popping the top off his beer or propping a foot up on the picnic table bench.

"Nice place you guys have here," he said, directed at Margie.

"Oh, thanks. We just love it out here, being in the yard. We're outdoor people, I mean when the weather gets warm, which in Texas, is most of the time! Well I would rather be closer to Dallas, to be honest with you. I'm more of a city girl, but we like the space out here. It's just wonderful really, especially for the children, even though there are a few more things we want to do to the house, both inside and out. We've been meaning to put shrubs over here, and maybe plant a peach tree over there..." Margie had a tendency to ramble when she met new people and she could feel herself doing it now. "So what in the world brought you to Prairie Mound, Texas, of all the places in the world?"

"I'm a bit of an explorer, a nomad, I guess. I sort of just go where the wind takes me."

"Must be nice," Margie said.

The children were drawn to his open and approachable demeanor, and they waited politely for the small talk to end before dragging him away to the turtle pond indentation, which was slowly filling with water, the garden hose snaking across the lawn and disappearing under the surface.

"We get to go to the pet store soon and pick out *six* turtles," Oliver said.

"Wow!" said Auden. "You should get yourselves some red-eared slider turtles. They make real good pets because they're hardy and adaptable, and they just love the Texas climate. The reason they call them sliders is because of the way they slide right off the rocks into the water, like a belly dive."

"I'm the one who put the rocks all around the edges," Aimee said in between cartwheels.

"They will love that, let me tell you. And of course they have fantastic red ears! Well not ears exactly but they have bright red streaks, kinda like war paint, behind each eye."

"Cool!" Aimee and Oliver said in unison.

Margie listened to their chatter as she set the food out. Jack was busy grilling the meat. She glanced over at the pond to find Auden staring back at her. Or rather, already staring at her when she looked over. So she glanced away. Friendly as he was, he made her anxious and she didn't know why. She twirled and twisted her hair, bit her bottom lip, nervous habits of hers that she was always trying to break. When she looked back a few minutes later, to see if he was still staring, he was not—but then he glanced back at her with a knowing look. Shit, why had she looked over again, probably giving him the wrong impression. She turned back toward the table, busying herself by cutting up some pickles.

They all talked and ate burgers sitting around the warped picnic table. Margie brought the men another beer and even opened one for herself, feeling slightly uncomfortable. Auden's eyes penetrated her, though not in an overtly sexual way. Even though it would be highly inappropriate, that she could handle, was used to even at her age. This was different. He seemed to see through her, into her most private places. Her normally perfect posture slumped; she cowered, drawing into herself and subconsciously trying to block him out, to protect herself.

He seemed so pure. She had secrets, more than ever, of which his mere presence made her aware. He was so confident, assured. While she did not have especially bad self-esteem, she questioned herself on a deeper level: her motives, her desires. Then again, to be a drifter—must be nice to be in your early twenties without a family to support. She was sure if she could rewind the clock and make different choices she would be pure, relaxed and carefree too! She guessed he was probably a trust fund baby, and how unfair was that?

While she might not have always made the best choices, some of the choices weren't hers to be made. Did she choose to have a drunkard for a dad? One who reached for the Bible after he reached for the bottle? One who didn't spare the rod, who didn't spoil the child? Always staggering home on Saturday nights and always shuffling into the front pew on Sunday mornings. When the Southern Baptist preacher raged on about sin and forgiveness, hell and redemption, she thought to herself her father must be begging for redemption every damned day. A religion made just for him, allowing him to continue his shameful and selfish behavior—and still get into heaven.

A welder by trade, he was fired for drinking on the job after many warnings. But when he called to tell her he could no longer pay for her college tuition, he had said it was God's will, and that's what had pissed her off the most. Said he was being called for higher purposes. Purposes other than earning a living, apparently, because he never worked another day in his life. And of course even before that they had been poor. It was in middle school that she learned a few of her friends weren't allowed to come to the trailer, either because of the undesirable neighborhood or her father's reputation—or both.

Then again, she dreaded having friends over anyway, so what had it mattered. She now recalled the time she had invited Sara Sanderson over after school, before remembering what had happened the night before. Something she had tried to block from her mind during the school day. Walking home with Sara, she was suddenly mortified. Her father had come home in the middle of the night. When she heard knocking and stumbling she'd crept into the living room to see what was happening, only to see her dad with his pants dropped to his ankles, peeing on the sofa. When he saw her he asked what the hell she was staring at and what she was doing out of her goddamned bedroom. His voice boomed, his eyes two vacant black holes. That was the last time she ever investigated any noises, hiding under the covers no matter what frightening sounds she heard. As she approached the trailer she panicked, worried the house would smell like urine as it did when she went to school, and wondered how on earth she could be so stupid inviting Sara over, fearing her mom hadn't cleaned it up. But of course she had. Upon entering they were met by the sickening smell of cheap air freshener.

Auden, she realized, was speaking to her directly, breaking her out of her dark trance, rescuing her from the painful memory.

"So Jack tells me you work at the hospital, checking people into the emergency room. That must be intense," he said, locking eyes with her. She looked around to discover it was just the two of them at the table; Jack was cleaning the grill while the kids raced back and forth across the yard.

"Oh yeah," she said. "I have seen some things you wouldn't believe."

"I always wanted to find a job helping people. I mean otherwise, what is the point? I guess now I help people with their lawns, but it's not the same. That's a luxury, you know?"

"Well, there's nothing wrong with a little luxury in life. My job is not rocket science, I mean, a monkey could do it. A monkey with a lot of patience, excellent organizational skills, and a stomach made of steel, that is!" she said, letting out a quick burst of usually contagious laughter. He was immune, smiling but silent.

"I can imagine. But at least you're serving the community, comforting them in times of need. I mean that takes a strong person…a person with ideals, I guess. It's all about karma in this life. What goes around comes around. To me it's about being real with people, transparent. I believe in total transparency, you know?"

She really didn't know. While she loved his warm positive energy, she didn't care for over-analyzing things and found the conversation oddly intense. Was this kid some kind of New Ager, or Buddhist? So she lightened the mood by asking him how he was settling in and gave him some advice on surviving the humdrum town. He said he felt it was a good change of pace for him and that the people were much friendlier than in the northwest.

"Damn straight we are!" she said. The beer was kicking in. Yet there was something in his tone that seemed judgmental toward her for judging the town. The longer they spoke, the longer the pauses between his statements. Which gave her pause. The whole exchange exhausted her and she retired early, excusing herself to begin her nightly makeup removal routine.

Margie had her work cut out for her the next week at the hospital, and on Monday morning she bustled around with nervous energy keeping busy with mundane tasks. She drank too much coffee, wiping down all of the break room counters on her second refill. She kept tidying her desk even before it was messy, shifting a stack of files slightly, moving the stapler just so. She emptied her trash can, containing only an envelope and gum wrapper, and then emptied her nearest co-worker's. She was in hyper-productive mode gearing up for what she had to do.

Throughout the day, she purposely placed herself in position to naturally run into each doctor, got involved in casual conversation, asked about their own families, and then wound her way into her fake medical problems. She started with Dr. Brighton, who was her cousin's wife's friend. She told her she had horrible anxiety, bugging her eyes out and trying to assume an expression of frozen terror, then made her way to Dr. Carter, stopping off at the bathroom beforehand and rubbing her eyes ferociously to make them red. She told him she was having trouble sleeping, yawning repeatedly. She told Dr. Nicholson her neck and back were aching causing chronic pain—and this is where she secured the Oxycontin—walking away hunchbacked. On a high, she had decided to go for Percocet as well, lest she need them in the future so she told Dr. Taylor she had tendonitis in her shoulder, squeezing one shoulder blade up to her neck for effect. She told the dermatologist she felt old and tired—and that was entirely true—and got a free Botox treatment as a bonus, something just for her. He had just treated a patient for the same ailment and had plenty of poison left in the syringe, which he plunged into her forehead again and again, leaving her pleasantly numb and tingly. The doctors really did like her! Some of them had prescribed refills and some had not; she really couldn't push the issue.

She would pick up a couple of the prescriptions at the hospital's dusty pharmacy and would have the others filled at two different pharmacies to avoid any red flags, one at the local drugstore near her home and one in the next suburb twenty miles away.

She secured the meds from good old Ed on two different days hoping he wouldn't notice the similarities between the medications. Not that he ever seemed to notice such things; he was more curious about how Aimee was doing in school and if Oliver was in Little League. She picked up the others at the drug stores, hitting horrible traffic on the interstate and adding an hour to her commute, but although it was an inconvenience, she rose to the occasion and secured a plethora of pills by Friday's end.

As such she sent out another email setting the stage for another girls' night out in two weeks' time, giving plenty of lead time so the ladies could clear their calendars. Again they would meet downtown, this time at a bar to mix things up—and so they could get right to the point without the pretense of a meal.

When she told Jack lying in bed that night he seemed a little less understanding than he was a couple of weeks ago, wondering aloud why she had to go all the way down to Dallas again. He said he had been working hard and she needed to pull her weight with the kids. Then he mumbled something under his breath, sounded like "just my luck," or "bitches suck" or "what the fuck." This annoyed her so she popped an Ambien, and growing impatient waiting for it to kick in, gulped down another. Then finally she floated, first just above tree level and then off into the azure night sky.

JUNE

Margie woke up to the sound of heavy rain hammering the roof that kept amping up in volume just when her ears had adjusted to the pounding, irritated and unable to fall back to sleep even as exhausted as she was from performing at work all week. The stubborn storm would not let up. She had been looking forward to the weekend but was now forced into a foul mood, as if the rain was pummeling her personally.

Falling from such a high high to such a low low, she had an Ambien-induced hangover. Her outlook was as dark as the nebulous sky. She hated her life. What was the point of it? Always at work, and then the weekends flew by—most of which were spent taking care of other people, namely her family—with hardly any time for herself. Having to practically beg to go to Dallas, to ask for permission. She felt trapped. By her house, her town, her job, her debt, her kids, and her husband. Of course she loved her family. But it was the actual act of loving she found difficult, and she most certainly did not feel lovable at the moment. She tried to direct her hostility at some external event or outside entity which would be much less depressing, but every single thing that she detested was in fact a part of her life or related to it—otherwise how could it exist in her sphere of thought? So it was an endless loathsome loop, leaving her despondent.

The hopelessness of it all combined with bad weather on her only free day, her "me day," was more than she could take. She had planned on lying out in her bikini on the back porch working on her suntan. Instead the kids were arguing indoors, and had been all morning while watching cartoons, which she also abhorred. Their squeaky voices, awful sound effects and childish story lines had held her hostage in her own bed. When she finally emerged into the kitchen Jack was watching sports, an equally annoying soundtrack.

"Hey sleepyhead. We were thinking of going to the pet store, now that the pond is ready. This rain will make the turtles feel right at home," Jack said to Margie for the kids' benefit.

Her animosity was now aimed at the paper towel rack, which, unattached to the wall, fell down and rolled on the floor. Each time she tried to pick it up it rolled further out of reach. It happened almost every morning, but today, while it seemed indestructible, she cracked.

"Turtles? Goddamned turtles?" Margie snapped. "Is that all you can think about?" Lately she felt they were ganging up on her. And winning, judging from the three heads twisting toward her in unison, all giving her the stink-eye. "How about fixing this paper towel holder? We have been living in this house for over ten years and you've never even mounted it. It's *ridiculous*. I mean, *who lives like this?*"

"Margie, it's no secret you're never happy with anything in this house, and that's why we never fix it up, except for all the silly and unnecessary crap you buy." Jack replied calmly, voice over-controlled.

They tried not to fight in front of the children but did not always succeed. Just a few words in, their blood was boiling. Like any couple married for over a decade who have fought the same battle over and over with no solution in sight, only stubborn resolve, they knew that things could—and would—escalate quickly, both struggling to search for well-chosen, cutting words, thinking maybe this time one would convince the other. On much-chartered territory, it was a nasty argument they knew by heart. The kids were all too familiar with it too and disappeared outside.

"You're *damn right* I hate this house," she continued, her voice rising, more shrill than she intended. "But we have to live in it because *you* refuse to leave, so we could at least make the best of it. Yes, I wish we could move to downtown Dallas and I don't see why you won't even *consider* it," she said.

"Margie, *you're* the only one who wants to move to Dallas. Business is good, the kids are doing fine in school, so why can't you just be satisfied for once? Why do you have to be so fucking selfish? Nothing would be different in Dallas."

"*Nothing* would be *different?* Are you kidding me? There are art museums and restaurants, for one thing. There are new apartments all over Harry Hines Freeway and I'll bet you haven't even seen the new stadium downtown. You haven't been there since the dark ages so how would you even *know?*"

"You'd find something to complain about there too, I'm sure. There's the horrible traffic, and out here we're close to our parents."

"Another reason to leave! How can you say it would be no different? *Everything* would be different!"

"Because I know you. I told you when we got married and I had just built the house that I wanted to have a family here."

"Yes, but I didn't know you meant here in this *specific* spot, on this specific plot of dirt out in bum-fuck-Egypt. How could I have known that you would *never* leave? It's like the freaking Hotel California!"

"You know I don't want to live in Dallas."

"It doesn't have to be Dallas. How about…Houston or Phoenix or San Diego or Portland?" Even in her highly agitated state she was able to spew out a few cities that she felt would be more interesting.

"We are not moving *and that is final*," he boomed, his voice dropping two full octaves.

"You sound like a psychopath. Do you know one of the definitions of a mentally ill person is someone who can't adapt to change? Google it; you'll probably find a picture of yourself," she said, getting in what she considered a good blow.

"Margie, you are the one who's delusional," he said, abruptly grabbing his keys and stomping out.

"I want a divorce!" she imagined screaming behind him before he slammed the door, which shook in its cheap frame. *Delusional?* Her so-called delusions were the only thing that kept her sane in this sorry shithole excuse for a town.

She heard him round up the kids and then the Manscaping van started up with a testosterone-filled roar.

And that is final? The phrase made her livid. When he laid down the law it reminded her of her father. According to Southern Baptists the man is the head of the household and therefore her dad always got the last word, ending many family arguments with that exact phrase. Another way in which the religion suited him especially well. But she and Jack didn't even go to church for crying out loud, didn't believe in all that mumbo jumbo—and yet here she was being told what to do like a child. She thought they were living in modern times, where men and women were supposed to be equals, yet Jack was no more evolved than a Neanderthal.

Not once, not twice, but thrice, her father had slapped her—hard, right across the face—for talking back, for disagreeing with his *final* decisions. The burn went beyond the physical, the sting went to the soul, making her feel stunted, small, as was intended. He had wielded his power to make her feel powerless, worthless and helpless, and undeservedly so. As a child she had no choice, no recourse, but she vowed then and there, the third time as a teenager, that she would never put up with abuse from a man again, not as an adult. Now Jack wouldn't hurt a flea; he took field mice found in the house out in shoeboxes and freed them in the farmland along the highway. But still, although not physical, she wondered whether this was beginning to verge on verbal abuse, mental abuse.

What infuriated her the most was how he refused to budge in every sense of the word, didn't know the meaning of the word compromise. Yet her whole life had been a compromise. Yes, her childhood had been compromised, but also, as an adult perhaps she had settled, which she considered worse in a way. They were certainly settled in Prairie Mound, and would remain planted there until the end of time if Jack had his way. But she wondered, had she settled when it came to Jack? She had made concessions for him, for her family, certainly; but what she had given up wasn't entirely clear. She had the same job more or less as she did before they met; she had not really had that many opportunities staring her in the face. She supposed what she had given up was *possibilities*—for a different life, for many possible different lives.

And Jack mentioning their parents? Well they were a blessing and a curse. Admittedly his parents, who lived only a few miles away, babysat the kids in the summers and sometimes after school, which was a huge help, but that also held them captive in a way. They visited her parents a few times a year mostly for her mother's sake, so she could see their grandkids, but she would certainly not mind being an hour or two—or ten—farther away.

This recurring conflict always made her dream of divorce. In her heart of hearts it's not what she wanted but she could see no other alternative. It seemed entirely unsolvable, and unfortunately it affected every aspect of her own personal happiness. Money was what they used to fight about, also with no resolve, until they gave up on that, replacing it with this.

Her compulsive spending had caused him so much anxiety, created so much worry. He had taken her spending, at first, as a personal affront, when Margie knew he was reading too much into it; she spent simply because she liked to buy things. So was *she* the problem? She thought not, maybe then but not in their current crisis. In terms of their money problems, it was easier to lie than to fight—and of course he didn't know the half of it. But there was no way to lie herself out of this situation; the only option was to leave. *And that is final* still echoed in her head. Yet she really did want to stay. Just not stay *here*.

She unwound with a long hot bath, scrubbing fiercely, lathering up again and again, attempting to scour not just her body but her mind. She nearly rubbed her skin raw, knowing vast amounts of moisturizer would be required afterwards. She used her razor as a weapon, combatting every unwanted hair, taking out her aggression on each follicle. She shaved her entire body smooth, to the top of her ample upper thighs—even her pubic area—she wanted it completely removed, just like she wanted to be completely removed.

A bowl of ice cream and several phone calls later, after venting about his soul-crushing stubbornness to multiple friends, some of whom she had recently reconnected with, and to Katie of course, she felt slightly better.

Calmer now, she instant-chatted Stevie, the first time she'd initiated it. She really didn't feel right complaining about Jack to him. And yet she did, a little bit. Not surprisingly, he sided with her. Said he understood completely, and that no, she didn't overreact, that he didn't blame her one bit. Told her she had a sense of adventure, a lust for life.

"Well exactly! It's like I was telling you the other day, I have big plans... aspirations, you know?"

"Like what?" he asked.

The particulars caught her off guard. *"brb"* she typed. She thought hard.

"Oh I don't know. Like living in a loft apartment with no dividing walls and floor-to-ceiling windows with golden light pouring in in the mornings and views of a city at night." He didn't type back so she continued. *"Like driving a scooter around the cobblestone streets of Italy and eating a slice of pizza on the Spanish Steps...or lounging on a huge yacht sipping champagne."*

"Yeah, well... I was serious about Paris."

Damn it, she couldn't "brb" him again so soon. And the truth is she did want to go. With Jack's inflexible attitude and unfair demands, which were in fact limitations, she thought, screw it, and threw caution to the wind.

"Really? Tell me more..." she typed.

"Coincidentally, I have a sales conference coming up in Paris."

"You do?!?!?" She typed.

"It's in Paris, Texas. Wish it was the one across the Atlantic, believe you me. I wish we could meet on top of the Eiffel Tower, but maybe we could meet there instead

and discover some local charm, go to dinner, reconnect in person, spend a couple of nights."

Margie absorbed first the bad news and then the good. It wasn't the real Paris, which was a real bummer. But still, the whole idea of it was kind of exciting. *Spend a couple of nights.* Even though it wasn't in France, just another crappy Texas town, the fact that it was any Paris at all felt like fate to Margie. And that was something she firmly believed in. It was romantic in its own way, certainly the most romantic thing that had ever happened to her. The conference was not until fall so she had several months to think about it. And indeed, she would think about it—a lot.

In fact she began fantasizing about it immediately, and asked him what the town was like; she was sure it would have upscale restaurants serving French cuisine. She asked him more questions about his life, suddenly wanting to know him more intimately. He shared things about growing up, about his parents, his family, his feelings. At the end of the conversation, she already knew the answer would be yes.

When her family came home, no one questioned her inexplicable mood shift, everyone wanting to put the morning behind them. She watched the children put the turtles in the pond, newly-born babies bobbing around, poking their tiny extraterrestrial heads up for air, and she had to admit they were pretty precious. Seemingly quite taken with their new environment, they disappeared to explore the depths and then rested on Aimee's rocks, inspiring in Margie a vague sense of hope.

She caught Jack's eye across the small pond. "I'm sorry, Jack," she said. And she meant it. Though she wasn't sure whether she was sorry for what she had just done or what she was about to do. Oliver, standing beside her, reached up and held her hand.

Margie went through the next few weeks in a fog, waiting and wanting. Her pill-infused nights extended into glorious morning daydreams. And once or twice, she prolonged that daydream with the help of a pill. Even though it was a big no-no for her, now and then she would allow it, but only on days that were easy, no-brainers, repetitive enough to float through. Or on especially mundane and monotonous days, just to make them a hair more interesting. She was just having trouble finding things in her own life engaging; and how could she, really, when it seemed like her main activities were running the kids to and from school, sitting behind a desk dealing with all of the city's infected, infirm and indisposed, then coming home to unload and reload the dishwasher.

She was becoming distant, and her haze made her mysterious to her children, and to Jack. Beyond that, Jack had misinterpreted her shaving her nether-regions—she had given herself a full-on Brazilian—and it had made him crazed, sending their sex life soaring. Some of the times she visualized Stevie, but often she thought of Jack. It was hard not to, him all over her, touching her, going down on her like an eager teenager. Sure, it made her feel a little guilty for carrying on with Stevie, but mostly it added to the sexual energy she was unconsciously radiating. Stevie seemed to sense it all the way through cyberspace judging by his recent comments, more forward than ever. She just couldn't believe things were finally going her way.

Hovering in her own mental sphere, even more disconnected from reality than usual, she was becoming spacey, absentminded. She folded laundry in the evening with a faraway look in her eyes. She cooked dinner carelessly, forgetting ingredients, but mixing things methodically, whisking the sauce much longer than necessary, seemingly lost standing over the pasta. Engrossed in thought, she didn't hear when the kids called her name.

On Thursday, when it was her day to pick the kids up from their after school activities, she forgot entirely, coming straight home to make tacos. Dicing mounds of tomatoes, she was elsewhere, enjoying the peace and quiet, which is what stirred her memory as she stirred the meat. She raced off to get them, two hours late. Looking at her phone in the car, she saw she had two missed calls from the school. How had she not heard it ring? She felt a little guilty as this was one of the afternoons she'd allowed herself to indulge in an Ambien. Maybe it's time to get Aimee a cellphone, she thought. Then she would have to get one for Oliver too, though Jack would probably nix the idea, say he was too young.

The kids were sitting under a tree leaning on its trunk when she arrived, looking forlorn, the only ones in the schoolyard after dark. She kissed Oliver's tear-stained cheeks, nearly making her own eyes well up. Thank Christ school was ending soon, she thought, one less thing to worry about.

"I'm hungry," Aimee whined.

"I'm sorry sweetie, I feel just awful. I forgot today was Thursday...I made tacos tonight and they're waiting for us at home. I'll give you both an extra big dollop of sour cream." Jack was waiting at home too and she sheepishly recounted what had happened. Instead of being judgmental or sarcastic or spewing out a string of curse words, he merely rolled his eyes, exaggerated so the kids could see. She was pleased to see that their renewed sexual intensity seemed to also have a mellowing effect. Always hard in the bedroom, he was becoming a softie outside of it, and she smiled to herself.

For part two of girls' night out, Margie suggested a bar that used to be one of her favorites, The Gingerman. Built in an old multi-level house packed with antiques, the clutter created a quaint ambiance. Beyond that the bar boasted hundreds of beers on tap, and there was a charming outdoor garden. She was less nervous than last time and only changed clothes once, wearing a trendy top and her favorite ass-shaping jeans, making her feel pert and perky all over.

Upon arrival, she was thrilled to see it hadn't changed a bit in twenty years. Unfortunately *they* had, much older than the rest of the crowd.

"Look at these wispy young things," Margie said. "What I would give to have a body like that again."

"This place is like a frat house; it seems like a real pickup scene. If only I was single!" Allison joked, having to nearly yell to compete with the raucous noise levels.

"I *am* single! But if only I was a decade or two *younger*," Janet shouted back.

However, after chatting and drinking for a couple of hours, their volume rose until they became one of the louder groups, contributing to the clamor, cackling wildly. Again toward the end of the night they shared their problems and frustrations freely, loudly. Margie handed out the pills, cleverly disguised in cute goody bags complete with name tags. And she exercised some restraint this time, not allowing herself to cover the bill. She collected the money while they were paying the check, another crafty move she had devised in order to keep her drug dealing on the down-low. She had made five deliveries, some ordering ten pills and some asking for twenty, and had to contain her excitement and control her bulging eyes, glancing away as wads of twenties piled in.

Driving back, Margie turned the music up and began to sing off-key. Then she stopped singing in order to concentrate, doing the math in her head, which she had never been good at. If she had added the figures correctly, with these women's new orders, she should have over 1500 dollars! She would need some of it for her upcoming trip, which she hadn't officially said yes to but knew she would accept. There were the expenses from her recent online shopping spree and the restaurant tab from the other night. At least she hadn't made that mistake again. Well she certainly wouldn't have much extra but she was determined to make more than the minimum payment on her credit card and that was a step in the right direction.

But unfortunately it was just a baby step and she began to doubt her plan. At this rate, would she ever really get ahead? And other than a few refills, she would be in a predicament soon. Already there had been an incident at the hospital a few days ago in the break room. Dr. Nicholson was getting a coffee. Upon seeing her Margie couldn't immediately remember what ailment she had made up. So she started to walk right back out again, pretending she forgot something, but couldn't figure out on the spot what she could have forgotten, forcing her to turn around again making a complete circle, an awkward start to the uncomfortable dialogue that would follow.

"Margie! How are you feeling this week? I hope the Oxycontin is helping your back; if that doesn't do the trick, I don't know what will," Dr. Nicholson said.

Dr. Taylor walked in at that exact moment, overhearing what was meant to be a private conversation—and looked a little stunned. "I was going to ask you the same about your tendonitis and the Percocet," she asked pointedly, gazing at her intently.

Margie blundered for only a second. "Yeah, I know, right? I am such a mess! It's like ever since I turned forty I just feel like such a wreck, I mean everything happens at once, you know? But I do feel better this week, I really do." she continued nervously, but somehow naturally. Thank god for her gift for gab.

"The tendonitis in my shoulder, well I think that happened in Zumba class. They have all these crazy arm movements, and me, I'm so dang uncoordinated, I'm just flailing around out there like a crazy woman—like a chicken with my head cut off—but I get into it, you know, I try." She had never taken a Zumba class in her life. "I just love the Latin music—I pretend I'm on a tropical island dancing the salsa, the mambo—or trying to—and just when I was getting into the groove, I throw my shoulder out of whack. Well, c'est la vie! And then my back, well that just started the last couple of months, and I don't know how, just from sleeping or maybe lifting Oliver. It's my lower back, like right about here. Do you ever get that?"

"Oh yeah. I get a lower back ache when I get my period without fail, ever since I had my second child," Dr. Taylor said. She was relieved these were female doctors.

"I've been meaning to try Zumba for absolute ages," Dr. Nicholson said. "Well go easy; you really shouldn't be taking two pain medications, one should do for both problems. At least now the prescriptions will last you longer."

In the end they were all smiles, yammering on about their menstrual cramps and workout routines. But it had been a close call and had invoked a deep panic that penetrated her core, even as she remained calm on the outside. When she returned back to her desk she was met by a disgusting whiff of body odor and assumed it was emanating from the waiting room. But once safely behind her desk, she ducked down and sniffed her pits, proving it was coming from her.

Pulling into the driveway just after midnight, she was still replaying the scene while absentmindedly biting on her bottom lip until she tasted blood. Walking inside to the quiet tranquility of a sleeping household, she noticed an unfinished Monopoly game left out on the coffee table of her unfinished house, figures frozen in time, abandoned when the kids grew tired of it. Well that she could relate to. She, however, was still overly alert, jittery and jumpy; her last drink at the bar had been a large coffee since she was driving. So she sat in the living room in the dark, surfing Stevie's Facebook page, examining some new photos closely. His face had aged well. It didn't look like he had a dad-bod, but he probably didn't have a six-pack either. His loose beachwear and khaki hiking shorts didn't reveal much, leaving a lot to the imagination. Luckily she had a vivid one, and pictured his best self, the most toned and cut version of his body that could fill the baggy shorts and t-shirts, while still matching the arms, which, not overly muscular, hung limply by his sides.

He often wore his signature cowboy hat, not the kind worn by rednecks or cheesy country musicians, but a straw hat, curled up on the outer edges, always slightly askew. In other photos he had a full head of dirty blonde hair with highlights. The slight orange undertones indicated that the color came from a bottle rather than actual beams of sun, possibly even hydrogen peroxide like they used in high school. And she wondered, was he younger in these photos with hair? To her relief she zoomed in to see his wonderful laugh lines.

She on the other hand had erased most of hers. She loved her freshly Botoxed face. What it lacked in movement it made up for in smoothness, serene and silky, like porcelain, her expressions as masked and limited as a doll's. Without it there were hairline fractures, cracks and crevasses, the deepest of which ran between her eyebrows, which she felt made her look mad even when she was not. And that could send the entirely wrong message on social media. She made a mental note to take another new and improved selfie, and thinking about what Auden had said about being transparent, she would edit it less extensively. Then again, with the help of the Botox she really wouldn't need to. As far as timing, she would regain some movement in three months giving her a more natural look and allowing for a wider range of expression, so everything would work out perfectly.

She daydreamed about what they might do in Paris. She could barely even fathom kissing another man and thinking about making love to him, or fucking him or just doing it—she didn't even know what to call it—made her anxious. Instead she fantasized about dining out together, sure they would choose the fanciest restaurant in town. The kind of place with an expanse of shiny silverware, crisp white tablecloths, a maître d' who shows you the bottle of wine, holding it up like an expensive gift to gaze upon, like a prize you've won, rather than a bottle you've just ordered. Then ooh-la-la, a dash of it would be poured for her to sample, which she would swish, sniff and sip slowly. She would not add ice cubes no matter the taste! They would drink in all that life had to offer, like the French did. She pictured walking through the town hand in hand, in front of the old beautifully-lit courthouse which it would surely have, and then heading to another cozy bistro for coffee and dessert.

She would wear a light dress on this autumn evening, short and full to show off her shapely, still athletic-looking legs. She was wider in the hips and middle than she used to be, not unlike Marilyn Monroe she supposed, though admittedly less busty—and maybe she would have a Marilyn moment with a hot gust of air!

Margie had always had an active imagination, developed mostly as an escape mechanism at an early age. When she played house with the neighbors, whether imagining they were orphans living alone with no parents, or pretending she had better parents, indulgent and sophisticated ones, she extended the make-believe beyond the relationships to the setting, including what the curtains and the chandeliers would look like, what shoes she was wearing as well as her sequined ball gowns, which she would describe at length to her friends.

And still it served her well as she visualized the dress she would wear: it would have fluttery short sleeves, which was a shame because it would hide her shoulders, which were well-defined; she had always had great shoulders but unfortunately they were now attached to an ample amount of upper arm flab which she could not get rid of no matter how hard she tried. Well she no longer tried, but she used to.

But never mind. What else would they do? Maybe take a drive—oh if only he had a convertible, that would take the cake—and she delved deep into his photos looking for any and all pictures of him with cars. She saw an old Camaro and a Cutlass Supreme from the eighties, again trying to figure out whether the car was vintage or the photo itself was. In any case he obviously collected cars; he had mentioned that he liked to work on them and so he probably had a couple of new ones not pictured on Facebook for fear of coming off too braggy, and therefore it was very likely he had a convertible. The fantastic vision of flying down the highway, going eighty, ninety, one hundred miles per hour with her hair spilling out of a floral silk scarf, blowing wildly, excited her, before she remembered he would probably be flying down. So then she hoped he would rent a convertible.

JULY

On a Wednesday evening, Margie received a massive package with the signature smile graphic on the side, and she smiled back at it, and then at the delivery man, tipping him generously for his welcome interruption to her rather uninteresting week. That's what she loved about ordering online: getting the shoppers high not once but twice, first clicking "confirm order," then forgetting about it only to hear a buzz at the door followed by a delightful delivery. Much better than buying it at a store, she decided, which involved no outer boxes or bubble wrap. The excess packaging and subsequent mess invoked Christmas morning, and she tore through the boxes like a child. Which reminded her of her own children: the fact that she had them.

"Oliver! Aimee! Come down to the living room; we got a big package and I ordered some presents for you!" She wanted them to share in the fun.

Inside the outer box were many smaller boxes, and the kids dug around, Margie helping find which ones she guessed were for them, a difficult task since the fact was only a few were for them; most were self-indulgent. She handed one to Aimee.

"What in the *heck* is this?" she asked, holding up the French coffee press.

"Oh, dear, that's for me," she said, then added "and for Daddy."

Aimee dug impatiently through the boxes, tossing one aside. It landed with a thud.

"Hold your horses, Aimee! And be *careful*. Try these." She handed her a couple of boxes that she thought were the right size to contain her gifts.

Meanwhile Oliver successfully opened his magic kit and complete magician's outfit, and screamed that he loved it, stripping down to his underwear in the living room, first sticking out his bottom and shaking it at them, then putting on the costume piece by piece, complete with the top hat.

"This is *so awesome,* Mom," he said and gave Margie a big hug from behind, his thin arms cutting into her windpipe.

"Oh, god. That looks ridiculous!" Aimee said.

"*Aimee!* What did you open?"

"A stupid package of coffee beans and stupid flower overalls, that's what. Mom, how many times do I have to tell you that I don't like flowers anymore?"

"Well I honestly don't know how anyone can make such a sweeping statement to not like flowers, in any way shape or form. That's a little sad."

"*Mother,* I *do* like real flowers but I do *not* like them on my clothes."

At least she seemed relatively happy with the jewelry box, perhaps because it was made of wood and looked very grown-up, like an undersized antique chest of drawers. She opened them one by one and touched their velvet lining.

Margie herself dug down for the ultimate treasure—the stainless steel cappuccino maker, its weight justifying its cost.

Handling it with care, she positioned it on the countertop, which she had wiped down thoroughly, thrilled with the way the sleek metal gleamed. The surfaces reflecting off each other really brightened up the room. She placed the fair trade coffee beside it just so, with its upscale packaging in earthy colors, running her fingers across the expensive-looking foil lettering on heavy craft paper. The cappuccino maker's outstretched arm of the filter handle reached out to her, the milk frother to the side beckoned, begging to be tested. She studied the complicated instructions and carefully made an espresso, delighted with herself for getting it right the first time. She knew it would keep her from sleeping, but she simply couldn't resist. Since Jack was working late, she would surprise him with a cup in the morning.

The drink was delicious but far too small so she made herself another. She had no idea how Italians could limit the rich taste to such a miniscule size; she wondered if they could even fathom the supersized venti Frappuccinos she was used to. The way the single appliance transformed the kitchen inspired her and the espresso buzz motivated her to do some tidying up around the house, to make some other positive changes. She would prove a point to Jack that even though she hated this house, she was capable of making it nice and livable, and as luxurious as possible, with or without his help.

Her first mission was to take down all the taxidermy in the playroom once and for all. Not up for another fallout, she didn't dare dispose of them. No, she had a much more ingenious idea. She would arrange them in his laundry-office-weight room. Looking around, she felt bad for Jack, with the ironing board looming over the desk, kids' socks strewn around underfoot. The room made her feel claustrophobic, surrounded by the sickly sweet smell of detergent and sour scent of used towels thrown in to fall where they may. At six feet tall and 190 pounds, he was too much man for the room. He had a naturally muscular physique even though he didn't use the free weights often, and how could he, really, without enough space to fully extend his arms.

She felt this would be an improvement, and grabbed a hammer and some long nails and went to it, hurrying to hang the carcasses before he returned. She wanted to surprise him and this was sure to, with two animal heads, the buck and the jackalope, protruding from the walls on either side of his desk, the armadillo standing on a file cabinet so close it was in dire danger of being whacked with an elbow. So close its exaggerated shadow fell across his small work space, drenching his laptop in darkness. In the scale of the small room, walls not even ten feet apart, the creatures looked larger and far more sinister, their eyes popping out of their sockets, their snouts protruding, their horns a wide thicket of branches. Yet they added an undeniable rustic ambiance to the area, and she considered it an overwhelming success.

Next on the agenda was to rid herself of those awful boxes of bubble bath and alleviate the sickening smell of dying flowers—no, death itself—and a dream deferred. It would do her good. With the house bathed in the stench for six months it was a wonder no one had mentioned it, but she supposed they had all grown used to it, the perfume aging at the same rate they aged, their olfactory organs adjusting in unison. Or perhaps it was only her own nostrils that had become offended by the odor. Yet she remembered the comments in the hospital waiting room. She wanted the remaining twenty-seven boxes eradicated from her home and put them in a large black trash bag, stuffed them in her trunk like a body to dispose of in the nearby Carbucks dumpster on her way to work the next morning.

Elated by the evening's achievements but still restless and wired, she tucked the children in. It was hard to wind them down when she was still amped up. Her voice came out shrill when she was trying to be soothing. Prayers were rushed, impatient, lending them a desperate air. Well what did it matter; praying was an act of desperation anyway—and in a way she was a desperate woman. Hell, she didn't even believe in it, but recited them anyway for the sake of the children.

When she leaned in to kiss Aimee, her daughter pulled away and scowled. In fact, both kids seemed less affectionate than they used to be. They asked where Daddy was, not once, but several times. Forcing out a high-pitched whine from Margie: "*How* many *times* do I have to *tell* you *Daddy's not here!*"

She retired to the sofa to try and relax. But by cleaning up the house she knew she was trying to clean up a bigger mess, to stay one step ahead. Of what, she wasn't sure. Jack was still at work, leaving her too much time alone with her troubling thoughts. And she was feeling more disconnected from her kids than ever. Of course, they were getting older, but did they love her less?

They were so different, Aimee and Oliver. The firstborn was more strong-willed, stubborn, overly-opinionated even, and so perhaps she was just asserting her independence. And Margie did want to raise strong, confident children. Oliver, on the other hand, was so sweet and considerate. He never uttered an unkind word, always wanting everyone to be happy, the slightest family tension reflecting in his eyes. He was almost too delicate, too soft, and unfortunately that often translated into being emotionally needy, which she found overwhelming. But then again she knew every child needed love and affection. What she couldn't figure out was whether the children sensed her remoteness and were distancing themselves as a defense mechanism, or whether they were pulling away first, and if so, if it was her fault.

On the other hand, she was feeling overly connected to Jack. He was still all over her physically. She had to admit she liked the attention and feeling desired, but lately he seemed to be looking for an emotional bond as well, nearly suffocating her, when she felt what she needed was some space. Again he had mentioned Florida and sensing her hesitation had suggested they take a trip just the two of them. To the Carolina Coast, no less. Sensing further hesitation he grew quiet for a while.

"Maybe we can get a sitter and go out just the two of us, get some good Mexican food or something," he had said. "Damn, I can't even remember the last time I had Mexican food. We could go to, oh what's it called, the Blue Goose because they have that salsa we like."

"Sounds nice sweetie, but I'm on a diet. You know Mexican food goes straight to my hips. I don't know how you can eat the most fattening food on the planet and never gain a pound. It's just not fair!" she had teased, poking him in the stomach, but ultimately blowing him off.

Now she conjured up ways to solve the problem of her detachment from the children and Jack's over-attachment toward her. She resolved to have Katie's family over soon for a cookout. She and Jack would have another couple to talk to, while entertaining the kids, while providing quality together time—all with the welcome distraction of another family unit. Beyond that, the small but symbolic changes she'd made to the house made her eager to entertain. And, *shit*, Oliver's birthday was in three days—she'd totally forgotten—so she'd allow him to invite a couple of friends, buy a cake, and kill three birds with one stone.

Unfortunately there was another issue she had to deal with. The cappuccino maker alone had been 1300 dollars and Jack was still sore about the iPads. She knew she had gotten kind of carried away with the Amazon purchases, and that this time Jack would ask the prices and where she got the money. She had fibbed about the tablets, saying that they were part of a buy-one-get-one-free promotion because they were last year's models.

All of a sudden she had another brilliant idea. She would take things a step further, using her advanced Photoshop skills to doctor the receipts. She rushed upstairs to use the scanner in Jack's office, the armadillo watching her work. The creature made her nervous—and she was already jumpy knowing Jack could walk in at any moment. So she worked fast and emailed herself the scanned files, careful to delete them from his desktop, then headed downstairs to modify the multiple receipts on her laptop. She changed the numbers, giving herself a substantial discount on all items. She matched the font perfectly, printed them on the thinnest paper she could find, trimmed them out and then scrunched up the paper for a natural worn look before proudly presenting them in a pile on his desk. All of this before Jack rolled in at midnight, when she was snoozing soundly with the help of a Valium.

"What the heck, Margie?" he said the next morning. "Why did you go out and buy all that stuff?"

If he only knew the real totals, she thought, still pleased with herself. "I didn't go out and buy it, I ordered it online. It's just some things I've been needing to buy for ages." She served him a dainty espresso.

"What the hell is this?"

"It's an espresso, silly. It's what they drink in Italy," she said, trying to lighten the mood.

"Well it was too damn expensive," he grumbled.

"It's actually a good deal, Jack. I shopped around for hours looking for the best price," she said. Which wasn't exactly true; she had done a quick search but did not choose the less expensive models that came up because they lacked certain features.

Jack sat at the table and stared at the massive machine, looking a bit defeated, and shrugged. But his good nature prevailed.

"What the hell, let me try a shot of that fancy coffee." He struggled to pick up the tiny cup with his bulky fingers, holding his pinky out, exaggerated for effect.

Aimee and Oliver giggled. They always laughed eagerly at their dad's antics when Margie could barely get them to crack a smile. They both begged for a cup too so she indulged them, serving them each a dainty decaf. She ran the idea of the birthday cookout by Jack as they rushed around getting ready, and he was up for it.

Probably induced by the strong espressos and cappuccinos that they were now chugging like water, Jack was fully energized on Saturday. He actually had a sense of humor about sharing his office with the stuffed varmints and their musty smell, said he found it homey, like a ranch house or lodge. Even the kids cleaned their princess room until every item was crammed in its place, like a magical, crazy castle full of clothes and shoes, bows and berets. Jack mowed the lawn patches, cleaned the grill and wiped off the picnic table.

Margie took a few minutes alone to inspect the turtle pond. She had to admit it had come together splendidly. The misshapen circle, she now realized, had been intentional, giving it an organic, native look. The rock rim Aimee had built looked almost professional; she had topped off some of the stones with gathered moss that was somehow surviving. Jack had surrounded the pond with plants and small shrubs leftover from projects, choosing tropical varieties. The slider turtles constantly rose to the surface in twos and threes stretching out their necks, pinstriped yellow, their bright red markings more vivid than ever. With their protruding eyes, dots for noses, and tight-lipped smiles, the expressions on their round faces looked pleasant—almost mischievous—as if they knew something, were holding in a secret. When they dove back under she got a glimpse of their undersized shells, with intricate brown and green patterns rimmed in gold that sparkled in the sun.

When Katie's family and Oliver's friends arrived, the whole house came alive, just as Margie had anticipated. Aimee and Oliver ran to their bedroom with the other kids in tow, deconstructing it, wreaking havoc. The adults settled into the kitchen. Their friends noticed the cappuccino maker right away, oohing and awing over it appropriately. Margie busied herself making four perfectly-poured little espressos.

Outside they all gathered around the turtle pond, of which the children had every right to be proud, everyone talking all at once. When the guys started to drone on about real estate, the women went inside to bring out the food: steaks to throw on the grill and burgers for the kids, homemade potato salad and a fresh side of greens. With the temperature nearing triple digits, cold white wine flowed throughout dinner, as did the conversation. The children were acting very grown-up sitting at their own table and seemed to be having a nice time as well, not requiring much attention, to Margie's relief. But after she brought the cake out the sugar high transformed them into little terrors, shouting and running and wrestling, and she was relieved when the two boys' parents picked them up, leaving just the two families. Margie and Katie went inside to put the food away, really an excuse to be alone and drink more refrigerated wine in the air conditioning.

It was there at the kitchen table Katie ventured to ask about the Stevie situation. And Margie divulged all that had been developing, even the Paris part. She didn't yet admit that she would say yes—that she already had said yes just a week prior.

"I don't think I'm going to do it, but it was just so nice to be asked," she said. "I mean, I guess it's fair to say that I'm thinking about it."

"Yes, but talk is one thing, to actually meet him is quite another."

"Yeah, you're right," Margie said. "I know. But it's just that, well I think one of my flaws is not following through with things, you know? To be all talk and no action, that's not good either, is it? I want to be, *need* to be, more impulsive. To take charge of my life and make things happen."

"Well it's certainly a slippery slope." Katie always got so solemn on the subject, after starting out all eager ears. *She* was the one who brought it up! In any case, the guys came in to refill their glasses and then lounged on the couch, halting the conversation.

The four of them gossiped about some of the locals, laughing loudly, growing more animated. Margie was enjoying the white wine, feeling refreshed and refined. Rather than the sleepy buzz of red wine or the headachy ring of champagne, she felt sharp, witty and warm. In fact she felt wonderful except that it seemed like Jack was giving her some peculiar looks. He had been ever since he came inside. She couldn't tell if she was being paranoid, so the next time it was appropriate, rather than glancing away, she gave him a full on close-lipped smile, her kindest look with a glimmer in her eyes, a private wink. He glared back at her. Shit. She wondered if he could have overheard her and Katie speaking earlier, but it was impossible; she had been continually glancing out the window at the men, keeping them in her peripheral vision at all times. Or did she get carried away as she was describing Stevie's good looks and dreamy life and not notice Jack come into the bathroom, possibly standing right behind her in the hallway?!

When their neighbors left after a drawn out goodbye, Jack put the kids to bed, shutting their door behind him. He came back to the living room and then spilled it, speaking rapidly, rare for him.

"Margie, when I was talking to Brett out back, he told me that you are supplying Katie, er, *selling* Katie sleeping pills. Not just sleeping pills, but *Valium*, for fuck sakes. What in god's name is going on here?" He didn't wait for her to answer. "I find this whole situation bizarre. I mean, it sounds shady. Why are you selling Katie drugs and what are you doing with the money? And why haven't you told me—your own *husband*— about it, because when the conversation came up I was stunned and it was awkward so I sort of pretended to know. I know *you* take them every now and then but I had no idea you were supplying the whole damn *neighborhood!*"

Now it was Margie who was caught off guard. Her first thought was to blame Katie, angry at the betrayal. It wasn't a secret, not where women were concerned, but she had thought they had an unspoken understanding about their own husbands: to not involve them. Margie certainly kept her drug use on the down-low; she didn't feel the need to tell Jack she used them almost every single night. What was Katie thinking? And here she was caught red-handed. She had given, er, sold her more drugs that very evening. She felt remorseful, or uncomfortable about being found out. She'd always had trouble differentiating those subtle emotions, but in any case, she felt awful. While her first instinct was to react defensively, she tried to answer calmly.

"Yes, Jack, she asked for some and I got them for her. It's no big deal. I mean you may not know this but she is not well, not mentally, and is having a hard time adjusting to life out here. And frankly I don't blame her *one bit!* Well, you know how I feel about *that*, but anyway, it's just something between friends. Women do it for each other at the hospital *all the time.*"

"Well if that's the case, why didn't you tell me, and why in the world are you charging her?"

She suddenly felt ill and her head began to throb. He avoided eye contact, focusing all his energy instead on a button that was coming loose on his shirt, twisting it this way and that.

"First of all it's not that much, but if you must know I'm starting a college fund for Aimee and Oliver."

"Yeah right," he said. "I don't know what's going on with you lately." They were both still a bit buzzed from the wine and he mumbled something under his breath. It sounded like "well I guess" or "you're a mess" or "just confess."

As she and Jack lay in bed, backs turned toward each other, she stared at the wall, painted a salmon color that she had never really liked even in the daylight, because it had turned out more reddish than the picture, and it looked especially sinister in the moonlight. The room was spinning, and she realized maybe she had had one glass too many. Was what she was doing so wrong? Jack certainly seemed to think so. Maybe the whole thing had been a huge mistake, just another one of her half-baked ideas.

And the way he looked at her, eyes weary with disappointment and worry, made her feel like she was not only wrong but bordering on bat-shit crazy. She was a mess, just like Jack might have mumbled. No, she was a hot mess—a selfish, conniving woman—and a bad wife and mother to boot. Knowing this train of thought, this self-loathing, was unhealthy, she got up and went to the bathroom, closed the door and slowly opened the medicine cabinet so it wouldn't creak. She took a pill, which forced her mind to drift into more pleasant seas, rocking her back and forth on the water. Inappropriate as it was, she thought about the other man in her life, the one who was not yet in her life but very soon would be.

Though she woke up fretting about the incident with Jack, and perhaps because of it—and in order to avoid thinking about the tumultuous situation altogether—it was Stevie whom she allowed to occupy more of her mind. She felt she had dreamed about him but the specifics escaped her. She struggled to grasp any detail but could not.

Now that she had said yes to the Paris trip, she wanted to speak with him face to face on a video chat. She thought it might make her more comfortable when they met, since typing to him on a computer now seemed a bit stiff. She wanted to hear his voice. She was no expert on it but assumed the idea of having an affair included sleeping together, and that she would be expected to whether she wanted to or not, and so she wanted to want to. Now that her sex life with Jack had been improving she felt a little guilty. And also confused. Although she was aroused by the idea of Stevie, she didn't yet feel passion toward him. She almost blamed Jack; how could she when she was constantly getting laid already?

Yet she was curious. Wasn't being desired by two men at the same time supposed to be every woman's fantasy? Being with someone else, another, an other. She used to easily recall the sexual qualities and quirks of all of her past partners, but now it took effort. Those memories had been crowded out by Jack, with his solidity, stability, and of course, proximity. Yet she now recalled one boyfriend's odd-shaped member, head too large for the shaft, which she always found off-putting, and how it mushroomed further when he was excited. She remembered his earthy smell—and how eventually he himself became a fungus she couldn't get rid of. Most of the others had been Southern boys: Texans, an Okie, one from Missouri. But then there was the one-night stand with an English guy she had met at a bar in downtown Dallas whose accent alone made her weak in the knees. She had invited the charming young man back to her place, which had brought on the most powerful orgasm her futon had ever withstood.

While some of the experiences had been good and some had been not so good, she was most definitely curious about Stevie and hoped for the best.

Losing her virginity the first time had been a farce and the second time, anticlimactic. She thought she had lost it with her high school boyfriend at the age of fifteen when they had tried. He had poked around but not actually been fully inside her, he later told her, answering the question of why it hadn't hurt. She felt a fool but it's not like she could twist her head around down there and watch exactly what was going on between his bulky fumbling fingers and his smallish penis. She thought he had known what he was doing and he had come, prematurely, apparently. She had broken up with him because a cuter guy was interested in her, and while she was waiting for him to work up his nerve to ask her out, she had screwed someone at a house party, easily, readily, something she would have never done if she had known at the time that she was still a virgin. She guessed it had made her more relaxed, because it didn't hurt that time either—but it too had been a letdown. It wasn't until her early twenties that she had had an actual orgasm. Well she was no virgin anymore. She was an experienced and worldly woman, and so her mission was to video chat with Stevie.

Which was no easy task the following week, with her family hovering around and the fact that they all lived in the same household. Every room she entered was usually already occupied, and in this house a closed door meant nothing; people just barged right in. Finding a time when she could be alone was a challenge. Short chat blurbs and one-liners popped up on her office computer throughout her workdays. She was getting good at firing off responses, and though their dialogue was sometimes disconnected and interrupted, it was almost continual.

"How about tonight?" he typed.

"That's no good for me. We're going to the movies."

"What about Wednesday?"

"No can do. Sorry."

"But Thursday Oliver has a soccer game..." she typed quickly. *"I could make an excuse and skip the game and be home by 6:30!!!"*

"Thursday it is."

"Can't wait!" she typed before she could stop herself, not wanting to appear overly eager.

"Can't wait to see your smiling face," he responded.

She sent him a winking panda bear emoticon. She had recently discovered a large library of them by accidentally right clicking on an icon. They covered every possible emotion and scenario.

The following day:

"Good morning sunshine!"

"Hi! Whatcha doing today?" she asked.

"Thinking about my date tomorrow night with a hot chick."

So he thought she was hot! She played along.

"What a coincidence. I have a hot date too with an incredibly good looking guy." She wondered if "incredibly" was too much. She followed up with a "feeling excited" emoticon.

He blasted back a *"feeling happy!"* emo.

"Feeling curious!" she added.

"Feeling amused!" he replied.

She was amazed that this kind of juvenile back and forth could go on so long between two grown adults, adults approaching middle age no less. Online flirting could be so much fun. She liked the lightheartedness of it, especially when things felt all too serious at home. Jack still seemed annoyed with her and had recently cooled toward her, sexually and otherwise, though he hadn't brought up the meds again and hadn't specifically asked her to stop. Perhaps her explanation of Katie's situation had been believable after all. Aimee was always annoyed with her lately and Oliver soon would be when she would have to tell him she couldn't come to his soccer game.

That evening she tested out the FaceTime camera on Aimee's iPad, with the pretense of teaching Aimee and Oliver how to use the software, turning it into a game. Positioned at opposite corners of the house, she invited them to a chat. When she opened the app, which automatically activated the camera, her face appeared on the screen, and she jumped back, startled—and repulsed. She had bags under her eyes, a heavier bag under her chin, and observed that even the corners of her mouth were giving way to gravity. She noticed age spots on her forearms that she'd never seen before; was the screen in HD? She touched her arms, sure they weren't there the previous summer.

In her mind's eye she always pictured a younger version of herself. And maybe this was for self-preservation, a necessary delusion that all women possessed to help ease the aging process, but it made for a very rude awakening. Yes, the Botox was holding, but even science has its limits. She felt old, especially in stark contrast to her beautiful children, their tight, smooth, young skin so fresh and perfect compared to her blotchy patches and huge pores.

But in a few moments she got used to herself. She chuckled as the kids jabbered away and made funny faces, and she studied her own reflection in the small box, practicing seductive expressions.

Aimee burst out laughing. "Mom, are you trying to make duck lips?"

Margie felt a bit ridiculous but continued to experiment with angles and positions.

"Mom, you are *so* weird," Oliver said. Margie bulged her eyes and made fish lips at him, but mostly ignored both children—after all, it was a learning experience for all of them. She pulled her shirt down exposing one shoulder, taking care to show a bit of flesh but exposing only what she wanted: a firm shoulder but no loose upper arm blubber.

On Thursday morning she told Jack and the kids she would have to work late, that she hated to miss the game. She was more nervous than she expected, glancing at the clock all day at work. In fact time was crawling by so slowly that she didn't trust the wall clock and kept double-checking her cell phone for accuracy. She wanted to see him but wasn't looking forward to being seen, au natural and totally un-retouched. Then time shifted gears in the late afternoon and flew by. At five thirty her supervisor kept giving her annoying little tasks, forcing her to run several stoplights on the way home. In her bathroom she was frantic, dabbing sweat and applying new makeup over the old.

Unhappy with the results she scrubbed off the old and applied it fresh, just in time to race to the couch and open her daughter's iPad at six thirty sharp; her own laptop didn't have the latest software. To her relief he wasn't online yet so she could calm her breathing. When six thirty-five and six forty-five passed her breath again became labored. She kept sighing audibly, wondering if he had forgotten altogether. How could he when they had been talking about it for days? She wanted to text him but realized they hadn't even exchanged phone numbers yet. Was that *normal?* He was almost always online, so this was unusual. The radio silence coming from her screen was deafening; her inner ears were pounding. She looked on Facebook to see if he was online there but his computer said away. *"Are you there?"* she typed three times just to be sure.

The iPad's clock now read seven fifteen. The family would be home at eight o'clock with take-out, which would surely cut things short. She realized being stood up in cyberspace was just as maddening as being stood up in real life. Especially with the effort it had taken her to make this happen. She was beyond irritated. She chided herself for being hurt by someone she barely knew and shouldn't even be talking to. What the hell was she even *doing?* The whole scenario was just ridiculous.

She closed the FaceTime app at seven forty-five and placed the tablet exactly where Aimee had left it. When the family returned she had to get through the long evening pretending that nothing had happened, hiding her bad mood and bruised ego. It wasn't until the next day that she received his long email with a lame excuse, saying he got tied up at work—the very excuse she herself had used on her husband—proving now how weak and uncreative it had been. Yet she had no choice but to give him the benefit of the doubt without coming off like a nag or a psycho, so they rescheduled for the following week.

A couple of days later Margie had to make a delivery to one of her local girls, Candace, at the usual spot and time, five thirty at Carbucks. Margie had noticed that not enough seating was provided at this tiny location, forcing people to line the walls and loiter around the bar waiting for their drinks, packed in like sardines sweating in the summer heat, adding to the odor even with the air conditioner blasting.

She spotted Candace, who had somehow managed to secure a seat in the middle of the room. Tightly wound and highly strung, Candace dominated the conversation at a volume for all to hear, which consisted mostly of her complaining about uninteresting topics: her trouble finding shoes the right size, something on her toe that she thought might be a bunion, and a lengthy back and forth with herself about how she didn't know if the growth was the cause of or the result of her shoe size trouble. Margie, usually chatty, felt like she'd been muzzled, both because she couldn't get a word in and because she didn't want to. Margie couldn't care less about Candace's knobby toe, be it a bunion, a corn or a foot fungus, and the detailed description of the growth was turning her stomach. *I hope this isn't how I sound to other people*, she mused. She thought she rambled about more interesting subjects at least. Yes, she was quite sure she curated her content better. Yet she attempted to be patient and polite for a full half an hour—part of her job, she figured—before handing off the Xanax.

Margie wanted to suggest she take some then and there, on the spot, handing her the orange prescription bottle, and not subtly, plopping it on the table with a thud. Candace continued to talk, making hand gestures more animated than the anecdote deserved. She was one of those storytellers who seemed blissfully unaware that she was unable to get to the point. Not taking the hint that the meeting was winding down, she was wound up—now about how she thought buying organic was total bullshit—when Margie finally had to cut her off, saying, speaking of which, she needed to get home to start on dinner. Candace still ranted as she gathered her belongings, absentmindedly spilling things out of her purse, putting the pill bottle back on the table, digging for her car keys. Upon standing and turning toward the door, Margie spotted Jack's assistant, Auden, who had already spotted her, sitting at a barstool not three feet away. From his perch on the stool she was sure he had seen everything that had just gone down.

"Thanks for the pills, Margie; you have *no idea* how bad I need these right now!" she belted, in case anyone else within earshot had somehow missed the transaction.

"Yeah, okay, talk to you later," she said, walking her halfway to the door before turning back. "*Hey*, Auden, how *are* you? How long have you been sitting there? I mean have you been here this *whole* time? It's just so crazy, I didn't even see you walk in! Well, Candace is a talker so I guess that's why. Did you get a load of her? That's why I give her Xanax; she really truly needs it to mellow out."

"I guess that's one advantage working at the hospital, getting good meds," Auden said, smiling awkwardly. "I mean believe it or not, I don't do any drugs. People assume I smoke pot because of my long hair but I don't even do that, not that there's anything wrong with it. I don't judge, it's just that I try to treat my body like a temple, you know? Not that I'm religious, just spiritual, I guess."

Margie really didn't know, as she preferred to treat her body like a thing to be indulged. And she didn't consider herself religious *or* spiritual, not really caring for organized religion—or New Agers. Beyond that, she didn't know if he was downplaying the situation or if by saying he wasn't judging, he was in fact doing just that. He invited her to sit next to him if she didn't have to rush off.

With the intensity of the conversation, she said yes, partly because she felt obligated to explain herself a little further. Only a foot away from him now, she noticed that up close his beard was so curly, so dense and impenetrable that even at this distance not a millimeter of skin was visible, except when he smiled, which he was doing now.

She ordered a tea, and then elaborated on how she sometimes gave, or, actually sold meds to her friends. She was sure he had seen the money pass hands. She told him how she wished she could give them away, but it was just that she actually really needed the money and that in fact she was in a bit of a predicament. He was the polar opposite of Candace, all attentive ears, radiating warmth and compassion. His piercing yet unpresumptuous gaze steadied her, egged her on. She hadn't felt so comfortable all day.

She told him about the bank account she had opened years ago, and how she had a credit card that had gotten kind of out of hand, and how since she didn't want to worry him or stress him out, she hadn't told Jack.

"Where is Jack by the way? And why aren't you working?" she asked.

"Oh, he's wrapping up a job on Oak Lane and let me off early because we're ahead of schedule."

She continued with the story, trying to justify her reasoning without over explaining. But he was such a good listener that she began spilling everything. And he seemed to absorb it, soaking up her stress like a sponge. His calmness coaxed it out of her. Or perhaps the fact that she had been nearly mute through her previous appointment now made her gush.

"I *admit* that I overspend, on myself, on the kids—not on Jack, who never needs *anything*—but on the house, on gadgets, you name it; I just love buying appliances and electronics. And clothes obviously. I guess it's just that I didn't have much when growing up, and so—if I can play therapist here for a minute—I suppose I'm overcompensating. It could be considered almost an *addiction*, and because it's also a sort of stress reliever for me, it seems like the more in debt I become, the more I spend."

He was so still and statuesque, like a saint, like a priest, and she confessed.

"Believe it or not I grew up in a trailer park…and my father was a total alcoholic. He was lazy and selfish, you know, and he wasn't a good provider and I guess I want to do better for my own family. Only now things are kind of spiraling out of control." Here she stopped and begged him not to tell Jack, that she was going to try to control her spending. That she just didn't know how things had gotten this bad.

He placed his large hand on her shoulder and looked into her eyes. "I understand where you're coming from, Margie, I really do, but what are you going to do about it?"

"I don't know yet, I'm just not sure."

"It's not my place to tell Jack; this can stay between you and me, but Jack is your husband and he really has a right to know. I know I'm not married, but I consider marriage a partnership, a sanctuary where you should share everything. I'm a big believer in total honesty." Well she believed in the *concept* of honesty too—who didn't?—but unfortunately sometimes life wasn't black and white, as he would later learn.

On the drive home it occurred to her how highly inappropriate it all was. He was the last person she should have divulged everything to. And personal things too, even about her parents, whom she rarely talked about even to close friends. She suddenly felt vulnerable. Nauseous. Besides, he was so young and naïve, how could she have expected him to understand? Talking to him had felt therapeutic, like opening up to a counselor, or Jesus himself—with his kind face, flowing hair, and Birkenstocks. She had no more solutions than before, and in fact she had more problems.

"Good morning! You're in the office early today," showed up on Margie's screen just as soon as she turned her computer on at work, before all the programs had fully loaded. She hadn't even had her coffee. It was far too early to be sharp and witty.

"Hi Stevie. I just walked in. Give me a few minutes to settle in…"

She rushed into the break room and chose the largest coffee cup she could find, filling it to the brim so that it jostled and spilled all over her wrist while she walked briskly back to her desk. She looked at the stack of paperwork that already needed processing: a sprained ankle, a head wound, a deep cut needing sutures, and a child with a high fever. She perused the relatively quiet waiting room, trying to visually match each patient to an injury, and spotted Dirty Hairy sitting at the far end of the room, inspecting his nails, which Margie could only assume were filthy. She didn't want to think about where those hands had been.

She called out the first name and handed the patient a clipboard of insurance information to fill out before getting back to Stevie.

"Okay, I'm back. How are you?"

"Guess what I'm doing?"

"I give up. Tell me." she said, not yet in the mood for games.

"I'm researching our hotel for Paris. I'll choose a nice one...I want to surprise you!"

This got Margie's attention. Her face erupted in a smile, like a sunbeam breaking through the morning's haze. Her sprained ankle patient mistook it as a smile for her. As such she held it for a second longer before turning away to focus on her screen.

"That's sweet of you. It would be great to find something historic. Don't you think?"

"Sure."

"Something really charming...with a big front porch maybe."

"Leave it to me Margie. You won't be disappointed!"

Margie was picturing the most fantastic hotel she could think of, like a historic manor or an old plantation. Even though she didn't think there were that many plantations in Texas, if any, it's the visual she conjured up in her mind, with lace-like trim and a full wraparound porch, maybe painted a bright color—pink or green perhaps—and a big deck out back...and a pool and a hot tub would be nice.

"Wouldn't it be great to find one with a hot tub?!" she typed.

"I'll see what I can do." Followed by three winky faces.

She collected the paperwork, snatching the clipboard back absentmindedly and calling the next patient.

She hoped the hotel was in the town square; she wanted to be right in the center of things.

She was about to suggest as much to Stevie when Dirty Hairy had a distracting coughing fit. She tried to focus on the man sitting in front of her, who was in construction and had cut himself with a carpet cutter, white paint still wet on his overalls, his wound bleeding through a rag that was wrapped around his arm and secured with duct tape. He held the clipboard out for her with his good hand, grimacing in pain. She took the chart, more gently this time, but could barely concentrate as her mind was still occupied with images of fancy hotels—and because the hacking was becoming even louder and more constant.

She perused the paperwork to make sure his insurance information was filled out correctly, but couldn't seem to think straight, couldn't focus on the words, staring at a jumble of handwritten letters without meaning. She contemplated digging through her purse to find her reading glasses, but she blinked hard and realized, that no, it wasn't her eyes that were failing, it was her nerves that were shot from the hacking sounds from across the room, emanating from a deeper place now. She hoped he wasn't hacking up phlegm and if he was, she hoped he would have the decency to not spit it on the carpet. Now Dirty Hairy appeared to be gagging between coughs.

Margie stood up abruptly. "You sit tight for a minute. I'll be right back and I'll get you back to a doctor as soon as I can," she told the contractor.

She walked over to the homeless man, hit by his familiar rank smell. She glanced out the front door and saw his overflowing shopping cart parked at the curb. Margie thought he might be choking. But had he even been eating? She had seen him biting his nails, and wondered whether a person could choke on a nail.

"Are you okay, Dir…, Mister, er, sir? Are you choking?" she asked, suddenly unable to remember his real name even though she'd checked him in hundreds of times before. Without the desk in between them it was the nearest she'd ever been to him in proximity and she was nearly knocked out by his reeking breath. His lips were curled back revealing stained teeth and he made the universal choking sign, putting his hand to his hairy throat.

"Were you eating something, Mr. Green?" She remembered his name now. He motioned to the floor where peanuts were scattered; the bag on the floor must have fallen out of his hand.

Again he made the choking sign, more aggressively now, like in charades when a player is missing something exceedingly obvious. But this was no game. Mr. Green's face was turning blue. His eyes were bulging, wild as always. But she saw that up close they were filled with an underlying kindness. She didn't think she would have time to run back and call a doctor or a nurse; most of the doctors hadn't even arrived yet. She froze for a second, unsure what to do. The old man searched her eyes helplessly but remained calm, so Margie mirrored his manner. But she had to act fast. For once she didn't think about the odor emanating from him, his rotting teeth, his filthy clothes, or the germs probably crawling all over him. Underneath the florescent lights in the cold, sterile room, a warmth washed over her and she considered only his life, and saving it.

She remembered her CPR class, kind of, or rather, the Heimlich maneuver, walked around behind him and placed her palm squarely between his shoulder blades. She gave a good hard pound and tried again two more times. When that didn't work she told him to stand. He was robust—and tall—and now his face was purple. She panicked inside only for a second. She then stood on a waiting room chair, luckily bolted to the ground, and wrapped her arms around his upper torso, directly under his warm armpits. Hands interlaced under his abdomen, clamped tight, she squeezed in an upward motion in clean hard bursts as hard as she could. She told Mr. Green to relax his arms, giving him another squeeze with all her might.

The nut dislodged and flew across the room landing at least fifteen feet in front of him, freeing another coughing fit as he regained his breath. The other patients clapped, surprising Margie.

"You're a strong woman, Mrs. Moore," he said. "I didn't know you had it in you!" She was surprised that he knew her name.

"Neither did I, to be honest!" She gave him a kind smile. She had never thought or herself as a strong woman before. And *was* she? The jury was still out on that one.

"Well thank you, young lady." He had the gentlest eyes she had ever seen, almost jolly, surrounded by constellations of wrinkles. Rather than a vagabond, he reminded her now of a deep sea captain, with his dark tan and rugged face.

"Oh, it's nothing. And you're very welcome. Just doing my job—and I'm happy I could help."

"*Help?* Hell, you saved my life, for whatever these old bag of bones are worth. Wish I had you by my side when I was fighting in Iraq!"

"A war hero? Well then *I* should be thanking *you*...I'll bet you've had quite a life, Mr. Green."

"Oh yeah, you're damn right about that...pardon my French." She wondered how old he was. He looked so haggard but the dark hair threw her off, and he'd obviously seen some hard times, which can age a person prematurely. Iraq was a rather recent war, she knew, but was he talking about Desert Storm, which she recalled started while she was a freshman in high school because she had known some recent graduates who had signed up and been deployed, or the Iraq War that was after 9/11—or any of the wars and occupations since then? She wished she was more of a history buff, but regardless, she realized he could be in his forties, not much older than she was. He had fought for his country and what had she ever fought for? She couldn't think of a single thing—literally or figuratively.

And she constantly complained about her house and yet his home was nothing more than a metal cart, a cage on wheels, one of which was faulty, stolen from the nearby Walmart. And still he had a positive outlook. Throughout the day she wondered what atrocities he'd been through to bring him to this low point, and in turn questioned her own trajectory. He at least seemed happy.

Since she had been screwing up so much at home lately, she was glad at the hospital she could be sort of a hero for one day. A nurse had heard the commotion and wandered out into the waiting room, catching the final moments of the action, seeing the peanut fly through the air like a bullet, and word had spread around the hospital. It was nice to be appreciated and recognized, especially by the doctors. But more importantly, she had done a good thing, which gave her a good feeling. And beyond that she had saved a good person. And maybe, just maybe, that made her a good person.

When she got home that night she had a story to tell, and a truthful one at that. Jack said he was impressed by her stealthy actions and her ability to think so quickly on her feet. The kids were fascinated by their mom's heroism, their jaws dropped in disbelief, a bit too surprised, Margie thought. In fact they made her reenact the entire scene with Jack, using a Skittle since they had no nuts in the house, which became a game of seeing how far Jack could spit the Skittle after a hard pound from Margie, then the children, providing the evening's entertainment.

Yet she hardly had time to bask in the glory when another disaster struck. Awakened by a blood-curdling scream at dawn the next day, she jumped out of bed thinking Oliver—no, Aimee—was being murdered in her sleep; no, she had been badly injured and was running through the house in hysterics. Jarred from her pill-induced dreamless sleep, Margie tripped down the stairs, becoming slowly aware of her surroundings. She made out a few words between Aimee's harrowing screams that at first sounded nonsensical: "Polka Dot! Poor Polka Dot! Dad, Polka Dot is dead!" Polka Dot, Margie remembered, was Aimee's favorite turtle. The kids had taken to feeding the turtles first thing in the morning before anyone else had stirred. Jack was jolted awake too, and both a bit disoriented they tried to calm her, but she wouldn't allow it, arms flailing, dragging them to the turtle pond to see for themselves Polka Dot's rigor mortised body frozen in her little round shell bobbing around upside down in the murky water.

Now Aimee was sobbing, inconsolably. "She's dead, Daddy, I can't believe Polka Dot is dead. What could have caused Polka Dot to die?"

Even though Aimee was looking to her father for comfort, Margie tried to help Jack out, but couldn't think of what to say. She was good with emergencies in the hospital—she had just saved a life—but often felt helpless when it came to her own family. She was used to illness and even death at the hospital in humans, but knew nothing of the turtle realm. She looked at Jack, who bent down to Aimee's level, took her hands in his.

"Death is part of the cycle of life, Aimee, it's just a part of nature. I know it's sad, but it's just one of those things...and unfortunately, sometimes—" here Aimee broke free and ran inside.

They followed her to find her face down on her bed having a magnificent tantrum, a real hissy fit, something she hadn't done for years. Oliver stared on silently, ruddy cheeks tear-stained, his mouth gaping open. Both parents sat on the bed and tried to comfort her, talking to her softly, saying that sometimes these things happened and they would get her another one.

Aimee refused to go to school, screaming that it wasn't fair.

"Life isn't fair, sweetheart," Margie said. She said it kindly but she meant it; it sure hadn't been for her. This drama with Aimee was the last thing she needed with all she was going through, and it couldn't have happened at a more inconvenient time. She was dealing with the stress of being stood up, the delicate dance with the doctors at the hospital, the dreaded credit card bill that would arrive any day, the disastrous meeting with Auden, and now a dead turtle on top of it all. But she felt for her daughter, who was finding out that life wasn't fair for herself firsthand.

Jack insisted that she go to school, but she cried over her scrambled eggs, cried while Margie braided her hair extra gently and washed her face with a warm washcloth, her blue eyes pools of water, looking genuinely distraught. Margie had never seen her like this. Tears continued to drip onto the backpack in her lap as she drove them to school. Margie kissed her red face when she dropped her off, promising the family would have a turtle funeral that night.

Aimee had overreacted, certainly, and Margie wondered if she was acting out. But she was only ten years old, and in truth Margie was upset too all day at work—and she was supposed to be an adult.

When she returned home, Jack had already scooped out the body and placed it in a shoebox, poor Polka Dot's coffin, which the kids had decorated appropriately with red polka dots. Jack had dug another hole, this one much smaller, in a dirt patch in the lawn near the back fence, but they had waited for Margie for the actual funeral proceedings. Aimee had written a beautiful eulogy and read it aloud dramatically.

"We are gathered here today to mourn the short life of Polka Dot Moore. She was only with us for a matter of weeks, but she brought each and every one of us joy. She was like a member of the family and always came up to greet us, the friendliest of all of the turtles, full of energy and happiness. She was the only turtle who was comfortable being held, who let us pet her without squirming. She was a beautiful, loving creature and she will be missed."

Still overly emotional herself, Margie was touched, and several tears slid down her cheeks. Aimee seemed proud of her speech, so powerful it had moved her mother, whom she embraced in a long, tight hug. But the truth was Margie had realized she was not like the turtle, not happy or loving, yet she *was* the turtle, an empty shell of a woman, bobbing in the water aimlessly, her world flipping over, trying to float but losing her balance, off kilter.

AUGUST

Several of the women had reached out to Margie asking for more meds by the end of the week, so it was time for another mommy meet-up. Calling it that made her feel less guilty and they *were* all mothers, and very stressed out ones at that. After all, that was part of the criteria for selection in the first place. This time she invited the ladies to meet in Addison, a larger suburb halfway between Prairie Mound and downtown Dallas, thinking now that she had them hooked they could come to her. And she knew Jack would give her a hard time about going all the way to Dallas yet again. So she chose The Flying Saucer, a lively brewery she had been to once before with Jack on a date night. The walls and ceiling were covered in plates and saucers, and the space was so cavernous with indoor and outdoor picnic tables that it reminded her of a German beer hall—not that she'd actually ever been to one.

She invited Katie, who didn't even need any pills at the moment, but who was happy to join because both women agreed that these nights out were turning out to be a real hoot. She picked her up and they gabbed the whole way, making the ride enjoyable even when the horrific traffic on the interstate slowed to a crawl, which normally would have caused Margie severe road rage. Last to arrive, looking at the hen fest gathered around a large picnic table, Margie prided herself on her organizational skills. And she enjoyed getting out of the house; her plan was working on so many levels.

In fact she was having such a good time that she ignored her self-imposed two drink limit, and had three imported beers—German, no less—with a much higher alcohol content than she was used to. The booze loosened her up and toward the end of the evening she was the life of the party, spewing out hilarious one-liners and cutting observations, some self-deprecating and others with Jack or the kids as the target. When she stood up from sitting so long, her bar stool was higher than she remembered and she was thrown off-balance, then swayed noticeably on her way to the bathroom. As such, Katie offered to drive.

After fumbling with the seatbelt, before they even left the parking lot, Margie began divulging all about Stephen Singleton, as giddy as a schoolgirl, slurring slightly.

"We chat *all the time* at work," Margie said. "I mean sometimes *all day* long!" She waved her hands around for effect, movements slowed but exaggerated.

"Are you *serious?*"

"I'm *totally* serious. I kid you not! And he is *so funny*. Sometimes I laugh out loud—right in the middle of the reception room full of sick patients. I try not to; I know it's not appropriate, but I can't help it. I *literally* laugh my head off. He is just *so dang cute*. I have to admit I have a *major* crush on him."

"*Really?*" Katie asked, then said no more. Being a bit drunk, Margie needed very little encouragement.

"Yeah, *totally*. I mean, I haven't told another soul, Katie, no one on God's green earth, so please, *please* don't tell anyone. Promise me you won't tell a living soul."

Before giving her a chance to answer Margie launched into the whole long-winded story about Stevie standing her up on video chat.

"What do you think that *means?*" she asked several times. "Why would he do that if he's really into me?"

"Well, it could mean anything. It sounds like he has a very active life and he very well could have been busy…then again maybe he has something to hide."

Margie was flabbergasted. "Well what could he be hiding? I mean everything's spelled out on his Facebook profile." She had thought he had been a bit insensitive but hadn't even contemplated this angle. She continued, defensively. "I don't know why he would need to *hide* anything from me. I mean we're old friends after all. And we talk about *everything*. And have I told you he has a great sense of humor?" She was beginning to repeat herself. "I'm trying to think of what it was he said the other day that just cracked me up…well I can't think of any examples right now, I guess I'm *too drunk!*" Here she laughed, as if it were a joke. "But he is *super* sweet and supportive too. Just the other day he said that I look *smokin' hot* in my latest profile picture. Those were his exact words, can you freaking believe that?"

"Wow," Katie said.

"I said *yes!*" Margie blurted out, "to the Paris proposal. Now it's Paris, *Texas,* mind you, not the real one, but it still sounds like such an adventure."

"Adventure indeed. But are you sure you want to go through with it? I just can't help thinking of Jack; he's such a good person. Have you ever cheated on him before?"

"Absolutely *not!* I wouldn't think of it; I mean I've never even considered it. Until now that is."

At work on Monday, between checking in patients and dealing with the paperwork that accompanied them, Margie called in a couple of the refills the doctors had previously prescribed. Several weeks had passed since the last time, so she thought it would look legit. At the end of the workday, Margie gathered her belongings, including a few new Pinterest pages she had collected of things she might need on the trip—new outfits, a Coach handbag, a fashionable wide-brimmed hat—and headed to the pharmacy on her way out. She stood at the counter for a few minutes, wondering if it would be rude to ring the bell, but knowing Ed was methodical and slow-moving at his age, and not wanting to interrupt him, she just stood there. She cleared her throat, jingled her car keys. She finally heard rumbling, then footsteps. But instead of Ed, a woman whom Margie had never seen before emerged from the back. She had her dark hair in a tight bun and was wearing black, thick-rimmed glasses, the kind most often worn by museum curators in movies, pushed forward so they mirrored her thick dark eyebrows. She wore bright red lipstick, which contrasted nicely with her skin, as smooth and pure and white as the driven snow. Margie wondered if she was from somewhere else, the East Coast maybe, because it looked like her face had never been baked or beaten by the strong Texas sun. She looked younger than Margie, but her mannerisms were that of an older woman, confident and self-assured. She was shockingly tall, close to six feet from Margie's calculation, judging by the way she towered over her even from behind the counter.

"Hi there. Are you filling in for Ed today?" she asked wearing her warmest, widest smile.

The woman pursed her lips, and responded, "I'm the new pharmacist, just started today as a matter of fact."

"Oh, well, *hi*," Margie said, looking at her nametag, "Doreen, I'm Marjorie, Marjorie Moore, and I work over at the registration desk, checking in incoming patients. So nice to *meet* you. Welcome to the hospital!"

"Well thanks, I appreciate that. I'm Dr. Renquist. How can I help you today?"

"I left a message earlier calling in a couple of refills from my desk," she said, suddenly anxious, fidgeting with her purse straps.

"Oh yes, I recognize your name now. Can you hold on just a second? They're already filled. I just need to grab them from the bin." She was gone a long time and Margie caught a glimpse of her in the back, checking her computer. Checking *what*, Margie wondered.

When she appeared again Margie made another attempt to befriend her. "Are you from around here? You don't look like it—and I mean that as a *compliment*!"

"My husband and I just moved here from Houston actually. He's the new surgeon, Dr. Williams."

Margie was perplexed. Completely baffled. No one had told her Ed was quitting or retiring or whatever had happened. But she said, "How *wonderful*." When the woman didn't speak and just stood there like a statue, Margie added, "That's just *terrific*."

"Now Margie, check that these refills are correct because I see that you have quite a few prescriptions on file."

Margie's face was glistening now and her armpits were slippery with sweat. She glanced at them quickly before shoving them into her bag, debating whether to thank her and walk away without another word or whether to make one final attempt at camaraderie.

"Yeah, these are the right ones. I know, right? You see I just turned forty recently and that's when everything started to go wrong, and all at once! Take it from me, the aging process is not pleasant. But you won't have to worry about that for a very long while!"

Dr. Renquist offered up a tight-lipped semi-smile. "Well hopefully not…" Margie was eager to get away now. Clasping her keys, she turned away from the counter, when the new pharmacist spoke again.

"I need to talk to you about the side effects. You know Ambien and Xanax are extremely similar and so I'm a bit confused as to why you need both medications. If taken together, these could have serious effects on your heart. Do you mind me asking what these prescriptions are for?"

Margie was annoyed at herself for extending the conversation in the first place. But she launched easily into the Zumba incident, then the story about her back and picking up Oliver, and realizing these meds were not painkillers, transitioned smoothly into the insomnia and anxiety she'd been suffering from for years—and that was no lie—rambling on, yet knowing she really hadn't answered the question.

"Uh-huh, okay," Dr. Renquist said, looking unconvinced, her eyes narrowed with one dark eyebrow arched into a sharp question mark. "Well, have a nice evening, Margie."

She couldn't wait to get home and put the whole event out of her mind. Too mentally exhausted to even think about cooking, she brought home Taco Bell for the whole family. They jokingly called it Taco Hell, but Margie actually liked the flavor of the meat, the way it made the shell soggy after the drive, the creaminess of the pintos and cheese, into which she dipped her tacos. The kids had their own taco rituals too, Aimee tilting her head sideways to almost a ninety-degree angle and taking huge bites, Oliver nibbling his way around the taco shell and working his way inward by half circles. After his last bite, he followed Aimee outside to play.

When Jack returned an hour later after a long day, she sat with him at the table while he ate. He seemed to relish the few minutes of attention. She was still trying to put her day at the office—and especially the new pharmacist, the behemoth of a woman, the Amazonian lady—behind her, and so she was happy to listen as he told her about his. How he and Auden had rented a bulldozer to take down a massive tree that would barely budge, making the huge tractor rear up on its back wheel until they thought it would flip.

"It's going so well with Auden; he really is a great guy. I'd like to have him over to the house again soon, being that he has no family around."

"Well, I'm sure he's made a lot of friends and would probably rather hang out with people his own age…doesn't he have a girlfriend?" she asked, trying to dissuade him, to change the subject.

"Not that I know of. I think he's a kind of solitary type, a bit of a loner. How about this Sunday? We could grill out again, and the kids can show him the turtles, since he offered such good advice on which kind to buy."

Margie was silent, lost in thought.

"C'mon, it'll be fun."

"Yeah, sure," she said finally, staring out beyond the pond, beyond the backyard, and even further beyond.

After dinner while Jack was up in his laundry-office-weight room, she absentmindedly checked Facebook. She tried to think of excuses to cancel the cookout with Auden. She had really said too much. Lately every time she opened her mouth she seemed to be digging a hole… or talking her way out of a hole she had already dug. It was becoming exhausting remembering which ailment each doctor thought she had, which they asked her about frequently. She had thought it was out of genuine concern but was no longer so sure.

And she had to remember to whom she had told which secrets: Katie about Stevie and Paris, and Auden about her spending and debt. Beyond that, she had to remember what she had revealed to Stevie and what she had not. And not just about her family life, which she tried to keep relatively quiet, but misrepresentations and flat-out falsehoods that had recently slipped out. For example, the other day she had told him that she volunteered in a soup kitchen—and why had she felt the need?— oh yes, because he told her he was concerned about the environment and had donated time to the cause, picking up trash on the beach. And another time she had told him she was up for a big promotion at work— and where had this fib come from?—oh yeah, when he mentioned how challenging it was to work in sales, she guessed she had wanted to seem important too. She was up for a raise, her annual raise, which usually wasn't much.

Of course that was nothing compared to the deceptions and distortions when it came to Jack—which was probably why she continued to push him away. Yes, now he was pushing her away too, but she knew she had started it. The more exaggerations and untruths she invented about how she spent her money and more and more of her time, the less she could talk openly about, until things had grown unusually quiet, even for them.

And how had she let this happen? Growing up she had considered telling a lie an unforgivable offense. She didn't appreciate her dad lying to her, promising to come to her birthday parties and then going to bars instead, or when he lied to her mother about how he spent the rent money. Or her mother's many lies trying to cover for her father.

And she knew deep down that lying to Jack was the ultimate betrayal. Maybe that's why when he tried to spoon her at night, which was happening less and less often, she was as rigid and prickly as a fork, or else rolled over and straightened out like a knife.

Equally troubling, she was becoming even more distant with the kids, forgetting things, not listening, their voices becoming white noise among the clutter constantly crowding every inch of her mind. A mind that was sometimes under the influence of Xanax. Not often, just now and then, when she wanted, needed, to turn the white noise into a beautiful buzz—and then make it sing.

And tomorrow she would have to miss another of Oliver's soccer games, and she really did like seeing him play, even as he ducked away from the ball, kicked dandelions and skipped around the field. She had enjoyed playing soccer when she was a kid, never on an official team, but with the neighbors in nearby fields. She and her brother weren't allowed to join any extracurricular teams or take any classes, dance, piano lessons or otherwise, except for free programs and activities. As such she always dreamed that Oliver would be the star soccer player in high school—and Aimee a cheerleader, the ultimate status symbol for a teenage girl in the South. But lately Aimee had no interests outside of moping around and so far Oliver didn't seem to have a natural aptitude for sports. Still, she hated to miss the game. But c'est la vie—she and Stevie had another appointment to video chat.

She logged off Facebook, went upstairs and said good night to Jack, who was busy YouTubing. She only wished she could be so thoroughly entertained by something so completely banal. Under the covers she felt comfy and tried to relax, but her mind tossed and turned, started and stopped, tripped and tumbled, until it was spinning out of control, making her dizzy. She replayed the entire scene at the pharmacy again and again, wondering if Doreen—or Dr. Renquist as she *insisted* on being called—had bought her stories. She seemed uppity, a better-than-thou type who probably liked to look down on people—then again she was a giraffe of a woman. *I see that you have quite a few prescriptions on file* kept repeating in a loop as she tried to reimagine and recreate the exact tone of her voice.

She thought about what she *should* have said. When it came to her video chat with Stevie, she thought about what she *would* say, wondering if he said this or that, how she would respond. By now they had a constant stream of dialogue dominating her computer at work, each tedious daily task mentioned as if it were newsworthy, each observation stated as if it were an epiphany, each comment packed with innuendo, causing her to constantly close the windows on her screen. But video was different, and therefore her mental conversations were lengthy and exhausting, forcing her, per usual, to take a pill until her brain came to rest, acquiesced. Unfortunately that night she felt none of the euphoric effects, just total blankness. Then blackness.

She raced home from work the next day, following cars at an unsafe distance, changing lanes often, overtaking every other commuter on the road. At home she changed tops, freshened up her make up, and settled into her favorite spot on the sofa, trying to assume a naturally seductive position. She turned on the video app and placed Aimee's iPad on her lap, which blew up her double chin, made her look bloated, exaggerated her still-prominent front teeth. Then she put it on the coffee table, also too low and too far away making her slump and crane her neck simultaneously, a very unattractive combination. She finally propped it on the toaster oven brought in from the kitchen, and thought that was just about right, minimizing her wattle, maximizing her smile, her face in the dead center of the screen.

Six thirty rolled around and nothing happened, other than her perspiring profusely. Six forty and nothing, other than the damp spot spreading. If she raised her arms she could actually see the dark patches on the screen, so she made a mental note not to do that under any circumstances. She dared not leave to change her shirt lest that was the exact moment he invited her. Plus she had painstakingly chosen this top after much debate. At six forty-five, his icon appeared on the screen, but in the instant messaging app, not the video chat.

"Hey!" she wrote.

"Hey back at you, darlin'!"

"There you are! I was beginning to wonder!" No more exclamation marks, she told herself, realizing once they started actually talking, she wouldn't have to use them!

"No, I'm here. I've actually been on my computer for a while trying to get the damn camera to work. I haven't used it in ages."

"Oh, well I just double-clicked the app and searched your name, and then when I clicked it, it tried to call you."

"Are you on a Mac?"

"Yep."

"I'm on a PC. Hmm. Do you want to try Skype?"

"Sure, that's fine. I'll try to invite you."

"That didn't work. I'll try you," he typed.

Nothing.

"Try to invite me again," he typed. *"The camera icon has an ex in front of it, that can't be good."*

"Now try me."

Nothing.

"Now you try me."

Getting frustrated with the technology and annoyed with the back and forth that had gone on for twenty minutes as he fiddled with his settings, Margie suggested an old-fashioned phone call. They still hadn't exchanged numbers, so they did this now. Her phone rang immediately. She jumped even though she was expecting it, and answered promptly. Upon hearing the sweet tone of his voice she felt fourteen again.

She had forgotten what it sounded like altogether and now she was transported by it, soft and sexy with a slight drawl, a little hint of his country roots. It was totally unique and yet instantly familiar, like hearing a favorite song you haven't heard in twenty years and realizing how much you've missed it, discovering that you still know all of the lyrics. They were shy at first, giggling at the sound of each other.

"I wish I could come pick you up in my old beat-up pickup truck like old times," he said.

"It was a classic! Whatever happened to that old thing anyway?" she asked. Once the conversation began to flow, it did so smoothly and rapidly, and they were full of questions, greedy to know more, talking about life in their twenties and past relationships. They hadn't actually spoken since college and tried to remember the exact time they had seen each other last. Stevie thought it had been Rodney's house party when they were both home on Christmas break, when a fight broke out and a guy from another school bit off part of Ricky's ear, which they all had to search for in the grass, while Margie remembered hanging out at a UNT football game followed by a wild after-party at her friend's Dana's apartment in Denton where she drank too much tequila, danced on the coffee table until it broke, and then abruptly passed out on the sofa. As they reconstructed their timeline piece by piece, Margie was so completely engrossed that she was caught off guard when the door burst open and the kids ran in, Jack close behind.

She panicked and changed her voice to a more gossipy tone. "Okay, Katie, yeah, I hear you. Okay, I'll talk to you later...uh-huh...goodbye."

Then addressing the room, "That was Katie. How was the game?"

They had won their game, and Oliver had kicked the ball three times, driving it towards a goal. This was a shocker and Margie regretted missing it, fearing it wouldn't happen again. They had lost the first four games of the season and Margie could only imagine the skill of the other team, or lack thereof. She silently questioned whether Stevie was really having trouble with his camera or if that was some kind of tactical ploy. But to hear his voice! It was so surreal. The energy in the room was palpable. She tried to shift her focus back to the big game. They had picked up pizza and all sat around the table chowing down, Margie making every effort to be present.

"Tell me exactly what happened, Oliver. I want to hear the play-by-play."

"Well, I was just standing far away in the grass, like usual, when the ball just came right towards me, and I gave it a good hard kick, then ran after it, so fast—the fastest I've ever ran in my whole entire life—and when I caught up to it, I kicked it two more times, real hard, right in the center just like Dad taught me, and it flew across the field to Donnie Davidson and he kicked it right into the goal. I couldn't believe my eyes!" he beamed.

"That's incredible," Margie said, then smiled at Jack, genuinely proud. But the moment soon passed and she was gone again, back with Stevie on the phone, back with Stevie riding around in his ruby red, '67 Chevy pickup truck.

Margie floated through the rest of the week not really succeeding in being present. Lately she was pulled in so many different directions and had so much trouble concentrating, she wondered if she had late-onset ADHD. She felt she definitely had developed some kind of disorder. What else could explain how she was always lost in thought and unable to focus?

Saturday, however, the whole family went to the lake, to one of their favorite picnic areas with a small strip of sandy beach, which did require her full attention. It was Jack's idea, and a nice one. Of course it was more work for Margie, who had to go to the grocery store and make the sandwiches, pack the towels and sunscreen, dig out the beach toys and floaties from the garage, get herself and the kids ready, and help Jack pack up the car. She liked the lake. Not nearly as much as the ocean, mind you, but unfortunately that was not an option available to them in Prairie Mound, and she still enjoyed lounging in the sun like a lizard, paging through magazines, perusing articles and dog-earing pages she would clip out later.

Although she was already exhausted, upon arrival she felt more relaxed than she had in weeks. Maybe months. Basking in the sun was one of her favorite hobbies.

And privately, lakes always reminded her of her happiest memories with her father, who would take her fishing at a neighbor's pond a few miles away. It was usually just the two of them; her brother found it boring since they never caught any fish. But Margie couldn't have cared less about the fish. She loved jumping off the rickety pier to cool down; she remembered the welcoming, lukewarm water, how it made her feel alive. Always a strong swimmer, she loved it when her dad called her his little flounder. Warned by her mother not to drink beer, he didn't, which Margie considered a special gesture in itself.

They would paddle out in the old rowboat and sit there rocking on the water for hours. He would actually ask her questions and listen patiently to her longwinded answers. She would let out all she had saved up to say, all that had built up, all that she had held in while he was in his near-constant, alcohol-induced moods, and the words would burst forth, spilling out like a waterfall while she had his undivided attention. When she finally finished, she'd ask him to tell her a story. Most involved bears, or bees, or tornadoes, told in gruesome detail with climactic but happy endings about surviving disasters. At those moments she thought maybe she too would survive: that compared to those stories, her life wasn't that bad. Until he came home drunk again, and then it was.

Thinking about how invigorating the water had felt then, and how heavily she was sweating now, she decided to take a dip to cool down. It felt nice even though the water was filthy. All the lakes in the area were. Her skin was coated with a smelly film and she wondered if the pond she had found so refreshing in her childhood had been this skanky. Probably so. Fortunately there was a public outdoor shower where she could rinse off the funk directly afterwards.

"Momma, will you come float on the inner tube with me?" Oliver asked with a wistful smile.

"I would, dollface, but I just showered—and it took a while to get all that lake slime off, believe you me!" she answered.

She was beat at the end of the day, tired from the sun, from making sure the kids showered thoroughly, putting food away and packing everything up in the car with Jack. And she still had to prepare for Auden's visit the following afternoon, physically—and especially mentally. She had to clean the house. She didn't much care for housekeeping and wasn't very meticulous, even though she loved when things were immaculate and orderly, scrubbed until they sparkled and shined. But the unfinished nature of the house made it somehow okay when the cleaning was left incomplete, and she tended to vacuum the center of the room but not worry about the edges, to dust only the front of objects, to sweep around the furniture rather than to move it.

She had already bought sausages and steaks, and Jack would prepare the grill and the yard, but there was so much to think about. Would

Auden mention her spending when it was just the two of them alone and check in and see if things had gotten any better? They had not. Even with selling the meds she was barely able to make much more than the minimum payment, because the minimum was rising at a rapid rate. Surely he hadn't said—and wouldn't say—anything to Jack because he had given her his word. And he was nothing if not honest. But she could well imagine him dying to ask her about it privately, out of a mixture of real concern, curiosity, and as a way to offer self-important advice. Yes, his problem was that he took himself too seriously. She had been fooled by his attentive kindness once already, and she would not make that mistake again.

With all the cleaning, Sunday flew by and she found herself getting all gussied up once more, primping and plucking at length. She wore cute denim cutoffs, a bit tight but not unflattering, and encouraged Aimee to put on a carefree sundress. With her being extra obstinate these days, Margie finally had to demand it. She dressed Oliver in cute khaki shorts with brown suspenders.

"Are you alright?" Jack asked Margie. She became aware that her face was clenched into a scowl, probably had been all day.

"Yeah, I'm fine sweetie," she said, softening her face with effort, relaxing her features one by one. "I guess I'm just tired." She hoped the Botox wasn't wearing off.

"Well it's been an action-packed weekend," Jack said, giving her shoulders a squeeze.

Auden arrived, knocking on the front door rather than walking around to the back where Jack was lighting the grill.

"Auden's here!" she yelled upstairs to the kids in the playroom. She didn't want to be alone with him for any amount of time, even just opening the door. They bounded down the stairs and beat her to it.

They all greeted each other warmly. Oliver jumped up and down. Aimee took Auden's hand, in order to lead him to the turtle pond, Margie was sure. She followed them out to the backyard, hanging back a bit, grabbing some condiments on the way.

Just steps behind them, she heard a shriek from Aimee. And not an excited squeal or an enthusiastic shout, but a bone-chilling, hair-raising, horrific scream that she knew could only mean one thing. Sure enough, when she neared the pond where they were all now gathered, another turtle had gone to meet his maker.

"Now Speckles is dead! Oh my god, Speckles is dead!" Aimee shouted.

Jack tried to console her and Margie tried to think what to say, to Aimee but also to Auden, a bit embarrassed by her tantrum. She was already in tears and she was really too old to keep doing this.

This was the last thing Margie needed. Even Jack was struggling as he'd used all of his good lines when Polka Dot had passed: the circle of life, death being part of life, that sometimes these things happen. Margie had to dig deep, to think hard.

"At least Speckles had a good life, I mean he was happy, of that I'm sure. He got to swim around all day in the warm sun, in a beautiful environment, the perfect place for a turtle. We should all be so lucky! And, Aimee, that is mostly because of the rocks and moss you gathered."

"Mom, who cares about the *stupid* rocks, the *stupid* moss? That doesn't make Speckles any less dead!"

"I know, honey. But we don't even really know the lifespan of these turtles. Auden, do you have any idea how long turtles are supposed to live?"

"They can live for years and years actually. You know the giant tortoises of South America can live much longer than humans, for up to 150 years. Can you believe that?" He looked at the kids for effect. "They migrate to Mexico each year and lay their eggs, and then walk slowly all the way home. Isn't that incredible?"

What a know-it-all, thought Margie. But at least his insights were changing the subject, cheering the kids up a little. Oliver at least, who asked him more questions about how the mothers protect the fragile eggs. Aimee pressed him on what could cause such a small turtle like Speckles to die. Finally, not having an answer, Auden grew quiet.

Aimee went inside to find another shoebox, this time not bothering to decorate it, and placed the tiny turtle corpse inside, asking if they could have another funeral tomorrow. Margie said of course they could. But Aimee continued to brood throughout the cookout, snapping at Oliver and making morose comments.

"This house is a death trap," she said in an unnaturally low voice, right in the middle of Oliver telling Auden about his exciting soccer game.

"Now Aimee, you interrupted Oliver. Would you like to be excused from the table?" Margie said.

She sulked off to her room to continue to pout in private. Shortly after, Oliver followed her inside to play. When Jack disappeared to try to console Aimee, Margie realized the mistake she'd made, leaving just Auden at the table—and leading to the moment she'd been dreading.

She busied herself clearing the picnic table, but to no avail.

"So how's it going Margie?" he asked.

"It's fine, you know, just same old same old, busy with work and the kids. We went to the lake yesterday. How are things with you?"

"Oh, I'm good. Just fine. I meant how are things going with the, er, situation?"

"What situation? Oh, you mean what we talked about the other day? Well I was just being overly dramatic, that's all. I apologize. It was probably just PMS or something." Here she laughed. "No big deal. I have a tendency to exaggerate—*in case you haven't noticed!*"

"Well, it sounded pretty serious to me, Margie," he said, leaning his bushy face closer, wild strands of his beard poking out inches from her face, his big brown eyes piercing hers. "If you ever need to talk, you can call me any time. I mean that. I care about you and Jack, really. I have a huge amount of respect for him, been trying to send positive vibes your way."

Positive vibes? thought Margie. *I need more than vibes to get me out of this mess. I need cold hard cash.*

"Thanks Auden," she said. "That means a lot to me. Now let's get you another cold beer. Jack should be out any second." She went upstairs to retrieve Jack, and the two men continued to talk late into the night, long after she retired. *About what?* she wondered.

The next morning there was another turtle carcass floating in the pond. This one she and Jack removed with a net before Aimee had a chance to notice, flinging it far over the fence instead of giving it a proper burial.

Margie moved through the next couple of weeks in a daze, preoccupied. Even the first week of school had been a blur. She had rushed around buying school supplies, selling meds, greeting the new teachers, meeting old friends at Starbucks—and even once in a shady parking lot. She juggled the women's needs, the children's needs, and her needs, which now included speaking to Stevie on the phone once a week. He had begun texting her as well, which she had sworn she wouldn't allow. It was too easy for anyone in her family to lean over and peer at the phone and see not only the sender's name but also the first few lines of an incoming text, even before she had unlocked her phone. But she had kind of been forced to text him back, for fear of seeming rude, and banter had followed, though she asked him to keep it to a minimum.

In fact, a text had come in that afternoon as she was driving home from work, which is probably what distracted her. Upon pulling into the driveway she remembered it was her turn to pick up the kids from Jack's parents' house—and when she arrived they hadn't been fed yet, to her disappointment. The kids really didn't like their grandma's cooking, and Margie didn't blame them. It was bland and the vegetables were overcooked and mushy, prepared by and for people with dentures. Margie couldn't stomach it herself, but it was a big help to her family. Their grandma explained that they hadn't eaten yet because the kids were having too much fun in the neighbor's pool. Now they were happy and hyper, both dark tan, with Aimee's stringy, sun-dried hair falling down her back and Oliver's dark curls wild and unruly.

Margie suddenly saw this as an opportunity. She asked the kids what they would like for dinner, said they could choose anything they wanted, listing their favorite fast food joints: Burger King, Sonic, Little Caesars. They picked Sonic and she jerked the car around back towards town, making a U-turn in the middle of the highway. She and Jack had both been making a special effort with Aimee—well, Jack always made an effort, she was making a special effort—who was still upset about the turtles.

And apparently, according to the principal, she had been acting out in class in the new school year. A few days prior both she and Jack had received calls; she had let hers go to voicemail whereas Jack picked up. The principal told Jack that Aimee had pushed a girl off the jungle gym, prying her legs off while she was hanging upside down, causing the child to scrape her hands and knees. Could have been worse, the principal warned: the girl could have cracked her skull.

"That was a bit melodramatic," Margie had said to Jack. "It sounds to me just like child's play, like innocent roughhousing."

"Yes, but yanking a kid's legs off like that? It does sound a bit cruel, Margie, don't you think?"

They confronted Aimee in bed that night, asking her if she did it and why.

"I don't like that girl, Becky Boddington, and that's why I had pushed, well actually *pulled* her legs off one by one," Aimee had explained.

"Is she a bully?" Margie then asked.

"No, not really," Aimee had said. "Her hair is messy and she wears ugly clothes."

Margie worried then, thinking about the hand-me-downs she and her brother had to wear, and told Aimee so, and how many others are less fortunate, that not every little girl had a closet overflowing with clothes along with matching hair bows and over thirty pairs of shoes. She seemed to understand and was especially empathetic about Margie's unfortunate circumstances growing up, but really hadn't looked all that sorry.

"It's not like you to pick on someone, Aimee, and we're disappointed in your behavior. Think about how she must have felt. And she could have been hurt. Consider this a warning," Jack had said, wrapping up the conversation. Afterwards Margie and Jack spoke about whether they should ground her from her tablet or TV, but Margie argued she had been through a lot the last couple of weeks, and as such she had made an unspoken mental note to spend more time with her daughter. Which she was doing now at Sonic.

Margie decided to get the burgers to go and entered the drive-through, but both children begged to eat in the car to get the full Sonic experience, where friendly waiters had once glided out on roller skates in the sixties and seventies but now sauntered out in sneakers, sulking from the heat. Many were pierced in places that pained her and copped attitudes, she remembered from her last few visits. But finally she indulged them, driving over a median to exit the line, pulling into a stall. The car was crooked and too far from the electronic menu, forcing her to stretch out her entire arm and then half her torso through the window.

"Damn it," she said having to open the car door to reach the order button.

It was far too hot in the car even with the windows down and she was sweating like a pig, barely able to enjoy her tater tots with cheese. So she blasted the air conditioner and the music, finding a radio station the kids liked. Between bites they sang along to a Katie Perry song. Even though Margie wasn't a fan of Katie Perry or this song, "Tiger," with all of its echo effects disguising what she didn't consider a great voice—she was no Madonna after all—she had heard it many times. She didn't know the lyrics, but they did, even Oliver who was only six, or rather, seven. The kids belted out the chorus about thunder shaking the ground, especially Aimee, who revved up to a powerful crescendo ending in *you're gonna hear me roar*. With the "you" being Margie, apparently, considering how Aimee was glaring at her. Yikes, Margie thought.

But it was so dang cute that she recorded it in order to post on Facebook later that night. In just a few takes, she got a perfectly precious video. At times she found her children so adorable that she wondered why she couldn't seem to really connect with them on a deeper level.

SEPTEMBER

With the Paris trip six weeks away, Margie knew she needed to talk to Jack, to tell him her alibi, whether it was a fake conference or a fabricated seminar. Fortunately she had been brainstorming on this for months. She had only travelled for work once in her career to a seminar on responding to emergency situations. She could tell him she had to update her certification, although she wasn't technically certified: it had been more of an overview of possible life-threatening scenarios involving gunmen, robberies, terrorist attacks, bomb threats, and blackouts. Unsurprisingly, not one of the scenarios had ever occurred in Prairie Mound.

Or she could tell him she was required to take a class to learn new software they were incorporating into the system, an entire hospital overhaul. Hell, it could be anything. She considered saying it was a class on political correctness—something she could benefit from with her big mouth, she would joke.

She was leaning toward the second option and needed to tell him in preparation, but instead she prepared another way, logging onto Amazon.com. The Coach handbag she wanted was 450 dollars. Margie wanted to look successful, sophisticated. Stevie knew her humble beginnings and it's not that she felt she needed to impress him, but well, it would be nice to. Stevie had lived in an upper-middle class neighborhood, which in those parts meant having a three or four bedroom brick house in one of the "nicer" subdivisions. She thought back to his block, trying to envision what his house looked like. Its faded beige brick and the cool tree house in front crystallized in her mind and she remembered his family had even had a pool, a sign of being rich in the outer suburbs, and the closest these small-town folks came to displaying wealth, or what they considered wealthy anyway.

Once Margie set her mind on something she really had trouble letting it go. Especially when it came to objects, like the Coach purse, she could be very focused. She would need a couple of new outfits, but for those she would go to the mall; she didn't like to buy clothes online with her challenging figure. She was a size six in dresses—which for someone five foot five wasn't bad—but an eight or sometimes even a ten in jeans, to her horror. Besides, shopping at the mall was more immediate, and therefore more satisfying, even though the crowds irritated her, and she knew it would be packed on a Saturday afternoon, especially at the Galleria, where she intended to go instead of the shitty mall across from the Olive Garden. Jack was working a half-day while she half-watched the kids, and when he got home, she asked him if he would mind if she went to the mall for a couple of hours.

"What in the world are you buying *now* Margie? You just had a huge splurge!"

She decided to tell him right then and there on the spot. "It's just that there's this seminar that I have to go to next month to learn a new software, a whole new system, really, that the hospital is switching over to. I've been meaning to tell you and I just found out on Friday for sure that they want me to go. It's from a Friday to a Monday, over a long weekend in Paris, Texas. The third weekend of October, I think."

"You've always wanted to go to Paris but that's probably not what you had in mind," he teased. "And why the hell did they schedule it on a weekend?"

"I guess they planned it that way so people will have to miss less work. Believe me, it's not how I want to spend my weekend. But I feel like it could lead to a promotion; a few of us from the hospital are going, and I guess that's why I want to make a good impression. I need a couple of new work outfits anyway." In fact she had been asked by her supervisor to meet on Monday, and Margie wondered if it was for the promotion she felt she deserved—and had told Stevie she had received—but kept that information from Jack for now.

"Well go ahead and get yourself a couple of things…but don't go overboard, okay?" he said.

The upscale shopping mall was flocked with people, but the clientele was so civilized and refined that the atmosphere was pleasant. Yes, she was in the right place and fit in well with the chic outfit she'd put together for the occasion. She decided to start big, at Neiman Marcus.

One of her "work outfits" was actually a bright yellow sundress, fitted in all the right places, flaring out below the waist and falling above her knees. Even though she wished she could lose ten pounds, it really did look flattering. The weather in October in Texas was so mild that it should be perfect, but she bought a little black cashmere sweater to layer just in case. She bought a second more casual outfit, though no less expensive, and then headed to the accessories section of the store. They had the Coach handbag she had her eye on in stock and in her desired color, which she considered a sign. Was 450 dollars going overboard, for a designer brand? She didn't think so. She tried to force herself to like one of the 350-dollar styles, but they were far too small to hold all of her stuff. She was the kind of person who had everything anyone could need: a hairbrush, an eyelash curler, tweezers, lip liner, Band Aids, gum, granola bars, pepper spray, a mirror, tissues, hand lotion, lip balm, disinfectant. No one working in an emergency room should be without these items; a simple stick of sugarless gum often cheered up her younger patients.

So she paced the store with purse in hand to debate the purchase further, the wad of heavy clothing clutched in her other arm so tightly that her hand began to cramp up. However, she passed the shoe section while she paced, and found two pairs of shoes that would complete her outfits perfectly. When the sales clerk rang up the total her items came to over 1200 dollars, a receipt she would have to perform some serious work on.

Returning home, she stuffed the items into her closet, not modeling them as she sometimes did, only showing the shoes, saying the work clothes weren't that exciting.

"Those are for the *office*? Won't the high heels be uncomfortable at work?" Jack asked.

"These are my power shoes! Welcome to the new millennium, Jack. People wear open-toed shoes to the office all the time now."

She thanked him for watching the kids, and now took over, plopping onto the sofa with her cell phone in hand. Jack was being nice enough, making an effort, but she could tell underneath it all he was annoyed with her. By his mannerisms and his movements, which seemed contained, smaller somehow, with his shoulders always slumped, and his tone of voice also overly controlled and solemn. That, and the fact that he seemed to be hiding from her in other rooms of the house, never settling in near where she was sitting.

Maybe he was still perturbed about her selling the meds to Katie, or perhaps because she had blown off his beloved Florida trip, on his same strip of sand. She just could not pretend to be excited, could not get on board, no matter how many times he mentioned it. Had he been more creative in his choice of destinations, maybe she would have been more enthusiastic, and she hoped it would be a lesson to him. And now that it was September, he had dropped the subject a few weeks ago—she hoped—saying, "It looks like we're not going to Florida this year." Indeed.

But she knew he was disappointed and decided to make his favorite dinner: steak, peas, and mashed potatoes. She was engrossed in cooking, a skill that took all of her concentration, the little bit she had left. The guys were outside and Aimee had just come in to cool off on the couch with her tablet.

"Mom? *Mom!*"Aimee squealed from the living room. Oh for fuck sake, thought Margie, I hope it's not another dead turtle.

"*What?*"

"Something weird just happened on my iPad. There's some random old dude on my computer, like a message box just popped up and it says: *Hey there, cutie, what's up?* Margie froze in her tracks, clutching a potato. Aimee continued. "*Mom*, it says his name is Steve. Do you think he's some kind of *creep?*"

Margie rushed over, leaving a pot on the stove that was boiling over. Her heart had jumped from her chest and her pulse was pounding loudly in her inner ear. She had to stop him before he fired off something even more indiscrete. She wondered if she could quit out of the application before getting caught or whether she would need to concoct a lie and what it should it be, maybe saying it was some long-lost crazy cousin, or a nutjob from the ER.

"Let me see that thing," she said, grabbing the device out of Aimee's arms. "I'll bet some wires just got crossed in cyberspace; I'm sure it's a mistake and he has the wrong email address."

"But it's not in email, Mom, it's in iChat and it seems like he has gotten into my address book, see?" she said, looking worried, unconvinced.

Sure enough Stevie's name—and a small photo icon—appeared in the address list. Of course. She'd used Aimee's iPad the other day, and she'd forgotten to close the app, to delete the name. How could she have been so careless?

"He looks kind of familiar...do you *know* him, Mom?"

"*What are you up to tonight, my dear?*" now appeared with a bling, invading the screen and assaulting Margie's senses. She was sure that

Aimee could feel her trepidation, would notice her frenzied movements.

"No, I have absolutely no idea what's going on." She put the tablet on her lap and tilted just out of Aimee's view, who leaned over to watch while she typed.

"Excuse me, but I think you're trying to reach someone else. This computer belongs to Aimee Moore, and I am ten years old."

"Almost eleven," Aimee corrected.

"???"

Silence. Margie hoped he grasped the situation, and quickly. But there was a long delay.

"Sorry kid, you're right, I was trying to reach someone else." He left the chat abruptly and Margie deleted his contact.

"That was so weird, right Mom? It was like he thought he knew me. That gave me the *willies.*"

It gave Margie the willies too, and she was a bundle of nerves as she cleaned up the mess on the stove and put dinner on the table. The peas were overcooked to a greenish-grey mush.

To her dismay, Aimee rehashed the story in detail over supper, animated in front of her new audience.

"Let's not relive it, Aimee," she said.

"What I don't understand," she continued, "is how his name got into my address book without me inviting him or him accepting the invitation. It just makes no sense!"

"What a pervert," Jack said. "We should look his name up and report him. See, Margie, I *told* you the kids were too young to have their own iPads."

Margie suggested a family movie afterwards, for any distraction, for any escape, and they all watched *Back to the Future*, which ironically hadn't stood the test of time, in her opinion. All the while she worried whether Aimee would put two and two together and remember him from before as "the man in the hat."

On Monday Margie dressed up for work, looking extra professional. She wore her new heels, which did in fact make her feel more powerful. The highest she had ever worn to the office, they tripped her up as she was manuevering to sit down at her desk. She ended up turning her ankle and fell hard into her chair. Her important meeting was at two, and after a short lunch break she went to her supervisor's office.

"Oh, hi Margie, can you shut the door?" Mrs. Jones said. A nice, competent woman in her fifties, she was called Mrs. Jones by everyone, even though Margie had been working with her for over a decade.

A closed-door meeting? This very well could mean a raise and maybe a big one. Margie sat up straight and smoothed her skirt, waiting for some acknowledgement and then the big announcement.

"Margie, how are you doing? Is...everything alright at home?"

Pleasantries were a necessity of course. "Oh, yeah, things are good. Jack's landscaping business has really done well this summer and the kids are doing just great. Oliver's excelling at soccer—nearly kicked in a goal the other day—and Aimee, well, she is becoming a preteen, almost eleven, and has the attitude to match."

"What I mean, Margie, well, the reason I called you in here, is that Dr. Renquist, you know, the new pharmacist, has noticed that you have several prescriptions from multiple doctors in the hospital, and it was kind of a red flag for her, so she brought it to my attention. We looked at your medication history here at the hospital, and while there have been many over the years, there are more than ever over the last few months, with two prescriptions for benzodiazepines, and two more for opiates. And a couple of the prescriptions are still active and provide refills."

Margie was stunned into silence. So Mrs. Jones continued.

"Now I need to ask you what's going on here. You do an excellent job at the front desk, and you don't seem impaired at work. But do you have a problem, Margie? Are you taking the drugs for recreational use?"

She felt her chest constrict as she knew lately she had done just that. Not often, maybe once a week or so, but still she would never admit to it, would flat out deny it. Instead she went to her usual spiel, which flowed out so naturally by now she almost believed it herself.

Margie took a deep breath. She explained the Zumba class and throwing out her shoulder, a story she drew out in order to buy time, as always, and mentioned how she had hurt her back lifting Oliver—and how big he was getting. She explained that both she and Jack had horrible insomnia, and sometimes took pills for that. But that only came to two prescriptions, and she wasn't sure where to go from there.

"Margie, first of all, those symptoms wouldn't require so many prescriptions. You know, a lot of hospital personnel develop addictions, especially the nurses. This is not uncommon. Do you take the pills at home to get high?"

Oh god, this wasn't what she was expecting. She couldn't believe it was happening, like something out of a made-for-TV movie. She had to think fast. She looked down at her power shoes.

"I suppose when I take Oxycontin for the shoulder pain and to help with my sleeping, it does give me a warm fuzzy feeling, but I don't take any drugs during the day, at work or at home. What it is, is that I have a friend who is a freelancer and has no insurance, and she is really going through some things, suffering from depression—and anxiety—and that is who the Valium is for, to be completely honest. And the Ambien is for Jack's dad, who is eighty-eight and forgets to go to the drug store to pick up his meds, and so I just thought it was easier to get it for him. I know it must look bad, but honestly I'm just trying to help a couple of people out."

"Well, I must admit, the healthcare in our country is atrocious. But still, it is not legal to get prescriptions filled for other people, and I'm quite sure you're aware of that."

"I guess I just thought these situations were kind of an exception, but now I see what you mean. Jack's poor old pop has so many issues, PTSD from Vietnam, high blood pressure and, oh, what is it called…"

"I feel for him Margie, but getting back to the subject at hand, getting meds for other people including your husband goes against federal regulations. After speaking with Dr. Renquist at length, I have decided to place you on probation."

"Oh, god, Leslie," here she slipped and called her by her first name. "I can't not work here, I can't lose my job. We are just squeaking by and I'm in debt up to my ears, to tell you the truth." Shit, why did she always take things a step too far? Lately she was over-sharing, and not just harmless gossip but information that made her look bad.

"This is a serious situation and you've put me in a precarious position. People have been fired for less. I am legally required to report this; if I don't, I could lose *my* job. Getting prescriptions from doctors on the side, without proper documentation or even an examination, well it makes us *all* look bad. It's only because you have been such a good long-term employee that I'm extending you the option of probation… but if you continue to break hospital protocol I'll have no choice but to terminate your employment here."

Margie could feel her pulse, reverberating through her body all the way to her fingers and toes. The room turned to television static, and she lost her peripheral vision. She wondered if this is what it felt like to have a panic attack, if she was in the midst of an actual panic attack. The top of her head tingled, and as Mrs. Jones continued the words sounded jumbled and distant, as if they'd traveled through a long tunnel before reaching her ears. But the tone came through loud and clear; she had never heard Mrs. Jones sound so austere, and her manner made

Margie grasp the seriousness of the situation. She took a deep breath, refocused, and changed her tune accordingly, making no more excuses.

"Thank you, Mrs. Jones, for giving me another chance to make this right. You will not be sorry and I won't let you down."

Mrs. Jones informed her that it was a temporary probation just in terms of prescriptions, that they would put a hold on her account for three months, and then they would assign a doctor to her—*one* doctor—and evaluate her mental and physical health at that time, that she should come to the hospital and perform her job as normal, and that no one else on the staff would need to know.

Her eyes burned as she walked back to her desk, fighting tears. Her job was one of the few things she took pride in. One of the few things she was really good at. She had never before even been reprimanded, and now she was being punished, making her feel unethical, immoral—and just awful. Not that she considered it a major crime—but she hadn't been careful. Like with Aimee's iPad, she had been reckless.

And now her very job was at stake.

Regardless of what Mrs. Jones had said, she worried that everyone in the hospital was already talking about her. In this two-bit town news like this would spread faster than a backwoods wildfire. Jack hadn't broached the subject of her selling meds to Katie again, but he would be furious if he knew she was dealing to an array of women stretching from here to downtown Dallas.

With her current stock and recent refills she could keep selling to the girls for a few more months, even sacrificing some of her own extensive stash if necessary. Besides, she still had friends at the downtown hospital where she worked in her twenties whom she could call if she was desperate for meds. The even bigger issue—and this was already a biggie, affecting her very employment—was beginning to see that the whole venture might not solve all her problems as she'd hoped. Especially with her most recent spree.

She would tell no one about this, not Jack, not Auden, not Stevie, not Katie. She would take this secret, this humiliation, to the grave. She was meeting Katie to catch up at Carbucks in a few days time and she would not divulge no matter what. She would give her a small amount of meds and say she was running low—maybe it was *Katie* who was addicted at the rate she went through them.

When she saw Katie, she didn't let it slip out, even though it had been on her mind nonstop. She hated getting in trouble, hated to disappoint, hated her situation, but she persevered, pushing through each day working harder than ever. While she waited for Katie she thought about the giraffe, whom, when she walked past in the hall the other day, had given her a brief knowing smile then turned away. She hated being snubbed, hated being seen as "having a problem." Although she knew she had many.

It was a relief to see Katie, to think about something else. And she listened, her minor problems a welcome relief, their laughter just the right medicine. While Margie didn't mention the incident at work, she did tell her about Paris and her alibi. She wanted just one person in the world to know the truth, in case there was an emergency, so she gave her the dates.

"Stevie's company is flying him down of course, and I'll drive. My plan is to arrive at the hotel a couple of hours before him to freshen up. I'm just a horrible traveler. I always look so exhausted—seriously, like hammered dog shit—and I'll text you the name of the hotel when I get it. He's choosing the hotel. Isn't that *romantic*? I asked him to find something historical and charming…maybe a little bed and breakfast. I've never stayed in one before, if you can believe that. I know, it's sad really, but anyway, I'll text you the name, in case he's a serial killer," here she burst out laughing. "I am a little nervous, but in a good way I guess."

"I can't believe you're really going to do it," Katie said. Margie couldn't gauge from the flat tone whether it was said in support or in disgust, but she had a suspicion it was the latter.

"Yes, I'm really going to do it," Margie said, equally matter-of-fact.

"Well, for the record, I don't think you should," Katie replied, eliminating any ambivalence.

"Hmph," Margie muttered under her breath. Not knowing what else to say, she put on her jacket and began to gather her things.

It was a busy month for Margie with preparations for her trip, not just her own planning but for the kids and Jack; she had travelled alone only twice since they'd been married. She made arrangements with Jack's parents to help out with the babysitting after school and printed out an oversized calendar, marking up after-school activities, birthday parties and the like.

And of course she had to coordinate with Stevie, to find a subtle, sneaky way to ask for his flight number; which technically she didn't need but she wanted in case there were delays, which was crucial to her plan to get there two hours early in order to freshen up. He would rent a car and drive an hour and a half from the nearest airport. She still hoped he rented a convertible.

She had scheduled phone calls with Stevie, along with their regular instant messaging, most of which took place at work, especially with the near miss that had happened at home. She had warned him about the severity of the situation, subtly blaming him for the slip up rather than herself for the indiscretion. She was paranoid about how much Aimee knew, being more careful than ever to shut down instant message windows at home and to monitor her expressions while she read incoming texts, keeping her face serious and even solemn at all times, teaching herself to let her eyes glaze over, like when she was on meds—vacant—to make sure they didn't reveal even a glimmer. She was at work now, when an instant message popped up.

"*Hey baby,*" he typed. *Baby?* He'd never called her baby before but the phone calls did make things feel more intimate.

"*Hiya, how you doin' Cowboy?*" using the new nickname she had recently given him.

"*Are you excited about the trip?*" he asked.

"*Hell yeah!*" she said. "*I really have a lot to do the next few weeks; it's just insane. Meetings and appointments, making sure to have a sitter while Jack is working. I guess I should make a casserole or two. You know what they say, a woman's work is never done!*" She really didn't have that many appointments, and no real meetings.

"*I'm easy. I just have to throw some clothes into a suitcase and I'll be good to go.*"

"*You are easy,*" she teased.

"*Well don't go overboard, Margie. You don't need to pack that many clothes yourself. Wink wink.*"

"*You are such a bad boy!*" She blushed; she wasn't good at talking dirty and wished she could take it back by pressing a key to "undo." She wasn't really comfortable with sexting, as the kids called it, but then again, she liked being flirted with.

"*But seriously, Marge, it will be fun. We'll just hang out. It will be casual, laid-back, relaxing. Nothing in the world to worry about. Won't that be nice?*"

It would be nice to have nothing to worry about, she thought to herself; that would be an absolute dream at this point, and probably an unattainable one. But she said, "*Yeah, I know. I can't wait. I love exploring new places.*"

"*And exploring new people.*"

"*Oh Stevie, you're making me blush...I have to go do some filing.*"

"Wanna talk on the phone tonight?"
"I don't think I can do tonight, but soon, okay?"

As the rendezvous grew closer and the days passed one by one, she was more and more anxious, and since the incident in her supervisor's office where her vision and her world had gone grey, she had experienced what she was convinced were more minor panic attacks. She would be momentarily paralyzed by a sharp instant of dread, as real as the feeling of cutting one's finger with a knife, which she had done recently while chopping celery, in that split second before the pain registers when one wonders how deep the cut is, whether it will draw blood, and if so, how much.

To get through these debilitating attacks she focused her energy on each task at hand: picking up the kids from school, running them around to play dates, putting food on the table, constantly doing dishes. She made it to a couple of Oliver's games, and she was making an effort with Aimee, who was fully aware another turtle had passed, keeping close count. She ran out to check the pond every day before and after school, monitoring their movements and analyzing their behavior, as if by doing so she personally could keep them all safe. Just the other day she had told Margie that Puddles was acting weird, coming up too often for air, eyes bulging, lips curled like a fish in place of his usual upturned line of a smile.

While driving Aimee home from yet another of Oliver's soccer games one evening—she was beginning to wonder if the season would ever end—Margie was trying to suggest activities that might take her mind off the turtles, provide a diversion. It was just the two of them, a rarity, as Jack and Oliver were riding home in the Manscaping van.

"What do you think about ballet lessons or tap dancing? That would be fun."

No response. Lately she seemed so apathetic, so gloomy, so moody, most of which seemed directed at Margie herself. She wondered if after the iPad incident Aimee suspected she was having an affair. Yet she was only eleven, almost, and Margie hoped she wasn't astute or perceptive enough to suspect such scenarios.

"Maybe there is a mother-daughter class. Can you imagine me trying to tap with how clumsy I am? That would be a riot."

"No, Mom," she said, rolling her eyes.

"Well what would *you* like to do? Maybe a music class or an art class? You're good at drawing. I can see if there are any programs through the local community college or maybe through the chamber of commerce."

"I don't want to do a *boring class*! I want to do fun things, like go to the zoo or Six Flags or an art museum."

Like mother, like daughter, Margie thought. "That's the spirit," she said. "I like to do fun things too believe it or not." She was thinking about whether there was something they could do before the trip—the trip!—or whether it would have to wait until after.

"Well you never do fun things with *me*."

The simple statement struck her to the bone, like a kick in the shin. Her cheeks burned. Aimee was right: she couldn't think of the last time the two of them did something "fun," or anything at all together. She needed to do something and she needed to do it now, so she jerked the car around. "Do you want to get a manicure and pedicure, just you and I, right now? A little pampering, just for us girls?"

"Yeah, sure, I guess," she said.

Killing two birds with one stone, she desperately needed one before meeting Stevie. While Margie sometimes painted her nails at home, Aimee had never had a professional mani-pedi, and she jumped and jerked as her toenails were poked and prodded. But she looked utterly relaxed as they massaged her petite ankles and feet. Margie tried to engage her in conversation, asking about schoolwork and her friends from school, hoping for girlie gossip about friendships and such, maybe even boys. But Aimee always answered in single syllables. Well sometimes just being together is enough, thought Margie.

"Mom," she said finally, "remember when that guy Steve showed up in my chat app and started talking to me?"

"Yes?" she said calmly. But her heart pounded and her face was on fire. She bit her lip too hard and drew blood, tasting the iron. Had it happened *again*? I mean how well did she really *know* Stevie? Was she being catfished, or worse, *was* he some kind of *pervert*?

"That was really weird, huh? That was so hilarious." Aimee laughed, caught up in a preteen-powered giggling fit.

Was that it, Margie wondered? She breathed a sigh of relief when she realized—or hoped—it was nothing more than a shared memory, a bonding moment, and then started laughing hysterically too.

When they got home it was ten o'clock, late for a school night. The two of them ate some leftovers, again in near silence before she put both kids to bed. Jack was in the living room, flipping channels.

Margie let out a deep sigh while dropping heavily into her section of the sofa. Even though she didn't love the living room, the new coffee table making everything else look dated by comparison, she always found her indention on the couch welcoming and sank into it, hoping that wouldn't trigger Jack to head off to his laundry-office-weight room. She was relieved when he stayed put.

Unwinding, they caught up about their days, exchanging random tidbits. Margie was just happy to have a conversation using full sentences and eye contact after her evening with Aimee. Jack mentioned that because he was still busy at work Auden was going to stay on through the fall, maybe all year. This made Margie tense up again, brought back the knife-slicing sensation in her fingertips. September was supposed to be his last month. She was ready to be rid of him.

"*Really?*" Margie questioned. "Shouldn't a bright kid like that be in college? I mean what if you slow down in the fall, which often happens? You'll feel obligated to keep him on. Be careful not to put yourself in that situation," Margie advised.

"Why are you always so pessimistic, Margie? This is the best the company has done in years and that's all you have to say? *God.*"

Margie really didn't feel like being alienated by yet another family member. "I'm sorry," she said, with a weary smile. "I *am* glad business is good. You should keep him if you think it's best."

Margie was juggling a lot before her trip and her mind was jumbled, trying to get everything just right, hoping she could pull it off without a hitch. She had to do lists within to do lists, which had spawned separate to do lists, with lines and arrows connecting them, diagrams in chicken scratch only she could understand. She fed the kids, fed her friends meds, and fed Jack more bullshit: details about the conference, going so far as to tell him the schedule, making up events and lectures filling up the entire four days. She knew she had gotten carried away but then she had never done anything like this before.

Adultery. She didn't like the sound of it, didn't like the biblical word itself and it kept her up at night, reminding her of the fiery sermons she had been forced to sit through growing up, about sin and unrighteousness, about burning in hell for eternity. She couldn't shake off the imagery scorched into her mind. Yet she didn't want to cancel the "conference." Because it would be an *adventure.* She did like the sound of that word, and it was the one thing that propelled her forward.

Meanwhile the following week there was a real conference she had to attend: of the student-teacher variety. Aimee had been acting out in school again. She and Jack agreed to go together, neither knowing what it was about, both taking off work on a Thursday afternoon. Aimee's teacher told them her behavior had changed of late.

"She is usually such an outstanding child who does well in school and gets along with others, but lately she is bullying the less-fortunate kids and lying to the more popular ones. She has been coming up with fabrications, well, at least I think they are fabrications. For example, Aimee said last week you were, or are building a huge swimming pool with gold statues and fountains, and was announcing who she would and wouldn't invite to a swim party, yelling out *you can't come, you can't come*, to the kids of...how should I put it...of a lower income, while inviting the kids she considers cool to a fantastical party."

Margie and Jack looked at each other, stunned, mouths ajar.

"Is this true, are you building a pool?"

"No," said Jack.

"She said you, Margie, were taking her to Disneyland over Christmas and she could bring along three friends, of course choosing two popular girls and a well-liked boy. Is this true?"

"Afraid not," said Margie.

She told them of another situation where Aimee pretended to lose a real diamond ring on the playground, getting three teachers involved until she finally came clean. "Just effing with you," she had said. The list went on and on. She told someone that her parents were buying her a prize pony during social studies, she threw a dodge ball right at Jenny Johnson's face at close range in P.E., announced that her dad drove a Porsche in the middle of math class, and pushed over a girl's bike after school.

At home that night they would have to have another family discussion with Aimee. Truth be told, Margie probably dreaded family talks more than her daughter. Her family had never had any, just drunken yelling and rage followed by unspoken regret and guilt-driven niceties. She supposed it was a good thing to have these talks, a sign of a good family, but it always reminded her of an episode of *Growing Pains* or *Family Ties*. She pictured Alan Thicke talking to cute Kirk Cameron, of whom she used to have an oversized poster taped up in her undersized bedroom when she was in junior high. But in real life it didn't always end in a family-sized lesson learned, a clear-cut moral of the story, followed by laughter all around, then more canned laughter.

She had no idea where Aimee got the bullying from. Margie had never bullied anyone in her life. She had some idea of where she was getting the lying from. Could she sense it? She knew kids were very observant, but what *exactly* had she observed? Maybe a suspect window left open on Margie's own laptop or phone? Or even a sparkle in her eye while she was daydreaming, fantasizing about Stevie? While she had tried to mask her expressions in direct communication, she had forgotten to control the times when she was lost in thought, especially the days on the rare occasion when she had popped a pill. Speaking of which, could Aimee possibly have overheard a phone conversation with one of her ladies about meds? There were so many indiscretions for her to choose from.

She and Jack had a serious talk with her that night in the living room after they'd put Oliver to bed.

"*Why* did you do and say all these things, Aimee? Why did you feel the need to *lie*?" She hated to see her own faults surfacing in her daughter and came off harsh, realizing she could ask herself the same questions. The to whom, about what, where and when she was all too aware of, and yet she had never asked herself *why*. But this was about Aimee at the moment, and she refocused on her.

Aimee clammed up, looking sheepish, staring down at her sandals.

"I mean I just don't see why you felt the need to make these things up. You have a lot of nice things already."

Margie wasn't getting through to her. Jack jumped in.

"Aimee, can you explain to us why you did it so we can try to understand? The stories about the swimming pool and the Porsche?"

"I don't know…I guess I just wanted the kids to like me more. I mean getting picked up from school in that beat up van, well it's kind of embarrassing. Mom, you hate it too."

"Well it's not that I *hate* it exactly, it's just that it's sometimes dirty with loose soil and gravel knocking around."

"That's my point."

"But that's how your father makes a living. And he has his own company, and a very successful one of late."

Aimee was silent and didn't meet their eyes.

"Aimee," Jack said to the top of her forehead. "Can you look at me when I'm talking to you? People will like you for who you are, and no one likes a braggart. That's not the way to make friends. It sounds to me like you need to appreciate what you have."

Margie didn't saying anything, knowing this was not her area of expertise.

"It's just that I don't think the popular kids like me that much. See, there's this group, called the Preteen Princesses, they made up the names themselves, with Anne and Kim and Claire in it, and they do everything together and won't let me hang around with them."

Margie recalled that this was a hard age when girls get very cliquish. "I remember being that age," Margie said. "You're growing up Aimee, and this is a difficult age for girls and will probably last until high school. It might take a few years, but you'll find your own group, people who you can be yourself with and laugh about the silliest things."

"But it sucks being left out."

"Aimee, it does suck sometimes, and life sucks sometimes," Jack said. "But we need to talk about the way you're treating some of your classmates, throwing dodge balls and pushing over bikes. That's not the way to deal with your frustration."

"That was an accident. I didn't mean to throw it that hard. And she was way closer than I thought, which is why the welt swelled up so bad."

"Well what about pushing over the bike?" Jack pressed. "That doesn't sound like something my sweet daughter would do."

"Well I guess I'm not that sweet anymore," she said, looking him directly in the eyes.

"Don't smart off to your father. You need to apologize to this girl, tell her you were having a bad day and you're sorry you took it out on her. And you need to find better ways to deal with your anger…and your disappointment when things don't go your way."

"Okay, fine. Can I please go to bed now?"

Unlike a sitcom, it was unclear whether any lessons were learned. Only time would tell.

Oliver was such a good child, her golden boy, never causing any problems. At least not yet. But even he had grown more solemn and pensive lately, always in his own world, daydreaming, a million miles away. Margie conceded that she herself was a million miles away, yet he had distanced himself further, floating away from her in zero gravity, as if pulled—or pushed—by some invisible force field. What went on inside that head, she wondered.

Late that night she snuck out into the back yard to be alone with her thoughts. She saw two blackish spots on the surface of the dark pond, like two small splotches of oil, shining in the moonlight. Walking closer she saw two more deceased turtles, to her dismay, their carcasses bobbing belly up. This was a dismal day indeed. Apocalyptic even. She realized only one turtle was left. And would it, could it survive? It would surely die of heartbreak and loneliness. Of sheer desperation.

Thinking about how she would tell Aimee, she began to cry. Between sobs she inhaled deeply, gasping for air. She too was suffocating. She wondered if she could endure what she was about to do. Part of her wanted to cancel the trip altogether, but another part, the darker part that was forever searching, argued that if she cancelled she would always be curious. Besides, the chain of events leading up to it were already set in motion, and she felt it was too late to change course.

In bed that night she allowed Jack to spoon her without stiffening up. Then she turned to face him and put her arms around him, holding him tight. She needed the comfort and knew she was using him for just this purpose. She wanted to absorb the strength radiating from him, to bask in his body heat and the comfort it provided. She told him about the two turtles, and more importantly, her concerns about the kids, discussing Aimee's bad behavior further and telling him how even Oliver seemed to be withdrawing from her.

"Sweetie, everything's going to be alright," Jack assured her. "It's just a phase, you'll see. Everything's going to work out fine." She wasn't so sure of that.

The sense of asphyxiation stuck with her throughout the next week. She felt her choices closing in on her, her insides seeming to squeeze tighter together on their own accord, her innards in knots, her organs gripping each other. She blamed it on nerves. But as she finalized every last detail of her trip, she was aware that the anxiety in which she was drowning was a direct result of her bad decisions even as she was making them. Knowing that her life would be forever changed, she was having a harder and harder time rising to the surface, getting enough oxygen into her lungs.

And night after night she kept having the same dream that even her meds couldn't suppress. In it she was digging a massive grave in the backyard and scooping up mounds and mounds of dead turtles, throwing them into the hole with her bare hands. But these turtles didn't have shells; they were slimy blobs of flesh covered in blood and gunk and no matter how many handfuls she hurled in, the pile of vile creatures never got smaller. The dream always ended the same, with her looking down to see the new yellow dress she was wearing smeared with blood.

OCTOBER

The Affair: Day 1

When the big day arrived Margie rose early, a whirlwind of activity. Still having trouble getting enough air, she took shallow breaths. Packing had been tricky as she chose outfits carefully, mentally pairing items and accessories and then slipping them in separately, secretly; it's not like she could lay them out all over her bedroom the night before like she normally would, with Jack lingering around. As a result she had not one but two suitcases, the largest one and the next size down, also large, far too many items for a four-day "conference."

"Holy shit," Jack said when he helped her with her bags. "Is there anything left in your closet?" But he knew good and well the answer was yes.

She was trying to get the luggage into the car before he noticed but kept having to reopen them, re-latch them, then open them again, to shove a necklace in the side pocket, to cram in a pair of high-heeled wedges, sandals, and then mules, and finally the floral silk headscarf she almost forgot, which was integral to her afternoon drive outfit, in case he had indeed rented a convertible. She was wearing cutoff denim shorts and a billowy blouse now, casual and comfortable but still cute enough.

She hugged the kids and kissed Jack goodbye. Unable to meet their eyes, she focused on a point beyond them above the porch, where a rickety light fixture hung out of its socket, a tangle of wires exposed. All three stood in the driveway waving to her, like a scene from an old home movie, standing there too long, she thought, making her feel guilty for wishing they would all just go back inside already. The entire morning had the hazy seventies hue of an aged photograph with saturated colors, exaggerated yellows and reds, evoking a warmth that wasn't necessarily there in the original. She looked away, glancing behind her shoulder as she backed out of the drive and then barreled down the block.

The end of October was usually still nice in Texas, and today was no exception, a perfect seventy-five degrees, sun shining. Yet a couple of miles in—before she'd even made it out of Prairie Mound—she was perspiring heavily and rolled down the windows, a very reckless move considering how much time she had spent on her hair. She suddenly jerked the car to the right and pulled over to the shoulder, lurching to a stop, opened the trunk and dug out her precious scarf. Tying it in a neat knot, she inspected her work in the rearview mirror before bolting back out into traffic. If she was going to do this thing, she was damn well going to do it right!

Besides, she could freshen up at the hotel. His plane landed at DFW at two o'clock, so there was no way he could get there before four, giving her ample time to settle in and relax. She hoped a bottle of wine would be waiting in the room, which she would dip into.

It had been ages since she'd taken a road trip, and upon hitting the highway she found a sense of freedom she'd forgotten. How she loved to drive. Finding an eighties station on the dial, she turned it up loud to compete with the whipping wind, and belted out tunes along with the radio. The sheer volume distorted the sound, which helped hide the fact that she was off key. As if she cared! She wailed along to a Journey song. She too was just a small town girl; she too felt she was living in a lonely world. Rather than on a midnight train she was in her sedan, *going anywhere*...but still it seemed written solely for her. Almost yelling the lyrics now, she took a short break to give her throat a rest.

Before she knew it an hour had passed. Many more songs had been sung and in some ways she didn't want the trip to end. She passed cattle ranches and their peaceful grazing made her introspective. She liked nature, especially cruising through it from the comfort of her air-conditioned car at high speeds. The once sparse landscape became spotted with skinny pine trees, growing denser as she travelled northeast. With only an hour to go, she wished she could just keep driving, leaving her problems farther and farther behind, her worries shrinking and then disappearing through her rearview mirror. Beyond the stress of marriage and motherhood, she was beginning to blame herself for many of her current predicaments. There were obstacles she wanted to outrun, to escape from altogether. She wondered if she really could leave it all behind. No, she couldn't fathom it. Or *could* she? Flying down the highway in two tons of solid steel, she realized that the thing about leaving a place is that you are simultaneously approaching something else, another destination altogether, a different destiny. "Destiny," she said aloud into the time capsule of her car, into the abyss beyond. These were deep thoughts for Margie and for a minute it blew her mind.

She eased up on the gas now, slightly afraid of the actual arrival. She hadn't allowed herself to google photos of the town; she wanted it to be a complete surprise, to approach it all with a child's sense of wonder. Like the time her family drove to South Padre Island. She was eleven actually, and no longer considered herself a child, and she'd declared it an injustice that she'd had to live for over a decade without seeing the sea. They had visited relatives in Mississippi and Alabama, but this was the only true family vacation in her memory. She and her brother had played in the ocean for hours, worrying her mother, pruning up, until the salt stung their eyes and coated their skin.

What would Paris be like? Wedged up at the top of Texas near the border between rural, redneck Oklahoma and illiterate Arkansas, it was not a sophisticated location by any stretch of the imagination. Stevie had booked the hotel as he had promised, which would be yet another surprise, choosing a bed and breakfast a few blocks from the town square called The Old Magnolia Chateau. It sounded lovely; she had never stayed in a chateau, and that's why she was hoping for a bottle of cold white wine in an ice bucket.

Cruising along desolate Highway 82, she finally saw a sign for Paris, the exit in twenty-two miles. Good god, at this speed she would be there in fifteen minutes. Her fingers wouldn't cooperate as she tried to type in the name of the hotel in her GPS, so she had to punch in the address a few times before she got it right, veering off into the shoulder with each attempt. She couldn't believe this was really happening. She had to pee like a racehorse, always did when she got nervous. She spotted a ramshackle gas station. Unsure if it was even open, she jerked the car into the parking lot at the last possible second, nearly slamming into the rickety building, which would have surely finished it off. She used the filthy restroom and applied lipstick, another nervous habit of hers. Then she plopped a Diet Coke and a dusty pack of chewing gum on the counter.

"Where you headed in such a hurry, darlin'?" the ancient attendant asked.

Margie became paranoid, thought about lying, but realized he was a just a harmless old man.

"I'm on my way to Paris, sir. Paris, Texas."

"Well, my friend, you're nearly there. Now you be careful out there, ya hear?"

As she climbed back into the car, the phrase reverberated in her head, sounding more like an ominous warning than a common greeting. She approached the town, wanting to look around but concentrating hard on listening to the GPS. Speaking too quickly in her English accent, the voice sounded anxious too, impatient: *in 200 yards take a LEFT*. Margie knew there were three feet in a yard—but who could think in feet at thirty miles per hour! *In forty yards take a LEFT!* Margie pumped the brakes and skidded around the corner. *In seventy-five yards take a RIGHT.* She made a wide turn into oncoming traffic and then overcorrected. *In thirty yards you will reach your destination!* She flew past it, then saw it in her peripheral vision, screeched to a stop and reversed to park near the curb, misjudging it so that one wheel was actually on the curb. Her nerves were shot.

The chateau was smaller than she expected, but charming nonetheless. She had hoped it would look more chateau-esque somehow, maybe with arched gables liked she'd seen in the movie Amélie. She thought the architecture might be more Victorian, stealing from the French in name only, but she was certainly no expert. Painted the palest shade of green with white trim, it looked clean, minty and fresh. Margie, on the other hand, felt anything but. The trip had been so freeing that she had allowed herself to sweat freely, the thin fabric of her shirt clinging to her back. She had worn flip flops, her preferred driving footwear and now her feet were sliding around as she walked to the front door, toes curled around the thong tightly, cramping up.

She was unsure how to proceed, whether to knock first. Just walking in would feel almost like intruding into someone's home. But she couldn't find the damn doorbell anywhere. She just stood there a moment, before finally knocking too lightly. When no one answered she creaked the door open. On the entryway wall was a huge clock, like an oversized stopwatch, which she hoped was from France. Upon closer inspection she saw that the cracks were printed on and it was just made to look old. In fact the price tag was left on and she saw that it was from Target; at twenty-nine dollars it was certainly no antique. It read two-oh-seven. She'd made perfect time. At least the purple loveseat upholstered in heavy fabric looked authentic, lush, next to a tufted green velvet chair.

She peered into the dining room and it was indeed elegant, with a black chandelier hanging in the center of the room—but was surprised to see only one communal table.

"Hello?" she said too softly, hearing footsteps in another room.

A few seconds later a grandmotherly woman walked in, buxom and bustling. "Oh, hey there, honey. I didn't hear you come in. My name's Bonnie, do you need some help with your bags?" Her drawl was pure Texan—nothing French about it. "Your gentleman friend is already up in the room settling in; I left y'all a bottle of champagne chilling up there, so I hope it's to your liking. It's a scorcher out there today, huh, especially for October, so I left the air conditioner on for ya. Just up the stairs and to your right, in the Oak Room, across from the Peach Tree room; those folks will be coming in later tonight."

"Oh, you mean my gentleman friend, er, Steve, Stevie, I mean Stephen Singleton has already checked in?" Margie asked, now anxious. "He wasn't supposed to be here for another couple of hours." She hoped the old woman was just confused, mistaken.

"He's here alright—arrived about thirty minutes ago. Maybe he wanted to surprise you and here I've gone prattling on, spoiling everything."

"Oh, no, that's alright," Margie said. But her face was a picture of pure panic. "I can get my bags myself, that's no problem. I'm just going to go out to my car for a few minutes, and sort of get organized, you know, well I've got a lot of stuff, too much really. I always over pack, so it might take me awhile, but I'll…I'll be back in a bit."

Margie opened the trunk and grabbed her bulging makeup bag and dug the desired dress out of her suitcase. She felt gross, grimy. There was nothing she despised more than sweating and just as she predicted traveling had made her look tired, her foundation mostly oozed off revealing dark bags under her eyes. She'd hardly slept the night before due to nerves. Even taking three Ambien hadn't helped. She unlocked the back door and crawled in, slouched down, rolled over and wiggled into her bright yellow sundress, which caught around her damp mid-section, until she forced her arms into the flattering sleeves, which now seemed tighter than she remembered as she inched her upper arms through. She moved to the front seat and closed the door, applying ample deodorant even as she continued to perspire. She touched up her makeup, hard to do without glistening again, reapplying powder on an as-need basis. This wasn't how she had planned it at all, dressing in the car like a homeless person, and now she was frazzled when she wanted to be fresh. Once finished, she sat in the car a while longer. Finally, she summoned all of her inner strength, opened the door and pranced up the walk, head held high, carrying only an oversized tote bag.

She knocked once and then walked right in. Bonnie was already there to greet her. Surely she hadn't been watching her this whole time in her car!

"I thought you had a lot of luggage dear, are you sure you don't need any help? I can call my husband from the back."

"No, I'm fine, I really am," she said, reassuring herself. "We'll get it later. Now do I need a key for the room?"

Bonnie placed an old-timey key in her hand with a knowing look. Margie marched up the stairs, rattled the key in the lock to give him plenty of warning, took a deep breath and walked in. Sauntered, really, monitoring her movements. She put down her bag and placed a hand on her hip, one leg slightly in front of the other like she'd seen women stand on the red carpet, wearing her million-dollar smile.

Stevie was leaning back on the bed propped on his elbows, shoes tossed off. He stood up to meet her, smiled back politely, eyes lingering on her a moment before embracing her in a warm hug. He was thinner than she expected, thinner than Jack's solid torso, and her arms looped around on the other side, hands not sure whether to continue around to squeeze his sides or hang loosely behind. His hat was on and when they separated, she was greeted by his dimples, deepened and weathered with time. She could see now that the photos weren't recent. He'd aged well, just more than she'd thought.

Now that she was standing there in the flesh she really didn't know what to say. After all the time she had spent picturing this moment, all of the hypothetical conversations in her head, all of the witty banter she had conjured up, her usually clamorous mind went completely blank.

"How was your trip?" he asked, breaking the silence that at first seemed intimate but was growing more awkward by the second.

"Well I should ask you the same thing. I mean, I only had to drive a couple of hours but it was actually *divine*. Being alone on the open highway was just…so therapeutic. Just *terrific*, truly." Along with her mannerisms her speech was affected, and she didn't sound like herself, not to anyone who really knew her. "What about you, I hope your flight was pleasant? I thought you were arriving two hours from now."

"Yeah, I know, I wanted to surprise you," he said with an impish smirk. "I cancelled my flight and decided to drive. I love road trips too and I just want us to have as much time as possible together. I mean every hour counts, right?"

Oh, how devilish! she almost said. But that really would have been too much. She was trying to be herself, to find herself, or if she was going to put on airs, at least figure out who she was trying to be. "No doubt. I just want to enjoy every moment, drink life in like a true Parisian, you know? Speaking of which, should we open the champagne?"

"Absolutely." He struggled with twisting and popping off the cork. It didn't shoot across the room like Margie anticipated, but plopped to the floor directly in front of him, disappearing into the wild print of the faded floral rug. "Here's to us. And to Paris," he said, and then whispered "Texas."

Margie let out a fantastic burst of laughter that kept echoing in little spurts before it died out. Stevie said he had missed that laugh. They sat at a small table in tufted chairs, more comfortable—and civilized— than sprawling out on the bed right away. Yet conversation really wasn't flowing that well.

But half a bottle later the effects of the alcohol kicked in and they began to loosen up and reminisce. They were old friends after all. Finally sounding like herself, she asked him if he remembered that summer when they'd climbed to the top of a massive oil tank in the dead of night. When he, Stevie, had ridden an oil pump like a steel horse, bucking in the moonlight, the only one brave enough to do so. Was it 1992 or 1993? The summer her cousin from Arkansas had stayed with her, sharing her tiny bedroom, oppressed by her parents' many rules, when they'd snuck out for six nights in a row, climbing out of the window and walking down the long unpaved drive. Night after night Stevie would pick them up in his beat-up pickup truck and then they would head across town to pick up Daniel, the preacher's son no less. They laughed hard about this now. The four of them, a band of teenage bandits, running around town committing minor acts of vandalism. They had snuck past a neighbor's big two-story house and swam in their pond in their summer clothes. They had gone cow tipping—to test out the urban but back-country legend of easily pushing the beasts over with a single shove while they slept standing up. It worked. Only they had chosen a smallish cow, which had tumbled to the ground with barely a shove and then jumped around wild-eyed and crazy, upset, braying, until they felt sorry for it, unsure if it was actually a calf. They had only tipped the one.

"I have such great memories of high school," Stevie said. "They were the best years of my life." Margie found this revelation a little disturbing.

"Well what about your twenties and thirties, they must have been pretty great too. I'm sure you've had many more adventures, and I want to hear all about them."

"They were okay," he said with a wink. He was so damn charming, eyes twinkling like saltwater stars. Well prepared, she pulled out an additional bottle of red wine she'd brought from home and they each poured themselves a glass.

"I don't usually drink this much, I really don't," she explained, "but when in Rome—or Paris—for that matter." She giggled, feeling light-headed. He laughed at her when she took a couple of cubes of ice from the champagne bucket and dropped them in with a plop. The cubes bobbed around and soon began to dissolve, as did her anxiety. The day was going fantastically well, she thought, in the midst of a beautiful hazy afternoon buzz.

They traveled back again to familiar territory, Stevie reminding her of things she'd almost forgotten and vice versa. How he'd warned her when she was a freshman and Wesley Grubbs, a senior, had asked her out, that Wes was bad news. She had said no. He was in jail now, a fact they both knew from Facebook. She remembered calling Stevie crying when she didn't make cheerleader her freshman year. He, the star quarterback, had made her feel better, saying "nobody gives a damn about those silly girls doing their ridiculous dances, least of all the football players." Hours passed as they reminisced, dappled light spilling in sideways through the lacey drapes, the stodgy antique furniture basking in a warm glow. They reminisced about stealing the street signs, first Steven Road, and then finding names of a few of their other friends: Randall Road, Amanda Lane, Monica Drive. There had been no Margie Street. How the next night they had grown bold and driven all the way to Texas State Highway 69, stripping it of five of its signs, larger than they looked, barely fitting in the bed of his pickup. All that before she'd even actually been in the sixty-nine position herself, she said, laughing so hard she nearly fell out of her chair.

At the mention of that number, Stevie's eyes began to dance, then morphed into come-hither bedroom eyes, lids growing heavy. He took her hands in his across the table, came closer, leaned in and kissed her. Maybe she shouldn't have brought up the signs, the position, because she didn't feel ready for this now. She kissed back, but barely. He guided her to the bed, not removing his hat. Yes, she was prepared, but it didn't feel right; this was not the right moment. Their reflections brought back a time of innocence that she didn't want to taint. This would change everything. Besides, she felt a bit drunk. Her head was spinning. The kiss had not been bad and was a nice little teaser of things to come, but although she was attracted to him, she still felt nothing on a deeper level. She had to think fast.

"Stevie, I can't do this right now, not yet, I mean I'm just too tipsy. I'm sorry, I'm such a lightweight these days—I don't know why in god's name I opened a second bottle."

"Sure, that's okay, I understand," he said, like the perfect gentleman he was. But his body language showed his disappointment, shoulders slouched, bottom lip protruding slightly.

"Hey! Let's do something *wild and crazy* like we used to do," she offered, the memories making her feel mischievous, the wine making her bold.

"Margie, you really are nuts. What do you want to do, search for an oil pump in operation? This time *you* can ride it…wouldn't *that* be a hoot. Would that be '*wild and crazy*' enough for you?" he asked with a flirtatious chuckle, using exaggerated air quotes.

He was right; it was ridiculous. But on second thought she thought it sounded like the best idea ever. It was brilliant. In fact she felt she *had* to do it, perhaps to prove something to herself, to signify her new lust for life—and the start of the big adventure that was sure to follow.

"Is that a *dare*?" she asked.

"I *double-dog* dare you."

She changed into a more casual outfit and they walked to his car. It was a royal blue Cutlass Supreme, a classic car but a real beater nonetheless. She worried Stevie was too drunk to be driving, but then again, they hadn't finished the second bottle. Even though her buzz was most definitely spurring her on, she hadn't been as drunk as she had let on. And finding an oil pump in these parts was no problem. The landscape was dotted with the rusted steel rocking horses, some in use and others frozen at all angles in varying states of decay. They drove down side streets that were not streets at all but oil roads built specifically for the purpose of maintaining the pumps and wells. With the windows down, the smell of oil, pine trees and rich manure filled the car. They spotted one rolling gently back and forth in a field, its view mostly obstructed by a few pine trees. She thought Stevie would pull over on the side of the road but he turned the wheel hard and drove over a small ditch, now off-roading. As if hypnotized by the rhythmic motion, the car pummeled toward the sound of the pump's squeaks and groans, bouncing across the lumpy earth.

Stevie stopped the car close to the base and turned off the ignition.

Up close it loomed over her, like the mechanical monster it was, sobering her up instantly. She felt dizzy and shivered in the heat. Didn't know if she could do it. Yet riding it represented a new chapter in her life, where she would grab life by the balls—like she used to when she was a young teen.

But unfortunately she wasn't as agile as she was as a teenager. She had a much stronger fear of death and much weaker upper arm strength.

"I just *have* to do this Stevie," she said, explaining no further.

"You have to do it," he agreed.

She walked around the base, sizing up the industrial structure. It stood at least twelve feet high by her estimation. There was a ladder, but it too was shifting up and down with the pumping head. Stevie instructed her to hold on tight when she climbed the ladder, to take her time, then to kick one foot over while on the down stretch.

"It's no different than riding a horse," he said.

"More like a *bucking bronco*."

She had ridden horses at her cousins' farm many times but not often enough to become totally comfortable with the creatures. And this most certainly was different; if she got a sandal strap caught in the wrong place she could be pulled into the bowels of the beast, churned around and bashed into the ground, bones crushed. She tightened her sandals, making sure nothing was sticking out. She emptied her pockets and put her purse on the ground. First they both had to scale the surrounding fence, ignoring multiple bright red "keep out" signs. Stevie boosted her up and then followed her over.

Grabbing the moving ladder would not be easy, and she stared at it for a while, eyes following the rocking motion. Then she thought of a crass but funny phrase Jack often used, whether waiting for a car to make a left turn or a client to give the green light on a project: "shit or get off the pot." She knew it was now or never. Margie grabbed the ladder and managed to place both feet securely on the bottom rung, hugging the rusted steel beams, hanging on for dear life. It was five full pumps before she dared move up to the next one, but then ever so slowly she inched up the ladder one rung at a time. Throwing her leg over was the hardest part, but she knew her legs were strong at least and she locked her inner thighs around it, squeezing with all her might. She held onto the steel beam in front of her with both hands as if it were a saddle horn. It was an exhilarating rush she hadn't felt in decades. The rise of each rotation sent her spirit soaring. She was on top of the world, had tamed the beast. She dared to wave one arm and let out a hardy whoop.

"Way to go, Large Marge!" Stevie yelled up to her, and she smiled at him, just like old times.

The problem was she hadn't considered how the hell she would get off; to catch the moving ladder in reverse would be much more challenging, in the same way it's way easier to climb up a tree than down. "Shit, Stevie, I can't get down. I'm stuck!"

"Fling your leg back over, and balance on your stomach, and I'll tell you when to grab the ladder."

She was petrified for ten minutes, working up her nerve. Stevie was beginning to worry. Finally, when he said "now" for the umpteenth time she grabbed the ladder. She heard a rip and panicked—had she lost an arm? But there was no pain. Her new casual but expensive shirt had gotten caught on a bolt, ripping open under the arm.

But she made it to the ground otherwise unscathed. She wished she could have had Stevie record a video of it to prove she'd actually done it, but it's not like she could post it on Facebook, unfortunately, as it was an event that wasn't even supposed to be happening and would have to be kept hidden deep in her tangle of lies. This would be their secret, among others.

Back at the chateau Stevie changed into a nicer shirt for dinner. "I'm so hungry—after all I drove all night long just to meet you a little early, and I guess I haven't eaten since breakfast." His efforts were incredibly chivalrous and Margie blushed, already flushed. She freshened up her makeup, changed back into her yellow dress in the bathroom and grabbed her little black sweater. It really wasn't that cool out, in the mid-sixties, but she had bought it and then brought it all this way, and she liked the way it elevated the outfit.

Outside, she was energized and couldn't wait to explore. It was still light out, dusk, and when they turned on Main Street a billboard read: *Welcome to Historic Downtown Paris* printed in a Western font with French flourishes. Historic, perhaps, but slightly less so than the real one, Margie thought to herself upon seeing it.

Sure, the town square was quaint, with intricate façades from another era butted up next to each other, some red brick, some painted white, some sandstone. There was an old theater with arched windows that looked like it had been impressive at some point, a jewelry store with a dusty window display, an antique store, and a grand old hotel. Margie couldn't help thinking she would have preferred to stay there, but upon closer inspection, saw that it had been turned into a museum—and was currently closed. In fact the whole area looked like a ghost town. There were a few parked cars but they were the only ones on foot, the only ones around at all. She supposed that it could be considered a romantic scene, having all of Paris to themselves, and she reached for Stevie's hand. At first it felt nice but moments later too intimate. His hand grew clammy and she casually released it.

Margie wondered aloud why nothing was open as they circled the perimeter. She was adamant about dining in the square itself, but the only restaurants were a burger shop and a diner, and neither would do. This was not what she had envisioned. She dug out her phone from her handbag and pulled up Yelp, searching for "fancy French restaurant." Finding nothing, she typed the same key words in on her map app.

"The damn app's not working," she said. "This can't be right." Her fingers pummeled her phone pad.

"Let's just have a wander and see what we find," Stevie said, looking slightly irritated at Margie's obvious frustration. But he was patient and faced her, brushing her hair out of her eyes, gently squeezing her upper arm. She tried not to flinch as this was the exact spot she was most self-conscious of. "It's a beautiful evening," he continued, looking into her eyes, "maybe we'll find something on Main Street; I saw several places that looked nice when I drove in."

They passed Capizzi's Italian. Margie loved Italian food, but this place had all the ambiance of a fast food joint. And further on, The Fish Fry.

"I *hate* fish," Margie said. She was suddenly boiling and took off her outer layer, holding the sweater in her hand swinging by her side.

A couple of blocks down they spotted a place that looked like it had potential from afar. As they approached it a dinky sign read Hole in the Wall. Aptly named, with each step it looked dumpier to Margie.

"This place is kind of a dive..."

No response from Stevie.

"I mean it's just that I really *really* had my heart set on French cuisine."

"Let's at least take a look at the menu." When they stepped inside, Margie saw that it was nothing more than a Texas roadhouse. But not without its charms, she supposed, old metal signs and antiques littering the walls. The limited menu consisted of all-American bar food: quesadillas, burgers, jalapeño poppers and potato wedges topped with bacon bits and cheese. In truth, these were some of her favorite foods and—stomach rumbling—she agreed that it would do.

So much for the maître-d' and fine wine. Then again, she'd already had plenty. Instead they each ordered a beer, which seemed more appropriate. Always trying to make the best of a given situation, Margie told herself to just have fun! When the appetizers arrived Margie perked up and they became talkative again.

"Tell me more about your family," Stevie said. "What are your kids like?"

"Oliver is the sensitive one and Aimee, well, Aimee has been a handful. She's been getting in trouble at school a lot lately, and I don't know if it's just that she's a preteen now…or if it's something more." Margie felt that maybe what she was sharing was too personal, and discussing family at all made Margie slightly uncomfortable—considering what they were about to do—so she tried to steer the conversation in a different direction.

"What do you do for fun in Charleston? The town looks so charming—I googled it! Do you go out a lot?"

"I have a couple of favorite bars, of course, and a handful of good friends, but I'm really more of a homebody to be honest with you. I just like being in my cabin, watching ESPN or Fox News."

Fox news? Margie wasn't that political herself but knew that station was ultra-conservative, geared toward rednecks.

"Fox News? *Really?*" Margie asked.

"Oh yeah, I'm a hard-core Republican—from a long line of Republicans all the way back to my great grandpa. What about you? Do you bleed red?"

"Um, I'm kind of undecided, I mean I don't like to affiliate with a certain party, but I guess I lean more toward the left these days. I've voted for Democrats in the last three elections. I suppose it's because I agree with them more on social issues."

When he asked which ones she said equality and women's health, and elaborated no further, not in the mood to get into a debate. Instead, talk shifted to light, neutral subjects they could both agree on: his love of all sports and gamesmanship, her love of tater tots, their love of the beach.

"Luckily I've had plenty of time for the beach, now that my job has ended," Stevie said.

"Ended? What do you mean? But you're here for a conference, right? That starts on Monday after I leave?"

"Well not exactly. I mean a conference was scheduled here this year, but I got laid off, fired actually, about six months ago. Couldn't stand working for the man and I hated sales."

"You mean…you made this whole thing up?"

"Well, it's just that when you mentioned Paris, it triggered the idea. I never thought you'd actually go for it."

"But what about all those times you said you were working late?"

"Well, I mean, I just never changed my Facebook status. It's kind of private, you know? And then you just assumed and I didn't want to disappoint you. And I just really wanted to see you…I just had to." He did seem genuine, peering up at her out of those baby blues. She hadn't noticed before how long and dark his eyelashes were, a quality she had always loved in a man.

She didn't know what to say so she ordered pie for dessert. She had wanted to go somewhere more upscale to finish the evening off, but didn't feel like traipsing all over town again, especially considering how dead it was, and now she felt she needed to remain sitting to process the information.

"You're beautiful, Margie," Stevie blurted out, taking her hand, tracing her fingers with his. "Always were gorgeous and still are. You know, I always had a crush on you all through high school, college too."

"You did?" Now she met his eyes. "But you were so popular, Stevie. Stephen Singleton, football player, prom king, student council vice president; everyone loved you: the jocks, the preps, the thugs. I can't even believe I'm sitting across from you right now."

He smiled, probably at the sound of his own name, and she was still savoring the compliment. Had he liked her all that time? He really was quite sweet.

They got the check, feeling it was the right time to go. Regardless of the rocky conversation and the recent revelation, Margie suddenly felt a strong connection.

They walked back through the square, stopping to kiss in front of the fountain, somewhat expected but entirely essential. Her desire was intensifying. The smallest of movements, like the brush of his lips on her neck, his hand on her lower back, even lower now, propelling her forward. She was ready for the culmination of her scheming, the payoff of her planning, ready for the happy ending, so to speak. She kissed him back eagerly. Then stopped abruptly, impatient to get back to the hotel, wanting more.

After fumbling with the key, he fumbled with her bra. They tore off each other's clothes, clumsily, hungrily. "C'mon, cowboy," she said as she reached for his hat, and he dodged, but not before she dislodged it, revealing a shiny head as bald as a bowling ball—and slightly too small for his body. He looked silly, seemed embarrassed, as if he had read her thoughts—and he very well could have from the expression on her face. Like Sampson who had lost his strength, he became a caricature of himself, and the whole scene felt rushed and animated like a cartoon. But she kept her focus, concentrating on the task at hand. She honed in on his gorgeous eyes and found his erect penis—smaller than Jack's—and stroked it, trying to further arouse his very manhood, pumping it harder and harder, as if performing a CPR of sorts, wanting to revive him fully, restore his confidence.

They floundered around a few more minutes and then he was inside her. He rocked on top of her, rabbit style, to her dismay. She wanted to want him. Still determined to give it the old college try, she flipped him over and straddled him, tossing her voluminous hair this way and that—somehow she felt like she was screwing herself now—and he came quickly, the whole episode over almost as soon as it had begun. He said he felt bad. Wanted to finish her off, as he so eloquently put it. After some time she managed to climax, but to be honest she had to picture her husband, who knew exactly how to touch her. Afterwards she felt dirty, the emptiness inside her growing to epic proportions. She realized in a panic what she'd forgotten to pack: she wished she had a pill to pop.

The Affair, Day 2

The next morning, rather than basking in the afterglow, all she felt was sickening regret. Horrible guilt. And since she knew she would feel guilt, she wished it had at least been good. She hadn't liked their lovemaking; it had left a lot to be desired.

She removed his arm resting around her waist, picking it up by the finger like it was some awful thing, as limp as a dead animal. Her head hurt. She was badly hungover. After a couple of hours of alcohol-driven, dead sleep, she had been awakened by a pang of anxiety that kept her tossing and turning until dawn without her crucial meds, and her body felt heavy. Knowing she must look atrocious, she slipped out of bed and went into the bathroom to shower and apply her makeup while Stevie slept. When he still hadn't stirred after that process, she crept down the stairs, craving a cup of coffee. They had missed the communal breakfast, thankfully—how could she look the other guests in the eyes, and the grandmotherly woman, the sweet geriatric, Bonnie, well that was the last person she wanted to run into. In fact she found the whole B&B experience bizarre, much too personal. With only three rooms to rent in close proximity, she knew everyone must have heard them. Not that she was loud when she came but Stevie had been, bringing to mind the braying calf—now in hindsight she was sure it wasn't fully grown—that they had tipped over back in the day.

She tiptoed down the stairs and into the dining room, where a large pot of coffee was waiting in a silver tray. She would pour herself a cup then pass quietly to the front porch to be alone with her thoughts, reflect. But the dainty metal spoon hit the side of her porcelain cup, calling Bonnie in like a cowbell.

"Hello dear, I hope everything in the room was to your satisfaction?" Hardly, she thought. Whether the line was simply the well wish of a kind old lady or a subtle judgment, she could not tell. Could Bonnie sense they were having an affair?

"Oh, sure, it was just fine," Margie said, putting on a pleasant expression, making her way toward the front door. "Thanks."

"Where are you two visiting from?" Margie wasn't in the mood for small talk, but was relieved she thought they were a couple, from the same town.

"We're down from Charleston, South Carolina," she said, subconsciously putting on an accent she associated with those parts. "Been there for about five years," which she pronounced "fav yeahs." "We just love it there, we really do, just went for vacation and fell in love with it, and well, we just sort of stayed. We're beach people, you know, just love the beach, I mean we actually live in a log cabin but it's not far from the ocean, a few miles, I suppose, about a five minute drive, give or take."

"Well that's just lovely. How nice."

Sitting in an Adirondack chair, legs stretched out in front of her, she felt the coffee kick in, helping to ease her pounding head. They had planned to have lunch in town and then go to the miniature Eiffel Tower, which he had told her about. She had done no research, so it would be another surprise. Another adventure to look forward to. She wondered how long he would sleep—he was even lazier than Jack.

A sunbeam warmed her, clearing the fog in her head, and she looked around the porch. An antique rocker nestled between two lush potted plants rocked slowly in the breeze. On the wall behind it hung a hand-painted wooden sign with the words "Carpe Diem." She thought that it too was probably also purchased from Target, but strained her aching brain to remember what it meant: ah yes, she had seen it in a movie, *seize the day*.

After last night, she didn't know how she would get through the day, much less seize it. Then it occurred to her, it was not just about *this* day but *every* day, and she thought of all the days that had passed back at home that she had not seized. Hundreds. Thousands. Then and there, she wondered if she had gotten it all wrong. If all along she had been looking forward to the wrong things in life, cherishing the wrong moments. Valuing the wrong things. The wrong people.

Beyond that, she pondered that perhaps it was a matter of willpower, choosing to be satisfied, choosing to be happy, flat-out forcing yourself to find beauty in the everyday, the mundane. She knew some days that would be hard in pathetic Prairie Mound, an ambitious challenge indeed, but maybe she could try.

Just then Stevie strolled outside, stretching. In a T-shirt and khaki shorts, he looked refreshed, holiday ready. Her current line of contemplation changed her outlook. She would try to enjoy this short time with Stevie as best she could, and then try to enjoy the rest of her life when she got back home. He rested his hand on her head, stroked her hair, caressed her neck. It felt good. Maybe last night's rendezvous hadn't been so bad, Margie mused; first encounters are always a bit awkward and certainly nothing horrible had happened. He asked her if she'd like to come upstairs and get ready to go out for brunch.

When she entered the room a football game was playing on the television, the volume too loud, and Stevie plopped himself on the bed, motioning for her to come join him. She told him she needed to finish getting ready, chuckling that her routine took a while, which was no joke. As she wrestled with her hair, she could see him in the mirror from his position on the bed. He caught her eye and winked at her.

"Last night was just great, Margie. I wish every night could be like that."

Really? thought Margie.

"I mean I guess my life is pretty lonely; it's nice to have a real connection, you know?" She wasn't prepared for the direction of the conversation, and cringed. She consciously relaxed her furrowed eyebrows, trying to resume a neutral expression, since he could see her reflection. She was relieved that it was something she had practiced before.

"But it sounds like you have a pretty great life, living in that cozy cabin in the woods? It sounds so tranquil compared to my life," again stretching for vocabulary she rarely used. And she wondered why she felt the need to continually impress Stevie, to prove how much she had changed.

"It's great and all, but you know, having that whole house to myself, being separated, well it's been a hard year."

"Why don't you just get divorced anyway? I've been meaning to ask you that."

"I don't want to grant her that because of all the *bullshit* she put me through. She really hurt me, to tell you the truth, and now she wants half the house in town, the house she kicked me out of, and child support for our *almost-grown* kids? The *bitch* is *crazy!*" In their chats, he had always implied that he had ended it.

"Well why did she end it? Was it mutual? Was it somewhat amicable?"

"Not hardly," he said with a cold look in his eye, dimples all but disappeared. "She just lost interest, said she loved me but wasn't in love with me, and all that crap. That was six months ago. I mean I meet women around town, young ones too, that's not a problem…but it's not really that meaningful."

There was a roar from the raucous football game, which he did not volunteer to turn off, even in the midst of their somewhat serious conversation, bringing her headache back in full force.

Young girls? Now that was a creepy thing to say. Was Stevie still a player? There was a certain desperation in his eyes. He seemed to be searching for something. Maybe they did have a lot in common after all, Margie observed wryly. Yet the difference between them, Margie put her finger on it in her mind, was that she was not a *has been*.

Or was she? She herself spent too much time dwelling on the past or thinking about an abstract future; the place where she spent very little time, it now occurred to her, was the present.

She turned toward him. With morning sun pouring into the room, even from a distance, she noticed a light wedding band shaped strip dividing the tan around his ring finger. Surely the tan line would have faded over six months' time, considering how often he was at the beach. Or said he was. Well whatever—she was married, too.

"Turn off the game and let's go," she said, grabbing her purse.

He *had* lied to her. About several things. He had said he broke up with the ex a year ago, and in truth *she* dumped *him* and not that long ago—if that story was even true. And the carousing: it sounded like he was sleeping with the whole town. His pictures were a decade old by the looks of it. Yes, her own photos had been retouched, but women's weight fluctuates all the time and removing the wrinkles was a non-issue made right by the Botox. *And* he was unemployed, and that was a biggie. It occurred to Margie that he had not decided to drive to see her earlier like he had said, but that because he had no job he probably had no money and therefore had no choice. The flight had been a fabrication. Sure, she had fibbed about her volunteer work, about getting a promotion, but she'd always wanted to volunteer and was in line for a promotion. Or she hoped she still was with the recent probation. But at least she had a job!

At the cafe, the menu was once again all-American. While she had been anticipating something more exotic, she scarfed down her scrambled eggs, famished. Margie realized maybe she had overreacted due to low blood sugar. Who's to say whose lies were worse, though she was pretty certain his were. Even so, flirtation floated in the air. Eyes searched each other, sending out provocative glances, settled into knowing gazes. She realized sex is sex, regardless of the quality, and they now shared a newfound familiarity, a private affection, whether she liked it or not. She replayed the best moments in her mind, thinking it might have been the best hand job she'd ever given, mechanical as it was, and felt secretly proud of herself. He disappeared to the bathroom when the bill came and was in there so long that Margie grew impatient and picked up the tab.

They got into his clunker of a car and headed to the Eiffel Tower replica. He explained that it was just off Highway 371 as you enter town from the north. Margie grew quiet as she wrestled with her conflicting feelings. He turned on the radio for any distraction, any sound. Margie surfed the dial looking for an eighties station, playing just the first few notes before searching and searching again, the jumble of sounds, the stops and starts echoing her state of discontent. Until she finally found U2, a band which Stevie had introduced her to when she was in the eighth grade. He was perhaps Bono's biggest fan, writing down all of the lyrics in his English notebook, showing them to her once at a baseball game. They both sang along now, Margie never self-conscious of her singing voice because she seemed not to hear herself. "With or Without You" was blasting and the music transported them to a simpler time. Yet the words resonated with her more than ever, *you give it all but I want more* echoing in her head. At first she thought of Stevie, who had proven to be a bit of a disappointment, but then realized it was really about Jack, and her singing trailed off. *And you give, and you give...* She had given herself away—and for what?

She was glad when the song ended; it struck too close to home. But it was a back-to-back playback, and Margie was relieved when a different U2 song came on. Oh, she really loved this song: "I Still Haven't Found What I'm Looking For." In high school, she found the lyrics painfully poetic. Now they were even more so. She sang the verses but when it came to the chorus, again she grew quiet. Her thirteen-year-old self could never have imagined she'd still be searching when she was forty-one. Married with two kids, living in a big house, and she still hadn't found it. She was as lost as a teenager.

Meanwhile Stevie began relaying some "fun facts" he'd read. "For a while it was the highest Eiffel Tower in the country at sixty-five feet, built to outdo the tower in Paris, Tennessee."

"There's a Paris in Tennessee too? Well how many fake Parises are there?" Margie asked, a little irked.

"Believe it or not there are *fifteen* in the country."

What a farce, thought Margie, her mood continuing to spiral downward. He went on and on, explaining that another replica was built in Vegas, still more impressive, at half the height of the original Eiffel Tower.

She was a mess of emotions when they arrived. As they pulled into the parking lot from the highway she saw something, a big red splotch atop the tower, and she squinted to try to make it out. Entering the surrounding park on foot, she saw that the tower itself looked more like an oil derrick, and that the blood-colored eruption was actually an oversized cowboy hat. Margie found this Texas twist in bad taste—just as ridiculous as Stevie's signature hat, forever wedged on his head—even though she would be the first to admit he looked better with it on. Standing at the base of the structure, rimmed by bushes exploding with yellow roses, could have been, should have been, a highlight of the trip. But like the city, the tower was a fake, would fool no one.

At least Jack had the courage to wear his lack of hair with pride, closely shaven, looking sharp. The balls to bare it all, to stand up tall and be a man. And really, it wasn't about hats or hair or the lack thereof, Margie knew that. It was about the substance of the man underneath, the person that head was attached to.

Beyond the off-putting observation—in terms of Stevie—it made her question her own substance, what she was really made of. After all, she was putting on a facade even now as they circled the tower hand in hand.

"Isn't this cool?" he said. "Our own Texas version. The hat's a nice touch, don't you think? Damn thing must be eight feet wide at the rim."

"Yeah, everything's bigger in Texas, right?" She burst into a fit of uncontrollable laughter at the irony of it all.

Back in the car, they discussed what to do next. Margie, feeling out of sorts, decided she wanted to do some antiquing, and asked Stevie whether he would like to come with her or maybe take a nap, hoping for the latter. He said he'd tag along.

They went back to a strip of Main Street dotted with several antique shops and vintage clothing stores, but after only the first shop Stevie seemed bored, while Margie was just getting started. They stopped off at a coffee shop, long baguettes propped in a bucket on the counter, the first hint of anything Parisian she'd seen so far. Rather than a coffee, she chose a caramel mocha from the menu, feeling worldly and thinking of her cappuccino maker at home. This one was watery—she could do better—but she swallowed it down, nearly choking on the grounds at the bottom of the cup.

"I think I will go relax in the room for a little while and do some reading," Stevie said when he finished his coffee.

Yeah, right, thought Margie, he probably wanted to waste the day away watching another game with the curtains drawn.

"Sounds good." She would explore, happy to go it alone. Feeling empowered, she fingered her wallet in her purse. Stevie seemed to misread this as her offering to pay, and just sat there waiting, so she did. Again.

Finally free from him—the lech, the mooch—she walked into a vintage boutique, where she tried on outfit after outfit: a flapper dress, a shapeless shift mini-dress, its colorful pattern contrasting with white go-go boots, and a brown jumpsuit with wild flares. She spent over an hour there, but for once wasn't in the mood to buy anything.

The next store sold furniture, beautiful objects—no, *pieces*—judging by the price tags. She meandered through the space, cavernous as a museum, taking it all in. She played one of her favorite games, mentally choosing the items she would like to have in her home, which she would buy if money was no object—she could only choose ten—more challenging than you'd think in a store like this. She loved this exercise, for her elevated to a sport, like hunting. She'd been playing it for years, invented it when she was a child. But for the first time, in her current state, she saw it for what it was, a game of greed, and stopped herself at nine items.

In a back room, here in this fancy shop, she discovered a whole wall of taxidermy. Lizards and snakes were on display, and huge antelope heads mounted with twisted horns. She was surprised to see an armadillo wearing a tiny red bandana, jackalopes of all sizes, in no better shape than Jack's menagerie. Maybe Jack's craftwork had been more valuable than she'd realized. A tiny chipmunk caught her eye from the bottom shelf. She didn't even know they stuffed such small animals, rodents no less. But this creature spoke to her, its curious expression captured perfectly. She had to have it. For Jack. Perhaps as some sort of symbol. She thought it would make a perfect paperweight. The price shocked her at 225 dollars, handwritten on a homemade tag, but she sashayed over to the salesperson and said she'd take the item, setting it on the counter, whipping out her credit card. The lady raised an already arched eyebrow and wrapped the furball in layers of tissue paper, mummifying it. She handled it as gently as if it was a piece of fine art, carefully placing it into a shopping bag.

Margie toted its dead body, the day's only purchase, from shop to shop until her feet grew tired. Unsure what to do next, she went back to the cute cafe for one more cappuccino and a tart, another little taste of Paris. She didn't want to go back to the hotel, for fear Stevie would be napping, and try to coax her into bed for another round. So she stayed away, killing time before dinner. She went on Facebook, but per usual no one was sharing anything of interest—and she certainly couldn't post anything about this lie she was living. She was disappointed; this wasn't how the affair was supposed to go at all. Yet she still hung on to the hope that things would get better, forever optimistic, at least when it came to abstract fantasies. She stared out the window long after she finished her drink until the waitress began to give her impatient looks.

She returned quite late, after seven, and to her surprise, Stevie was still napping. Fox news blared on the television. She sat in the chair farthest away, busying herself with her phone. Probably sensing her presence, he awoke, stirred, spread out on the bed. He smiled, looked at her longingly, trying to shift into a seductive position. She ignored it, launching into a lengthy monologue about her day, about the outfits she tried on, about the items in the shops, about eating the raspberry tart with whipped cream on top, listing every single insignificant detail in order to dampen his desire and diffuse the sexual energy he was attempting to radiate. It was effective and he got up, realizing accurately that it just wasn't going to happen. He told her he'd found a charming little four-star Italian restaurant a couple of miles from the square that he would like to take her to tonight. She wondered if that meant he'd pay.

Margie began getting ready for their eight-thirty reservation. She went through the motions. She put on her makeup, a routine she was good at, and was as methodical as ever, giving herself sultry, smokey eyes. She slipped into her nicest little black dress, squeezed in, really. She stood in front of the full-length mirror, noticing a muffin top in the middle where her spanks cut off and two mini-muffins where the armholes squeezed the dough of her upper arms. Yet with her jewelry and high heels on she felt attractive, or attractive enough. She smiled at her reflection, masking her frustration, another thing she was good at.

"You look stunning tonight," Stevie said as he opened the clunky car door for her. Upon entering the restaurant she was pleased to see that it actually had ambiance, and she wanted to try to enjoy it. Stevie ordered an appetizer and a fifty-dollar bottle of Bordeaux, the evening scene suddenly unfolding just like she'd originally imagined. The wine was smoother, richer, than she had ever tasted, the quality so high she didn't even add ice cubes, wouldn't dream of diluting the delicate taste. The libation warmed her insides and had the power to improve her outlook.

Stevie looked nice with his button-down shirt and army green dinner jacket. He was full of witty one-liners. But as Jack often said, you can't bullshit a bullshitter, and thus she was full of feisty comebacks. Their banter was straight out of a movie, a romantic comedy, judging by the way Margie threw her head back exposing her elegant neck, releasing charming chuckles throughout the evening, refined this time, containing outright outbursts. She thought this might be her best performance yet, getting so involved in the role that she was actually beginning to enjoy herself. They talked about old times and abstract ideals. Life's memories and possibilities.

When dessert came, they giggled and nibbled on it, in no rush.

"I could get used to this," Stevie said. "I love spending time with you. We should do this again. And again and again and *again*." He winked.

The conversation had shifted from the hypothetical to the concrete, jolting Margie back to reality. She was unable to reciprocate, couldn't think of a response, with the commitment to her family she'd made just that morning, and the change in tone made her uncomfortable. She felt claustrophobic, the low neckline of her dress suddenly crushing her chest.

"We should get out of here," she said, with no hint of flirtation. She really wanted to get the hell out of there.

Stevie of course, read it another way, and shot his hand up, catching the waiter's attention, impatiently motioning for the bill.

Once again Stevie excused himself to the bathroom right as the check came, and Margie wondered if it was intentional, then tried to reverse the thought, chiding herself for always thinking the worst. Of course he would have to use the restroom as they had finished off a bottle of wine and then had ordered an aperitif with desert.

"Aperitif," she said softly aloud, a bit tipsy. She loved the sound of that word and whispered it a few more times, each repetition calming her nerves.

Just then his phone announced an incoming message alert with a bling. It was sitting right in the center of the table, so near that all she had to do was lean forward without touching anything, and she couldn't help taking a look. "Hey Cowboy," it said, "you coming over tonight?" With three winky faces to the right and to the left a tiny profile picture, a head in a circle, with long dark hair, surrounding a perky, pretty face. She looked half his age. Margie fumed. She felt stupid, and vulnerable, thinking about the line she'd used just last night. Probably half of Charleston called him Cowboy.

Shit. He would know she saw it unless she left now to pay the bill, which she refused to do. Instead she watched him return to the table to see the phone face up, message exposed, anxiety unveiled on his face. He looked at Margie—who was still looking at him—and then down at his phone, before sheepishly putting it back in his pocket. Neither knowing how to react, they ignored the incident. But it made its presence felt, renewing tension between them, further straining their already delicate dynamic.

The food and the service had been excellent, and the very competent waiter had brought the bill promptly. Yet Stevie seemed in no hurry to grab it, eying it and then Margie, suddenly chatty but saying nothing of substance. Margie certainly wasn't going to volunteer, for the principle of it, and thus the standoff began. The conversation, already forced at that point, piddled out completely.

"Do you want to settle up so we can get out of here?" Margie boldly suggested, not really a question at all. She'd had about enough. He took out his credit card in slow motion and covered the bill.

There had been a brief time when she had felt almost amorous while sipping the fine wine, but the moment had passed, perhaps when he tried to pass on the bill. She had wanted to have passionate, great sex with Stevie at some point, but now didn't think it was possible.

With all of the lies, with the incoming text he had not acknowledged and not explained—though it really needed no explanation because it was clearly a booty call; to go through with it, to have sex that she hoped would be hot but probably would not be, judging by the previous evening, probably forcing her to fake an orgasm, would just be too much. If he couldn't be bothered, neither could she.

So she blamed alcohol again, saying the red wine with no ice cubes gave her a headache, which she was surprised by since the quality was so high. Yet she knew she was faking it even as she laid there, resting her head on his chest while he flipped through the channels searching for a movie. The next night she would not. She would simply tell him it wasn't working out, and then dump him. Not only was he a *has been*, but he had been for some time. He was a phony. What's worse, she saw herself in him, even though he surely was a more pathetic version.

The Affair, Day 3

On Sunday morning, Margie woke up to Stevie's hard-on pressing against her thigh. He traced her eyebrows while she was still pretending to sleep. Before she even opened her eyes she could sense his face looming over her. When she dared open her heavy lids he was inches from her, just as she feared, and it reminded her of zooming in on his eye on her screen almost a year ago. She thought about how that moment had led to this. How she had allowed it, encouraged it. His eyeball up close in real life, bloodshot, crust-caked, was even more disturbing, yet he touched the tip of her nose, stroked her cheek. Margie tried to hide her grimace and popped out of bed with an enthusiasm she didn't feel, heading to the bathroom to shower and shave. She was in there a full hour, letting a near boiling stream of water wash over her. She scrubbed her tidy landing strip with a vengeance, which she had let grow slightly and pruned into a perfect V-shape, then her vagina, and her butthole too, not that he had been too near it, but because she felt like a filthy human being. Afterwards she ran the bath as hot as she could stand, and soaked a while, stewing at Stevie, mad at herself, reflecting on the choices she had made as of late and how she would put an end to the whole affair.

She wondered if she could get through the day, the night, and then the following morning. What would they do today? They'd exhausted many of the restaurants, and she assumed even less would be open on a Sunday, as if that was possible, with church in session in this run-down, Bible-belt town.

Stevie called to her that breakfast downstairs ended in thirty minutes and that they should try it, that Bonnie was an excellent cook based on the reviews. He's determined to get his money's worth, thought Margie. But she was in fact starving and needed to get out of the steamy water lest she faint. Once she got out of the tub she was unable to cool down, complaining incessantly about how hot it was in the room. She applied makeup in her bra and panties, Stevie staring like he'd never seen a half-naked woman before. It was only seventy degrees out but she blasted the air conditioner until it was almost arctic, freezing him out. He said he'd wait for her on the porch.

Down at breakfast, taking the last spots at the communal table, the atmosphere was as excruciating as she presumed, like having dinner with an aging relative, who in the grips of dementia accidentally invited a bunch of complete strangers. Bonnie introduced them to a couple with two small children who were staying on the top floor and an older couple staying in the Peach Tree room, who seemed to glare at her.

Of course Margie was skilled at small talk and she worked the room. She told them all about their cottage in the country, how much they loved Charleston, and how they loved the beach. She needed to divulge what she'd told Bonnie the previous day, for Stevie's benefit, and did so practically verbatim. Then she took it a bit further talking about how happy they were, and how she'd finally found her soul mate in Stevie, the man of her dreams.

"Well how long have you two lovebirds been married?" the older lady asked. Margie sensed she was being sarcastic. She still had her wedding ring on, and Stevie had the deep tan around where his had been.

"We've been married about five glorious years," she said. "Stevie's ring is being resized as we speak…because he's lost a bit of weight recently. He was big—not fat mind you,—but heavy for sure, so he started Weight Watchers at Christmas and the pounds just melted off. But anyway, I digress. We actually knew each other in high school…we found out later we secretly had a crush on each other all through high school *and* college, and we reconnected through Facebook—thank you very much Mark Zuckerberg!—and eventually he invited me to visit. He'd just gone through an awful divorce, just really nasty." Here she squeezed his hand. "So I visited, and we fell in love, and well, the rest is history."

"*Really*," said the woman. "How wonderful."

Stevie was quiet through breakfast, either unwilling to play along or unable to get a word in.

Back in the room, they googled things to do in Paris, Texas, and the results that came up fit onto one page. Margie would have liked to go to a museum to get a bit of culture, but the few she looked up were closed. Stevie suggested they go to a historic home, the Sam Bell Maxey State Historic House. Since it seemed to be the only thing open, Margie agreed.

They arrived at the site just in time, a tour starting in fifteen minutes. Not much of a history buff, Margie grew bored quickly as the chipper tour guide, dressed in a period costume from the 1800s, explained life in the Civil War era. Her big bustle and girdle nearly squeezed her in half in the middle, shifting her chub above and below it, forcing her hourglass figure. Just looking at it made Margie uncomfortable. But she did enjoy the antiques and period pieces sprinkled throughout the estate, busying herself by mentally rearranging the furniture. As the tour stretched to forty-five minutes, she grew antsy. General Maxey had owned this home for three generations and was an important historical figure, but an uninteresting one. Besides, it seemed more geared towards children and she felt the guide was talking down to her. She was especially restless knowing she must speak to Stevie and break things off, or to somehow steer the relationship back into the friend zone.

When it was finally over they were free to roam the grounds. Jack would have loved the beautifully manicured gardens, a thought that made her feel sick. Bonnie's breakfast seemed to reverse its flow in her system, triggering her gag reflex. She swallowed an oncoming belch, silencing it.

Stevie said he had loved the tour, and she feigned enjoyment. But she had to stop pretending, and prepared to launch into a speech, which she had mentally rehearsed in the shower.

"Last night was so special," Stevie said. "The nice dinner, then cuddling afterwards. Margie, you take my breath away."

This took her breath away and she inhaled deeply. His comment threw her off and she was having trouble focusing on what she had planned to say. She knew she had to dive in before he expounded further.

"Stevie, I, I, well, this has all been really lovely. I mean, I appreciate you making the effort, booking the chateau, finding the restaurant…all those gestures were so thoughtful. But it's just that I'm going through some things, things I haven't told you about."

"Margie, what is it? You can tell me anything. Aren't you enjoying yourself?" He looked at her with concern and pursed his lips, exposing his dimples.

"I truly am," she lied. "But I just feel like we haven't been totally honest with each other." To say the least, she thought; she felt like she was wearing a mask even now as she spoke, and he was an absolute imposter.

"Maybe so, but are these things that really matter? I mean who cares if you're a little heavier than your pictures, if you've gained a few pounds? Certainly not me; I like you exactly how you are."

She most definitely hadn't prepared for that response, forcing her to improvise.

"Well, Stevie, some things do matter. I mean, you have no job. And you've recently been dumped." She let that soak in for a minute before she continued. "But it's more than that. I mean, I have a family, and I guess it's just a little more difficult than I thought. This whole experience has made me realize that maybe I should work a little harder on my relationships at home."

He was taken aback. "Sure, I understand, Margie…I'm sure it's not easy for you. I just wish you'd thought about that about *three months ago*, before we started planning this trip. I thought you were into the whole damn idea as much as I was," he said. Then his face softened and he looked her right in the eyes. "I really care about you."

"Well I care about you too, Stevie."

"We have a history, and I have been in love with you ever since high school, ever since that time we parked in the Walmart parking lot—remember how everyone would hang out there? And when you drank your first beer, and said your head was so heavy and you laid it in my lap—and I'm sure it was heavy, you had like two tons of permed hair!" They both chuckled. "And we talked for hours under the stars, when you were scared to go home for fear your father would be waiting. And watching MTV videos at my place because your parents didn't have cable, and listening to Prince's "Erotic City" in my basement, replaying the cassette single again and again, dancing until we collapsed."

She had loved that song, with its illicit lyrics and funky beats. She had felt so free and uninhibited. But she forced herself back to the present.

"Stevie, that was a long time ago."

It was then that she got the text from Jack.

"Margie, call me immediately. We need to talk. Now."

She read it again and again. While she had not forgotten Jack on this trip, she'd forgotten to call him. Maybe that's all it was, but the urgency troubled her. Had he found out about the affair? This was serious. This was breakup worthy, an end-of-marriage scenario, and she didn't want to call. What if he had run into Katie in town and she had spilled the beans—or maybe she had told him on purpose; after all, she did really like Jack. Jack would be so devastated. What if he said he wanted a divorce? As Stevie droned on, she walked through the grass in a panic-driven daze. What was she supposed to say to Jack, what was she supposed to do, and for that matter, what was she actually supposed to be doing? She was in a seminar, that's right, and she could say she just stepped out to a nearby park for a coffee break. Well, she *was* in a park. She found it easier to lie based on just the thinnest thread of truth.

"Stevie, I need to use the ladies room," she said. They were so far out on the grounds that walking back would give her the time alone she would need.

"I can come too. Are you about ready to wrap it up out here?"

"It's just that I need a moment. I got a text from Jack and I have to call him. Sounds important. Do you just want to meet me on the front porch in twenty minutes or so?"

She turned toward the manor, not waiting for him to answer. She reached for her phone but her fingers felt frozen. After several deep breaths she finally pressed return call.

"Jack? Hi sweetie, it's me." Did she usually call him sweetie? She couldn't recall.

"Why the hell didn't you call me yesterday? Is everything going alright?"

"Yeah, I've just been busy in conferences, it's been nonstop, but I've been learning so much, it's really more interesting than I thought it would be, well, there was this one speaker who was kind of boring, going on and on about statistics, boring me nearly to dea—"

"Margie, I need to talk to you," He interrupted. Followed by silence.

"Okay."

A long audible exhale was followed by more silence. "Margie, I found a bunch of your files on my computer, dumped into the trash. A folder full of old receipts, and I know that you've been changing the receipts, lying about money. I need to know what else you've lied about, where you're getting the money, and how much you're spending. You need to tell me everything."

Shit, shit, shit. She was busted. She considered lying around it, or through it, or out of it, but couldn't think fast enough. Plus she really didn't want to. "Jack, I'm so sorry," she said. "I wanted to tell you but I didn't know how."

"How long has this been going on?"

"For a long time, I mean, for years, I guess." Tears streamed down her cheeks. "I'm so sorry. Remember when I got that bank card and my own account ten years ago? Well, it became a credit card soon after, and I'm in kind of a lot of debt. I have been for a while, and I just don't know what to do. I've really screwed up, Jack. I'm so sorry."

"And what about the phony receipts?" His voice was cold, detached, pained.

"That's more recent. I haven't been doing that all along, I swear to you, little fibs and half-truths, yes, but the receipts are something new, I promise."

"Un-fucking-believable. How can I believe a word you say? How much is it, Margie? What's the damage?" The words stung. The words that he had every right to say, that she had brought on herself, that she deserved to hear, carried a weight and gravity beyond what she could have ever expected.

"It's a lot Jack, I'm sorry. I want to change, and I'm really going to try. Please give me a chance to try to make things right. It's not just that, I want to try to have a new lease on life. I've been thinking, and I want to try harder, to work on myself, and I don't mean like a day at the spa. I want to—"

"We're going to talk about this when you get home," he cut her off, "and I want to know everything, numbers, access to the account to see if we can even get out of this mess, this clusterfuck you created…and we're going to talk about *us*."

"We will, Jack, we'll talk about everything. I'm sorry, Jack. I love you, I really do."

"*Do you?* Text me when you're on your way home."

She had caused damage. She wondered if it was even possible to tally the amount. She had damaged his trust, more than he even knew. She had damaged his very happiness by discounting him, by disparaging his home, their home. She had damaged their children by being distant. She had damaged them all.

She would change. She had never wanted anything more in her life, and she had wanted a lot. Now what she wanted went beyond the material—to repair what she had destroyed, to be more connected to her family, to be fully present in her own life—and she hoped if she wanted it badly enough she could achieve it. She sat for a long while. Finally she saw Stevie's sad, small figure across the ample lawn. She wiped her face with her sleeve.

Should she make up an excuse to go now? The rest of the weekend would just be wasted time, and she had wasted so much time in her life already. Yet if she came home early she would have to make an excuse, another lie in her tangled knot of lies. But how would she fill the time if she stayed? She certainly could not shop. She didn't want to nap or be anywhere near a bed. Or near Stevie for that matter. But he approached her now.

"Is everything alright?" He was out of breath for someone who surfed so much.

"It's fine," she said, "Nothing for you to worry about." She couldn't think of an excuse to give except for the truth, the intensity of which she didn't want to deal with. Like Scarlett O'Hara, she would think about it tomorrow.

Stevie suggested they take a drive to a lake about an hour away and take a walk or sit by the shore. She did like the lake. And this was another part of the trip she had envisioned, even though her mind was clouded, even though her mood was somber, even though his clunker was a far cry from a convertible. Again Margie went silent. Even with her vast skills in the areas of denial and dismissal she was not able to put the phone call out of her mind. The ride cleared her head, maybe too much so, as her mistakes became obvious, her misjudgments evident. All she could think about was Jack and how she had been taking him for granted. While yesterday she had blamed Stevie for the disastrous affair, now she blamed herself for being so naïve, so careless and so cruel. And that wasn't even to mention the spending, the reason for Jack's call, *"how much is the damage"* running through her mind.

Upon reaching the shore, they sat staring across the water. Spindly pines crowded the rim of the expansive lake, some covered in Spanish moss where a nearby inlet grew swampy. Stevie misread the silence for joint comfort, a connective quietude, and leaned in to kiss Margie. She turned her head away.

"Stevie, I'm really sorry. I think I've made a big mistake."

"How can you say that, Margie? I can't believe you don't feel *anything* for me."

"I do feel something, something that I've always felt...you really were a very good friend to me growing up, and I'll never forget that," Margie said. "Stevie, can we just finish the weekend off as friends?" He looked utterly dejected, didn't respond. She hadn't broken up with anyone in years and found it hadn't gotten any easier. She had no idea Stevie— Stephen Singleton, Mr. Popularity—would take it this hard, that he would even care about little old her. He had been used to getting any girl he wanted in high school and maybe that was part of it; but that was a long time ago and life hadn't been as kind to him since. That being said, he still seemed to get laid.

"I don't even know what to say," he said, the light in his eyes extinguished.

Margie didn't either, and she sat motionless for a while. She felt awful about hurting him and far worse about hurting Jack, and wondered how she would now put out the fires she had kindled.

His disappointment seemed to turn to irritation in a slow burn, the embers of anger making his cheeks glow. Though she could see he was trying to control his tone, his voice came out strained. "I just don't know how you could do this to me, lead me on. You're nothing but a *tease*. Just like you were in high school."

"*Me* a tease? It seems to me that you're sleeping with the whole town of Charleston! So don't give me this whole spiel about being in love with me since high school. That's probably just another lie in this whole string of lies you've been feeding me."

"It's the truth, Margie, and you don't have to be a *bitch* about it."

She was emotionally exhausted and didn't have the strength to argue with someone she now understood she didn't even care about. She saw that it had been easier for her to connect with a virtual stranger than make an effort with her actual husband. She would never know whether Stevie's feelings were genuine; the only thing she knew was that after this weekend she would never speak to him again. Maybe he was right: she was a bitch. And a fool. A fool who had been in love with a fantasy.

"Stevie, I'm sorry if I hurt you. I don't want to fight with you. Let's just try to get through this evening. How about we just go back to the hotel and get something to eat in town and call it a day, okay?" She secretly decided she would drive back home after dinner, inventing a clever excuse for why the seminar had ended early on the way.

"Okay," he said, barely audible.

It was dark out, and as they approached the hotel late after the long drive, she checked the time on her phone. It was nine thirty, and she had three missed calls from Auden. She also had a text from him and didn't want to look, not with what happened earlier, but felt she must, because of what happened earlier. It said to call him as soon as possible. He hadn't left a voice message. He had never called her and only had her number from when they had exchanged them in her backyard in case she couldn't get ahold of Jack. This was not good. Not good at all.

Maybe Jack had told Auden about the receipts, the debt, and the spending, which of course Auden already knew about, with the exception of the receipts, purposely omitted. But now that the cat was out of the bag, Auden might have felt compelled to finish the story, with the selling of the drugs and the depth of her debt, not that she had mentioned an actual number but she had admitted that it was a very dire situation that was spiraling out of control.

Or maybe Auden had found out about the affair somehow, and taken it upon himself to tell Jack everything, thinking it was the last straw, that she had crossed a line, and that Jack had a right to know the depth of her deception.

Back at the chateau, Margie waited with baited breath for Stevie to get in the shower before what would probably be a very awkward dinner. When she finally heard the sound of running water, she went out to the porch to call Auden.

She dialed the number, terrified of him answering.

"Margie," he picked up on the first ring. "I don't want to upset you, but, uh, I wanted to let you know that Jack is in the hospital, in the ER. We were, uh, finishing up at the Johnsons' place and he just collapsed out of the blue while hoeing some weeds and I carried him to the Manscaping van and drove him straight to the emergency room and they are doing some tests."

The knife-slicing sensation came back to her fingertips, which went numb, and now pierced her whole body, her very core, the final plunge penetrating her heart. Margie's head felt like it was splitting open, her thoughts shattered in a million directions. She was in shock, trying to absorb the news, to attach meaning to the words, sentence by sentence, trying to form one of her own.

"Oh my god. Is it serious? I mean it sounds serious but have they found out what caused it? Is he conscious?"

"I don't know, they rushed out to meet us in the parking lot with a gurney and used those paddle things, so yes I believe he is conscious but they have him in the back and the doctor hasn't called me in yet. I've been sitting here in the waiting room—your waiting room—and he's been back there for over an hour and nobody has told me a damn thing!"

"Auden, I'm going to pack up and get out of here in a few minutes. I'm in Paris—Paris, Texas, and it's a two-hour drive to the hospital. Has anyone called Jack's parents? Do the kids know?" She realized she hadn't thought of the children once in three days.

"I don't think so. They are with Jack's parents. I just wanted to call you first because I really didn't know what to do," Auden said, on the verge of tears by the sound it.

This made Margie well up but she did know what to do and she stayed strong. "Auden, I want you to stay right there in the emergency room. Can you do that? Call me and tell me any and all updates, and I'll call his parents once I get there and understand what's going on." She was an expert on emergencies, even if it was much more difficult when it involved her own husband. She wanted to sob but needed to stay in control and take care of the situation. She could cry later in the car. And she would.

Yet a couple of tears had escaped. Hearing the shaky, serious tone in her voice, Bonnie had made her way to the screen door, and still stood there. She asked if everything was alright.

"Yeah, it's fine, it's just that…my dog died. I have to leave right away."

"Will you both be checking out then?"

"No, my husband Stevie will be leaving later and he will take care of the bill," she said.

She sprinted up the stairs, and shouted into the direction of the shower over the sound of pounding water. "Stevie, Jack's passed out or collapsed or something and I have to get to the emergency room right away."

"God, Margie, are you serious? That's awful," Stevie's muffled voice floated through the room. "Let me get out of the shower; I just got in because it took forever for the water to warm up. But give me just a second."

"I don't have a second to spare, Stevie. We don't know what's wrong with him yet. It could be anything, a heat stroke, a real stroke, a heart attack, an aneurysm. I've got to get out of here."

She had never packed so quickly in her life, throwing all of the accessories, jewelry and shoes scattered around the room, and panties— oh Jesus, what had she done—into the two large suitcases. She barged into the bathroom and gathered the makeup and ointments covering every inch of the counters, stuffing everything into bags, piling her luggage by the door.

She paused before darting out the door, then turned and went into the bathroom. Stevie was still showering, his thin frame blurred through the translucent glass, with his small shoulders, flaccid little penis, and bald spot glistening. But he wasn't really a bad guy. No, *she* was the bad guy. She put her hands up to the glass door and their fingers touched, their eyes met.

"Thank you, Stevie. Thank you for everything." Though she knew he might misinterpret it, she was thanking him for *not* being the man of her dreams, for all that had gone wrong, for allowing her to see things more clearly. She grabbed her bags and rushed out, her luggage so heavy it nearly pulled her arms out of their sockets. But full of adrenaline, she hoisted them into the trunk.

She slammed it shut, slammed the door, and slammed her foot on the gas, hurling toward Prairie Mound at ninety miles an hour. She pulled her hair into a ponytail as she drove, deciding she would no longer waste time on superficialities, thinking about her ridiculous morning and evening routines and how many hours, days, weeks, months of her life she had wasted on such trivial matters.

What is the damage, Margie? At this point the damage was immense. He was her rock and she had been chipping away at him all this time. What if it was the recent discovery that had made him crack, collapse? She knew good and well stress could trigger most medical emergencies. And now that for once in his life he needed her, she was absent. She had helped the whole town with their traumas, but not the one person who mattered the most. In fact he had unknowingly rescued her from this disaster of an affair, and she would come to his rescue in turn, nurse him back to health no matter how bad the diagnosis. She hoped he would then save her, once again, from the disaster that was her life, and she would save him once more by bringing him the happiness he deserved.

The drive was long and she felt desperate. She wanted to pray. Wished she believed in God. But when she thought of him, which wasn't very often, she couldn't take him seriously. Not after being raised in the church seeing how he'd failed his congregation time after time, her parents and herself included. All the while his believers seemed to spend a lifetime waiting, wishing and wanting God's will to reveal itself. She recalled the drawn-out benedictions, the preacher practically begging someone to come forward to justify his preparation, and the testimonies from members about overcoming all kinds of hardships and horrors. Like the one gentleman, a coach at her school and her history teacher, who felt called to confess to an affair—and Margie had wondered if his wife felt the need for him to tell the whole congregation the gritty details. With all the hell-fire and brimstone sermons she had withstood, which really wasn't a choice at all, could she choose to reach out to God now? Would he remember the sad, fidgety, knobby-kneed girl doodling on a sketchpad in the pew?

God didn't stop her daddy's drinking, still hadn't, to her mother's dismay. Didn't answer her nine-year-old prayers begging Jesus to not let her dad come home falling down drunk for her friends to see when she had sleepovers. Even in Sunday school religion hadn't clicked for her; even then she knew it was a too easy answer in a complicated world. She saw religion itself as a crutch, a false comfort, with everything explained away as being God's will. She had used her own will to get through life. But then again, she clearly hadn't done a very good job of it.

And what if in this current crisis she needed that crutch? She had nothing to hold onto, nothing to clutch except Jack himself. Without him she had nothing. The hand that wasn't on the wheel was clenched in a fist, and her perfectly manicured nails drew blood. She wanted to pray but she knew she would feel as hypocritical as the pathetic people in the pews.

"Oh God, Oh God, Oh Jesus, help me!" she said aloud anyway.

Saying the words, however, did not offer the peace of mind she had hoped for. The peace that surpasses all understanding, a line she remembered from a Bible verse, still eluded her. Stevie had been a joke; and she had been the punch line. Thinking about the ridiculousness of the entire weekend, she threw her head back and laughed. Laughed at herself. Laughed in spite of herself. She was hysterical, her shoulders shaking, her entire body erupting uncontrollably, convulsing so hard she could hardly hold the steering wheel as the laughter transformed into shuddering sobs.

What she had at home was so much better. She thought about Jack's big strong hands and the way he held her. She thought warmly of Aimee's otherworldly eyes and Oliver's gentle soul. She pictured his dance moves. These were the important moments. Many of which she'd been missing.

And why hadn't Auden called? She desperately wanted to call him but had to first will herself to calm down until she was only sniffling, and even then she could barely get the words out, the syllables getting caught in her throat, her voice cracking at the edges. And all he could tell her was that they wouldn't tell him anything. No nurse or doctor had come out and when he inquired they said they couldn't disclose the information to a non-relative. Margie thought that must mean it was serious; couldn't they, wouldn't they let him know if Jack was doing fine and in stable condition? She called the hospital repeatedly, but no one picked up. She continued to call frantically, swerving more wildly the more agitated she became. Afraid she was going to have a wreck, she gave up and tried to focus on the dark highway ahead through teary eyes.

Finally she pulled into the hospital and parked in the circle drive reserved for ambulances, pulling up to leave them room and flew inside. She wanted to scream out *Why didn't anyone pick up the damn telephone?!* and looked to see who was working reception. But she kept calm, putting her training to the ultimate test. She was allowed to go back immediately, and a nurse told her that Jack had had a minor heart attack, gone into cardiac arrest for a short time but was now doing fine and they were running some tests to see how bad the damage was and choose the best method of treatment. *How bad is the damage* now took on even more meaning.

She rushed to his bedside and held his hand. "Oh baby, oh sweetie," she said. "How are you doing? Are you in pain? I got here as soon as I could."

"Hey Margie. Thank god you're finally here. I think I'm alright now," he said with a weak smile. "But it scared the shit out of me. I've never been so afraid in my whole life."

"I'm here, I'm here," she said. "I'm really here now."

And she stayed by his side for the next thirty-six hours in the hospital. She called his parents, who brought the kids and they all sat together in the waiting room, taking rotations with Jack. It felt surreal to Margie, and she walked around in a coffee-fueled, sleepless blur. But for once in her life, minute by minute, hour by hour, and still without access to her pills, she was fully—and painfully—present.

NOVEMBER

The heart attack could have been worse in terms of long-term effects, the current condition of his heart, and the treatment. To Margie's relief, at least Jack hadn't needed double or triple bypass surgery. Since the blockage wasn't severe, after several days recovering at home he had been scheduled to go back in to the hospital to the cath lab for cardiac catheterization. Margie knew that the procedure wasn't that serious and could be done in a day, followed by a couple of days of bed rest at home. She knew that they would run tubes through the blood vessels to his heart, opening up the arteries and inserting stents where necessary to clear the passages.

Yet Margie felt she was the real blockage, and ironically it was Margie's heart—and her eyes—that were opened up. They would well up and overflow at the slightest prompting: at a thought, a memory, a regret. She was constantly rushing to the bathroom and locking herself in to cry in private, careful to be strong in front of Jack and especially the children. Her mascara was always running, always smeared, requiring additional dabs of under eye concealer throughout the day. She started carrying her cover-up in her purse, never knowing when the floodgates would open, whether in line at the grocery store, at the bank, or dropping the children off for school. She told them she had allergies, or something in her eye. She felt certain she was the one who had attacked Jack's heart, jeopardizing everything, causing it to finally collapse—and he didn't know the half of it. She was sure the failure of his heart was a direct result of her failure as a human being.

After Jack returned from the cath lab, Margie tended to his recovery closely, taking a few days off from work, hovering by his side, anguishing over his every need.

"Can I get you anything, sweetie?" she asked repeatedly throughout the day.

"I'm fine," he would always say. "Maybe just a glass of orange juice." Or a Coke, or a magazine, or a pillow, his simple needs easily satisfied.

She enjoyed playing nurse, but wondered if she was overdoing it out of guilt, for which she felt even more guilty. However, he seemed pleased with the attention and was growing stronger. She, on the other hand, didn't know if she would ever fully recover, what the process would be, or what treatment could rid herself of the shame she felt. So she often just held his hand in silence, temporarily calmed by its warmth.

She occupied her mind with the children, bearing more responsibility than ever, not just taking care of them but actually *caring* for them. She consoled them, talking to them about what was happening with Jack each step of the way in terms that they could understand. And sometimes she just listened.

She thought often about her epiphany on the porch of the chateau, about happiness being something you make happen, not something that happens to you. She now felt sure that it was a choice. So she would make that choice every day, finding pleasure in the small things, the quiet moments. And if that came down to holding Jack's hand for five minutes or relishing a kind word from Aimee, so be it. On days that came up empty, she would have to dig deeper, or try again the next day.

Feeling responsible for the family's bad eating habits, which she knew also contributed to Jack's heart attack, she prepared well-balanced meals that now always included a side of vegetables, organic ones bought in the produce section of the supermarket. She remembered with a pang that she hadn't known what fresh vegetables tasted like as a kid, until spending the night with a friend and watching her mom chop fresh mushrooms.

"What are those?" she'd asked.

"You've never seen fresh mushrooms before?" the mother had responded, surprised. While she had been kind, handing Margie a paring knife and asking if she'd like to help, Margie had felt stupid and stared down at the table, too embarrassed to respond. She had never really thought about it, but if she had, she would have assumed vegetables grew in cans. And yet she hadn't done much better than her own parents, too busy, or too lazy to prepare healthy food, relying far too often on fast food and prepackaged meals. And her parents had the excuse of being poor whereas she was not; in debt, yes, but fully capable of providing. Instead she had simply been apathetic. She was determined to try harder. So even with her lack of cooking skills, she struggled to prepare healthier dinners that were not half bad. And the family ate them without much complaint.

She toted the kids to and from school, and patiently helped them with their homework, a chore she loathed. She hadn't realized just how heavy a load Jack had been carrying in terms of the family's day-to-day needs.

By the second day of Jack's recovery, he was feeling well enough to watch some online tutorials in his laundry-office-weight room. But on the third day a red swollen area had developed overnight on Jack's inner thigh, a puffy spot throbbing on the meaty part of his upper thigh, inflamed and hot to the touch. It was the entry point of the catheter, and Margie could see that it had gotten infected, despite her efforts to wash the wound and carefully disinfect the area. When his fever went up to 103 on Thursday morning, Margie insisted on driving him back to the hospital, overriding his protests. It was a wise decision; the area had gotten so badly inflamed that he was promptly readmitted to the hospital and forced to stay overnight. Margie was worried and upset; the infection was a serious complication.

And like his wound, the shame she felt grew more inflamed by the minute. She wished she could cleanse herself of her indiscretion entirely, but although she wracked her brain constantly, she had no idea how she would ever get through it, or if she could ever get past it.

She let the kids sleep in the bed with her, something that used to be reserved for when she and Jack fought, and they all enjoyed the comfort of the additional body heat sharing the king-sized bed. They stayed up too late watching television.

"Can we eat popcorn in bed?" Aimee asked.

"Well I don't see why not." Margie popped two bags in the microwave and brought in a big red bowl overflowing with a heaping cloud of popcorn.

"This is better than going to the movies, because we're under the covers," Oliver said as Margie flipped channels.

"Yeah, but you're on my side. Scoot over!" Aimee giggled, wiggling her legs and play wrestling with him.

Oliver snuggled up with Margie.

"I sure hope Daddy's okay," Aimee said when she turned off the lights.

They were all tired in the morning, but Margie managed to make scrambled eggs and to get themselves to school and to work on time, shortening her own morning routine as she'd promised. Leaving out steps of her familiar routine took effort: not plucking those stray hairs took restraint, lathering up only once in the shower took resolve, not fussing over her hair with a curling iron took willpower.

But with Jack still laid up in the hospital on Saturday, two full days later, Margie became restless. Felt helpless. Minutes crept by after breakfast and she had to think what to do with the kids, who were loud and hyper; she wasn't used to playing with them, entertaining them, actually spending time with them. It was hard work, she realized, and she wondered how Jack did it so naturally.

While one minute she felt warm and maternal, the next she felt cold and incapable—and questioned whether she had it in her. She wished they would just shut the hell up so she could think straight as she tried to concentrate on gaining a more positive mindset.

Sensing her discontentment, they were now arguing nonstop. Margie sat in the kitchen drinking her cappuccino, staring ahead blankly. She walked over to one of the walls in a trance, stopping in front of a spot where the collage was densest, multi-layered with products of all shapes and sizes. She stared at the intricate images until her eyes blurred, hypnotized. The pictures seemed to taunt her. Or maybe they were trying to tell her something, like the web of clues tied together with thumbtacks and string she sometimes saw on crime shows. She was unsure of how long she stood there. The kids had grown silent, watching Margie watch the wall. She suddenly ripped one photograph from the wall—of the precious pendant lights—and wadded it up and threw it on the floor. Then she picked it up from the floor, spread it back out and ripped it up in as many tiny pieces as she could, decimating it, throwing fistfuls of papers this way and that, pieces fluttering to the floor in all directions like confetti. She pulled off another and another, now a woman possessed, ripping and tearing and grunting.

"*Mom*, what are you doing to the pictures of all of our *things*?" Aimee asked in horror. When Margie looked over she could see the fear and confusion in their eyes.

Margie burst out in a fit of laughter, trying to calm them—but it was too uncontrolled at first—so she consciously toned it down a notch and then tapered it off completely to a soft smile.

"It's okay, kids. Come here." She hugged them close. "We're going to tear down these walls. You can help me—it'll be fun! Let's rip everything down to the bare paint."

The kids went wild and all three of them ran around the dining room and living room removing the clippings one by one, careful to remove the tape as Margie instructed, then shredding them, crinkling them, and crumpling them. They scattered the remains all over the floor, Oliver stomping them flat.

"Can we do *our* room too?" Aimee asked eagerly, probably ready to be rid of the constant reminders of things she didn't have. Things Aimee didn't even want, since they were not her own desires, but her mother's, Margie realized. They all charged into the bedroom together, the children extra energized to rid their own room of the ridiculous façade.

"I hate this stupid dance costume," she said. "I always hated this ugly sweater." She ranted and raved, but smiled all the while, catching her mother's eye to look for a reaction. Margie grinned and admitted that she didn't like them anymore either. While Oliver was certainly enjoying himself dancing and flailing around, obliterating the pages, Aimee seemed to be enjoying it on a more profound level. Behind the layers and layers of pictures, a room that was almost as pretty as a palace was revealed. Even though Aimee was now too old for the decor, she said it looked magical.

They went through every room of the house, eradicating the imagery, destroying haunting reminders, ghosts of past longings and future promises. When Aimee tried to pick some of the scraps from the floor, Margie told her not to worry, she'd do it later, not wanting to break the cathartic momentum.

Margie was pleased to see that at once the house appeared larger, with white walls expanding in all directions. She was thrilled that their home instantly looked newer, like they'd just moved in. A fresh start, she thought to herself.

"I can't wait until Daddy gets home and we can show him what we've done," Oliver said. "Do you think he'll like it?"

"I think he'll love it," Margie said.

And with that she made grilled cheese sandwiches, sat and ate with them at the table, and then started around the house with the vacuum, a broom and a wastepaper basket and tidied up for hours until there were no signs left of her trivial pursuits and all-consuming consumerism.

When she entered the kitchen the next morning, the newly uncluttered space seemed lighter, so bright, in fact, it gave her a slight headache. The angst of waiting for Jack's fever to go down made her feverish. Trying to cut down on her meds, she had fought the impulse to take a pill and therefore had not slept well. Always prone to sweating, that night her heavy excretion saturated the sheets—not once but several times. Her heart was racing and she was cranky, and she had to stop herself from snapping at the children. She and the kids could visit Jack in the hospital for a couple of hours, but there was still so much additional time to fill. She was already flushed and fatigued—plopping down into a chair for fear she might faint—yet she asked the children what they would like to do today, looking from Aimee to Oliver, and back to Aimee.

Her daughter beamed. She contemplated it as if it were a trick question. They weighed options. Aimee suggested a picnic in a beautiful park. Oliver suggested a boat ride on a river. Since there were no beautiful parks or rivers in Prairie Mound, they had to keep brainstorming. Finally the children decided they wanted to buy new turtles, to have friends for the sole survivor, Starlight, named for the radiant pattern on her shell. So Starlight had survived! Margie hadn't thought of it once, hadn't had time. She took it as a sign, found it marvelous, as if it was the best news she had ever received.

The pet store was usually Jack's domain; the smell of feces and fish made Margie nauseous. Not even a cute pet store with puppies and kittens, it carried only the less evolved animals on the food chain, like rats and snakes and disease-ridden birds.

But still, Margie thought it a wonderful idea, and she wanted to act fast, not knowing how much longer Starlight could hang on. They would go see Jack first and then to Petland. She wanted to take the most direct route from the pet store to the pond, lest the new turtles should perish in the car.

She stopped herself from choosing outfits for the children even though she wanted them all to look nice visiting Jack to cheer him up. Instead she let both kids pick out their clothes while she got ready—quickly. Aimee wore overalls with a well-worn T-shirt, and Oliver, to her delight, or to her dismay, chose his magic trick outfit, top hat and all. But she didn't want to waste time and both kids were shocked when she told them to grab their coats and go get in the car.

Jack was awake when they walked into his room. Margie pulled the divider curtain across and Aimee ran to him. It was obvious by the way her face lit up that she preferred him. They had been getting along splendidly the last few days but with Jack in the picture it was clear he was her favorite. Well, Margie supposed she had been overbearing. Their relationship wouldn't change overnight; it would just take a little more time, she hoped. She wondered if she could ever get along with her obstinate daughter when they didn't have that much in common, but she was determined to at least make an attempt.

"We have a terrific surprise for you when you get home," Oliver said. "We have—"

"Shh, Oliver, don't say any more or it won't be a surprise anymore," Margie warned gently.

"Spoiler alert, you blabbermouth!" Aimee taunted.

Jack had more energy and looked stronger and the four of them jabbered away, or at least the three of them did. Sometimes when Margie was with them she felt like a ghost. Invisible. But she was attentive, and listened, overcoming the temptation to retrieve her cell phone from her purse and check Facebook.

Dr. Taylor came in and informed them Jack would be released the next morning. Margie wondered if they had him on any meds and if they had told him about her, uh, situation. Her probation would be ending in a few weeks, and she would assure Mrs. Jones that she would never do it again—and she wouldn't—making sure not to reveal too much about what it was she'd actually been doing.

Margie sent the kids to the vending machine, wanting a moment alone with Jack, then regretted it. They looked into each other's eyes but even this was hard for Margie considering what she'd done. His eyes were open and warm, like pools of devotion she could fall into. But what did hers reveal? Even with all the lying she had done, she didn't feel like she was especially good at it, not at close range, inches away from each other, breathing the same oxygen in the airless room. And she knew he must still be angry with her about her spending. She wished she could be honest about everything, to start new and fresh like the walls, to strip out her insides and begin again. Instead she just sat there like a lump, not knowing quite what to say.

When the kids came back, talk turned to turtles. Jack seemed surprised about the pet store outing, knowing how Margie felt about the smell and funk in the cages. He looked at her with a loving smirk. The children were raring to go and they said their goodbyes. She lingered and kissed Jack goodbye on the lips, finally able to hold his gaze.

In Petland, they took their time, looking at each creature as if they were in a fantastic zoo rather than a seedy store. They studied the geometric patterns on the smooth snakes' skins, watched hamsters interact in human ways, and took in the intricate colors and textures on the feathers of birds. They chose five turtles thoughtfully, taking their time, giving each one a name based on physical attributes and personality traits.

Lying in bed that night, Margie couldn't sleep. She was determined to stop taking meds every single night, and was weaning herself down. She struggled to fight the urge. They called out to her constantly, like a foghorn in her pounding head, announcing their presence. Other times they whispered in her ear, promising peace. Whether it was withdrawal that made her pulse pound, or whether it was real anxiety based on her previous actions, she did not know. As her heart raced, her mind accelerated to keep up. She was panicking about whether to tell Jack about the affair, what the right course of action was. But what good would it do and how would they recover as a couple, a couple already skating on very thin ice, ice that was cracking at the edges. And they hadn't even talked about the issue of the debt and the lies. Instead of swallowing a pill, she swallowed hard, her mouth dry, and knew what she must do. She shifted in bed, trying not to wake the children who had rolled toward her weight, appendages intertwined with hers, searching for any nook and cranny to lock onto. She crept out of bed and downstairs to her computer.

She was going to look into her finances head on and attempt to come up with a plan. A chill spread over her sweat-soaked body and she shook it off as she logged on to her credit card account and looked directly at the amount of her debt, which she usually tried to avoid, purposely averting her eyes from the totals and focusing only at the minimum amount due. Good god, the amounts were awful, inducing a fresh layer of perspiration. She started tallying numbers. Even though she wasn't good at math she was very competent with a calculator. She would control her spending so the debt would stop growing. Like an infection, she would need to stop its spreading, then shrink it. At the hospital they had drawn a circle with a marker around the red spot on Jack's thigh to monitor the spread of the infection, and she would draw a hypothetical circle around her debt, contain it, then eradicate it. It might take years. But by re-budgeting their monthly income, if Jack helped her a little, they could make a big dent. That was if he would stay with her and try to work things out, not leave her. When Jack had discovered the receipts he had said "we have to talk about *us*" and they had not yet done so.

Before picking Jack up the next day, Margie prepared a quiche. She had found the recipe on a gourmet cooking website, having to dig up a pie pan from deep in the cupboards, a wedding gift she had never used. Hers didn't look anything like the picture, with its uneven crust and drooping center, but she hoped it would taste okay. The kids made welcome home posters with colorful magic markers, hanging them in the foyer, Margie wanting to leave the rest of the walls clean. It was a grand entrance indeed when he came through the front door, kids on either side, holding him at the elbows; although he didn't need their help he indulged them.

Jack looked at the posters and then looked past them, to the rest of the house. Margie watched his eyes and saw that he immediately registered the changes, the lack of potential possessions plastered over the home he had built.

"What the heck? I think I'm hallucinating here," he joked, blinking, she thought, to hold back tears.

"It's gone, Jack. All that crap and clutter is gone! The kids helped me rip it all down and boy did we have fun. You should have seen this place—it looked like a war zone."

"Talk about home improvement," he said. And they sat down to a nice brunch, the quiche flavorful, if a bit gooey in the middle.

She told Jack that Auden had called wanting to come by and say hello, and Brett had phoned yesterday checking in on him. Said she wanted to have them all over soon, but wanted to wait until he felt up for it. In truth Margie had to wait until *she* felt up for it.

Auden had been a godsend the last few weeks, taking charge of all of the Manscaping himself and doing a pretty good job of it, according to Jack. He had called Jack daily in the hospital or at home, keeping him informed and asking his advice on all their active jobs. Jack said he had risen to the occasion, was a natural. She was glad Auden was still here, and upon seeing him the first night in the hospital, when they had embraced and Margie hadn't been able to control her silent tears, she could see that he really did care about their family, that she had misjudged his being judgmental.

On the other hand, she dreaded seeing Katie, but knew she must. Brett and Katie had come by the hospital on the day after the heart attack, and Katie had hardly looked at her. It was tense and Brett seemed to give her dirty looks too; she was sure Katie had told him everything. After all, couples usually do tell each other everything—healthy couples at least. Because of the things that couldn't be discussed, Katie had commented on the curtains, the view, which was nothing more than a patch of grass muted by dingy gray light on the overcast day. Brett had fought the awkwardness with news of motorcycle repairs and techie talk about some sound equipment he'd just bought that went over everyone's heads.

It was obvious Katie blamed her for everything that happened, a blatant reminder that she blamed herself, as if she could for one second forget. Before having the entire family over, she wanted to have some one-on-one time with Katie, to set things right, if that was even possible. Jack was advised to take a few more days off of work, but seemed to be doing well, so Margie asked if he minded if she met Katie on Monday afternoon. At Carbucks, of course.

Waiting for Katie amidst the exhaust odor, Margie was exhausted and realized she was running on fumes. She felt light-headed and had to sit down while she waited for her drink. It was the first time she'd had any time to herself in weeks, other than in her bathroom with the door locked. She had been working hard, and had been strong on the outside, regardless of the turmoil she was feeling inside. Physically and emotionally depleted, she tried to regain her focus by savoring each sip of her Frappuccino.

Katie rushed in and plopped down with hardly a hello.

"So what happened in Paris?" she asked, not a question but an accusation. "I'm sure that's what you asked me here to talk to me about. To get it out of your system."

"Oh Katie, it was a disaster. I should have listened to you," she said, eyes welling up.

"It's certainly been a disaster here with what poor Jack went through," she said, not trusting the tears. "What happened?" she asked coolly.

"Well, everything and nothing happened. Stevie lied about lots of things."

"You haven't been exactly truthful." Margie wondered exactly which lies Katie was referring to, but continued.

"It wasn't just that. The whole thing felt like a farce. I mean I slept with him, I did, just once, on the first night and I felt just awful; I felt sick about it and knew right away I'd made a terrible mistake."

"I can imagine." Katie certainly wasn't making this easy for Margie.

But Margie didn't expect it to be easy. She didn't even know if she was capable of expressing what she was feeling, but pressed on. "No, it was more than that. I realized what I have here at home, I really did, and I'm really trying to change. I've come to understand that, that I have not been able to be happy in my own life. I want to stop looking elsewhere, you know? I'm not making excuses, but I think I needed the whole horrible weekend to realize that. I broke up with him before I left, ended it entirely…"

Here she paused but Katie didn't speak.

"I just don't know how to get past it, to get past the guilt. Not to make it all about me, Katie, but I really don't know what to do." She took a deep breath. "Do you think I should tell Jack?" She really wanted Katie's opinion, ironically, insight she had ignored in the past. Although she was afraid of receiving another cutting remark, that she could handle; she was more terrified of what her honest answer would be.

Katie pondered the question at length before she responded. "No. It would destroy him. It's already destroyed you and now you need to fix everything and make it right. But, like you said, you do have to make a change. Not who you are because I know deep down you are a good person, but your actions, your outlook…Margie, do you love him?"

"I do. I really do."

"Then you are going to have to show him that."

"I want to show him…and the kids too."

"And eventually, maybe not now, but eventually, you are going to have to forgive yourself."

"Oh, Katie, I don't know if I can." Tears flowed freely down her face now, and she sniffled and dabbed at her raccoon eyes, going through a thick stack of napkins, wiping and re-wiping her eyes in silence, until she was able to continue.

"I want you to know I appreciate your friendship. To me it's about more than the family barbeques, the affair, the meds—which I'm going to stop selling by the way, and I'm going to *try* to stop taking; I just don't feel right about it anymore—but I genuinely enjoy your companionship. I guess I don't really have enough true friendships, and I need you in my life right now more than ever."

Rather than respond with words, Katie reached across the table and held her hand. Once the barrier was finally broken, they backed into small talk and then caught up on the day-to-day challenges of life, the neighborhood gossip and minor family dramas, woman to woman, girl to girl.

Back at home Margie struggled with her new resolutions. Some days she succeeded and others she did not. Aimee was still giving her attitude, more now that Jack was around, and Margie lost her patience more than once. Oliver was needier than ever, constantly reaching for a hand or clinging to a leg.

Did some mothers actually like this level of dependency? She fretted that she wasn't all that competent at raising a family; there was no guidebook to follow and she certainly hadn't had a good example where her parents were concerned. Although she had birthed the children, she had been frightened when they were born in the hospital—didn't know what she was doing then—and hadn't really known ever since.

But waiting on Jack and wanting to pull up the slack, she tried to cover more of the workload. When Jack went back to work and they fell into a more normal routine, she fluctuated between feeling overwhelmed and then underwhelmed, still questioning at times if this was her true calling in life.

Was doing load after load of laundry, forever searching for matching socks supposed to satisfy her? Was slaving over the stove making a healthy dinner while Jack surfed the internet slouched on the sofa supposed to sustain her? Was struggling over difficult math assignments with Aimee until her brain ached supposed to placate her? Was constantly rinsing dishes until her fingers pruned up supposed to fulfill her?

Sometimes life felt so repetitive. She missed her meds at night, her one true escape. Without her mind-altering medications life was too sharp around the edges. And too dull in the middle.

She wondered if a person could truly change. She believed one could alter behaviors, overcome things, but not necessarily change characteristics inherent to one's personality. Her father had never changed. But now she saw that alcohol was his one fix, his serum to treat the intensity of life, and she herself had reached for remedies—and not just one, but several: the pills, the spending, the affair.

She almost felt sorry for her dad these days, as he was aging, growing smaller and more frail. Until, that is, he opened his mouth, constantly complaining, blurting out something misogynistic or harping on his backwards political views, which he never failed to do.

Unlike him, she would find joy in the little things in life. But this mindset was a struggle, didn't come easily to her. Yet she had done it at the pet store. She had taken to going out to the turtle pond and taking five deep breaths, meditating for ten minutes each evening. Yet she felt she never truly reached transcendence. She tried to savor a well-cooked meal, but that was difficult after the tiresome preparation. She tried to find beauty in the everyday. But sometimes she didn't know where to look.

Adopting this outlook, Margie realized, was a skill that must be learned. She had to practice gratification, to study the very concept of it, something she had failed to grasp in the past. She had to analyze how to feel satisfied, life giving her lessons daily, and to learn how to achieve the desired reaction, understanding what would produce it.

Just yesterday she had taken pleasure in helping out an elderly man with dementia at the hospital, but only after first feeling frustrated with him when he kept repeating the same nonsensical statement. She had felt a warm glow when Oliver had walked up to her and kissed her cheek for no reason, when admittedly her first response was wondering what in the world he needed now.

She found that she liked taking short walks around the block to clear her head. Even after living with herself all these years, even as she approached middle age, she felt like she was just now getting to know herself. Or rather, rediscovering herself. On her strolls she would reach down to pick up a red feather dropped from a cardinal, or a colorful leaf, like she had collected when she was a kid, pockets always full when she returned from following the creek that ran behind the trailer park. She was trying to quiet down and really see things, to take notice of the environment around her, and to feel with her senses.

And yet still, she struggled with whether these small moments were enough.

Sometimes she felt that life was like one of Aimee's complicated math story problems, where you are looking to define X, but you have no freaking idea what X is. Or, if X is anxiety and it is on a train twenty miles away moving at eighty miles an hour and panic is coming at you from the other direction from forty miles away at sixty miles an hour, what the hell does it take to stop both trains in their tracks and exist in the present—minus the use of pills, which would solve the problem instantly. Or, like on some days, if X is monotony and Y is boredom, how to find e, where e is the constant desired exponent, perhaps enjoyment.

Margie was giving herself a headache. Then there was the problem of Jack. Now that they were past the emotional intensity and connection based around the heart attack scare and back to a normal routine, he was pulling further away, seemed weary of her. They hadn't slept together since the accident. She pondered shaving her pubic hair again but didn't want it to be something so superficial that brought them together.

She had told him about the new budget she had put together and he seemed appreciative of the effort. But when she showed him the exact amount of debt, his eyes bulged like a deer in headlights, then flickered and died, like he had been hit by a Mac truck—and she knew she was the driver. He had looked so tired, so utterly hopeless, the contoured lines of his forehead like an impenetrable terrain. When he recovered he said he would help her but his eyes conveyed doubt, mistrust. And could she blame him?

She was making little attempts around the house, starting with the quiche, and since then had made many new dishes, like hamburger stroganoff and a ham and leek casserole. She was keeping the house tidier than ever. She and Jack hadn't been fighting, per se, but there was something indefinable between them, some blockage like a dam that kept everything festering on the stagnant surface. It was too difficult to broach anything of depth, and thus even pleasantries seemed extra shallow. What's worse, sometimes his comments were dripping with sarcasm, swimming in a sea of resentment. Margie didn't want another fake relationship, like she and Stevie had, like she and Jack had in the past due to her deception. For the first time in her life, she wanted something real, something that really mattered.

She wanted to be transparent. But if he really saw inside of her, would he—could he—still love her?

In any case, the things left unsaid made the things that were said fall flat. Entire conversations seemed to dissipate into thin air, and certain subjects seemed out of reach altogether. Margie remembered the forced conversation they had had just last night, skimming the surface as usual.

"How was work?" she had asked, after he returned from a long day, arriving home after nine p.m.

"*Wonderful*," he said, sarcastically, she thought.

"How are you feeling?" She realized it was too general of a question, and afraid of the answer, added, "any shortness of breath or chest pain?"

"Margie, I told you a million times, I'm fine. Save your questions for the whack jobs in your waiting room."

She didn't think he meant it as a joke, judging by his tone, but gave a chuckle to try to make it one.

"Speaking of patients, Dirty Hairy came in again today. Thanked me again for saving his life but said unfortunately he was now experiencing chronic gas."

"Poor bastard," Jack said, staring into his laptop.

Trying to shift the conversation to a more serious tone and show she was trying to make a change, she shifted the conversation to finances, something the old Margie never would have done. "I paid bills today, and we had a pretty good month. There were a few hospital bills, of course, that our insurance didn't cover, but I made the credit card payments just like we talked about."

"Now you're going to blame the money problems on me? God, Margie, you've gotta be kidding me."

"No, I didn't mean it like that. I was just saying, or trying to say, that I didn't spend any extra on me and the kids…that I think our plan is going to work."

"I hope so. But I'm exhausted. I'm not in the mood to talk about this right now."

"Fair enough. Well, you won't believe who I ran into at the supermarket, Pamela Pearlman, you know that woman that used to live down the block? She looked really awful, her hair was wild, totally unkempt, died this horrible brassy yellow, and she told me they moved to Plano, and the only reason she was in town was because her ex-husband, you know, Jim? Well, he still lives here, in those run-down apartments on Deer Run, across from the highway?"

When she glanced over to look for a reaction, she saw that he had put his ear buds in at some point to tune her out, leaving her in a vacuum. Well, c'est la vie, she said to herself.

And yet she longed to be closer to him, to connect with him again.

DECEMBER

Yes, Jack was retreating from her, of that she was certain. Since she couldn't seem to reach him, she searched harder within herself, trying to figure out what made her tick: who she was, who she wanted to be. And what, if anything, brought her joy.

Margie felt very alone. She had Katie of course, and they spoke on the phone often, but their busy lives made it hard to get together. She had the kids, with whom she was spending more time, but they were not exactly on the same level intellectually or emotionally, and too immature for the adult conversation she was craving.

Though she hated to admit it, what Margie missed most of all were her prescriptions, hundreds of tiny friends in different shapes and colors from the plastic bottles in her medicine cabinet that could cheer her up in no time, lifting her spirits like no one else could. She hadn't taken meds for two weeks, abandoning them completely—and they her. She missed the instant and deep comfort the pills offered her, requiring nothing in return, true unconditional love. She sometimes wondered if the same kind of love could exist for her outside of a bottle.

Three of her real friends, in human form—the women she had introduced to her little bottled friends—reached out to her about meeting up with the pretense of catching up but which was in actuality, Margie knew, for filling up. She decided to come clean to them. Over the phone she told them one by one that she had decided to stop selling the meds, explaining that she had never meant any harm by it and was only trying to help them, then admitting that she herself had had a problem with pills. She had never acknowledged this to anyone before, much less herself. Well how would she know she had a problem when she had never before tried to stop? But the proof was in the desire she felt for the drugs, which was strong. And the withdrawal was stronger, still causing her heart rate to fluctuate: skittering, skipping beats, or seizing up in a state of panic.

With all the additional anxiety she was experiencing, no longer masked with the meds, her nervous habits were worse than ever. Her constant hair twisting, which sometimes now resulted in her plucking out the hair, even when her voluminous hair was her pride and joy, and biting her lips, nibbling and peeling pieces of loose skin until they bled or at least required generous applications of lip balm until they healed. But only until she unconsciously did it again.

She found sharing the truth with the women therapeutic. So much so that after one such conversation she threw her pill bottles—all seventeen of them—in the trash and then emptied all of the trash cans in the house into a large black trash bag which she disposed of in the plastic bin at the curb. She regretted it immediately. Watching the sanitation truck come by and haul them all away brought on the most gut-wrenching panic attack yet, activating her sweat glands to spout even in the cold of winter, sending her to the end of the driveway to search the grass for any bottle that might have spilled, further proving the addiction, as if there was any doubt left.

She was glad the kids were in school and Jack was at work so she could sit on the curb and cry. Of course she wondered what the neighbors might think. But she didn't care. Knowing she would never again experience the pleasant, intoxicating benefits of taking benzos or relish the immediate relief it provided, she cried for her loss. About her past. And about the uncertainty of her future. Thought maybe throwing them out had been a mistake, premature. She certainly couldn't get more at the hospital. Her three-month probation period had finally ended, and Mrs. Jones had just called her into her office and again closed the door, complimenting her on her competence and diligence at work and her overall good behavior—and Margie would not, could not, jeopardize her job again.

Even the giraffe had warmed to her recently, maybe hearing good reports from Mrs. Jones, with even good gossip so rampant in the hospital. Dr. Renquist had come right up behind her in the cafeteria line. They hadn't spoken since the incident, and Margie faced forward, prepared to pretend she hadn't seen her, looking straight ahead as she always did when they passed in the halls, which happened several times a day to Margie's horror.

"I hear the potato salad is good today," she said. "The food in here isn't half bad, compared to the hospital where I used to work."

"Really? Must have been pretty awful then. This is certainly not fine dining in my book…but a person's got to eat, I suppose."

"Yep. And I'm so hungry right now I could eat a horse."

"Well, thanks for the heads-up. Maybe I'll try it—the potato salad, not the horse." She laughed and Dr. Renquist cracked what appeared to be a genuine smile. Even though she had wanted to not care what the behemoth thought of her, it did make her feel better—and it kind of annoyed her that it had.

In a slightly better mood now, she pulled herself together and stood up from the curb with a loud sigh, and went inside to check Facebook to take her mind off things.

Here she faced another challenge: every time she opened her laptop she was bombarded by ads on her Facebook page, on Pinterest, which she rarely logged on to these days, and ironically even on her online banking page. Ads directed at her, targeting her based on algorithms and her search history, trying to sell her things, things she had wanted, things she had needed, as well as "similar suggestions." They seemed to know her, feeding on her weaknesses while appealing to her excellent sense of style. Flashing, moving, blinking ads were all screaming for her attention in headers, sidebars, and pop-ups.

For example, she was surrounded by pendant lights of all styles and colors. Even after she'd ripped them from the walls, the temptation remained. But instead of feeling greedy desire, she was becoming irritated. A cabinet here, a Coach purse there, a soap dish here, a side table there. In light of recent events, the bright green side table seemed ridiculous, the birdcage filled with candles, frivolous. No, she didn't want things, she wanted Jack back, and that was something she couldn't get with the click of a button. She closed all of the windows that were open and searched for something else instead—rather than a thing, a thing to do with Jack.

Margie wanted to plan something special that they could do together, and she continued searching online when she had angst-fueled insomnia at night. She eventually decided on a cooking class—Provincial French cuisine, no less—at the Culinary Institute downtown. She still had a lot to learn in the kitchen and thought it might feel like being on a cooking show, almost like reality television. She read in the description of the class that each couple would be responsible for a dish or two, and then they would all sit down to the fantastic multi-course meal they had prepared with fine wine pairings. Other than grilling out, Jack didn't do much cooking, but she knew he loved to create, to work with his hands. When she told him, while not overly enthusiastic, he was up for it.

On the evening of the class she struggled with what to wear. She wanted to look elegant for their evening out. But realizing it might get messy and knowing she was a klutz in the kitchen, she chose dark jeans, a nice comfortable sweater and knee-high boots—fuck-me boots, as she used to refer to them when she was single. And she hoped her husband would. It was a "date night" after all, as much as she hated the cheesy term. To use it on Facebook pretty much announced to the world that a couple was making a desperate attempt to save their marriage. And in her case maybe they were.

They didn't talk much in the car, reduced to small talk as they were lately. Unfamiliar with gourmet cooking and yet knowing they would have to perform, they were slightly nervous when they entered the massive kitchen. Both a bit competitive in these kinds of situations, they chose a station at the far end of the room and whispered and giggled privately about the other couples—the uptight couple to their far right, whom they could tell right away would be overachievers, already brown-nosing the instructor. There was a pretentious couple at the table to the left who looked like they jumped off the pages of a Neiman Marcus catalogue; an older woman that they nicknamed the Silver Fox with her long shiny mane and five-inch heels; and the frumpy, earthy couple that, according to Jack, had the sickly look of vegans.

They grew quiet when the instructor began speaking. Knowledgeable and engaging, she talked the group through each dish, giving tips and explaining techniques. They were assigned Coq au Vin and Crab Cakes, using fresh crabmeat. Margie liked the sound of their dishes, but hadn't understood all of the preparation as it was a lot to retain and she wasn't familiar with many of the cooking terms. When the teacher announced it was time to begin, Margie and Jack split up the ingredient list, both darting around in search of obscure items, shouting across the room at each other. Other couples were frantic too and the stainless steel work kitchen came alive.

Jack hunted for the pancetta in the fridge among the proteins, unsure what it even looked like, while Margie rummaged through the produce, digging for herbs, finding parsley but having trouble with the tarragon. They scoured various industrial-sized pantries and fridges for cream, butter and breadcrumbs.

"What the heck does a crimini mushroom look like, Margie?" Jack shouted from across the room, pronouncing crimini to rhyme with Gemini. Margie had a flash of that childhood moment of not knowing what even a button mushroom looked like, and smiled to herself that she now found herself in—no, actually arranged to be in—this magnificent kitchen surrounded by these top-quality ingredients. He called her over as he foraged through five mushroom varieties: portabella, oyster, shitake, chanterelles, and enoki, proclaiming the latter "disgusting-looking" in a whisper, before the instructor finally came over and pointed them out.

"This is going to be a clusterfuck," Jack mumbled under his breath to Margie at their station. That word always made Margie laugh—with the exception of when it was directed at her and her life—and when their eyes met Margie saw a glimmer in his she hadn't seen in quite some time. She couldn't contain loud outbursts of laughter when they spilled flour on the floor and butchered the pancetta. Margie was hovering over him now, telling him to *hurry*—as he minced the garlic too slowly and methodically, the small sticky cloves slipping out of his bulky fingers. Margie wanted to take over but she had never known how to do it properly. At home she always grew impatient and smashed the cloves with the side of her knife, or to avoid the problem altogether used pre-cut garlic from a jar. Margie smirked at him when the instructor came over and showed him a much more effective technique, rolling her knife back and forth in a continual motion that effectively divided the cloves into hundreds of tiny pieces, emitting a wonderful aroma.

One would have thought they were Michelin star chefs the way they fretted over the mushroom sauce, worrying when the reduction wouldn't reduce. Their crab cakes were loose, not holding together properly so Jack mashed and muscled them together forcefully, the final shape more ball than patty. They worked themselves into a frenzy in a race against the clock in order to complete each dish at the proper time. "Coordinating the timing is one of the biggest challenges of cooking," the instructor had said. Unfortunately the only things happening simultaneously were the disasters striking all around the room sending the poor teacher rushing around to each station.

Finally they were finished, and while not achieving perfection, their dishes were done at least, as good as they were going to get. They took off their dirty aprons and watched as other groups finished up, feeling self-satisfied. Feeling happy, Margie thought. She couldn't remember the last time the two of them had done something like this, even when they were dating. In hindsight, they hadn't had much of a courting period.

She had just fallen into a comfortable situation, and she had been needy after the debacle with her ex. Maybe she had taken him for granted from day one.

At the large table they sat next to the kiss-ass couple who turned out to be hilarious. Maybe they were just truly friendly, Margie mused. The table setting was beautiful, utilizing full sets of heavy utensils, and the food was delicious. The entire evening was unlike anything Margie had experienced, and she tasted everything, savoring the many different flavors while she sipped the fine wine.

Driving home, they talked. Really talked. Margie was honest, if not about everything, about her feelings.

"The heart attack scared me to death Jack, it really did, and it made me realize how much I love you. I know I don't tell you that enough, and I've taken you for granted, but I don't know what I would do without you."

She continued, rambling on a bit, but it was the good kind of rambling she thought, and Jack seemed to really be listening. "I feel awful about the spending, and lying to you about it, but I just know I can control myself…"

"Margie, you have made mistakes, and it will not be easy, but what we need to focus on is how to move forward."

So he did want to move forward! Hearing him say it was a huge relief, and she did too, even though she wasn't sure how. She did, however, the only thing she could do, and that was share with him what was on her mind, which she realized she hadn't done in a very long time. She told him about the carpe diem sign she had seen in Paris, and shared her epiphany with him, searching for the words, stuttering through it even though saying it out loud made it sound corny, even though she worried he might think it was juvenile, discovering something so blatantly obvious, to him at least. Yet she told him how she wanted to seize every day from now on, how she hoped it wasn't too late, how she had been focusing on the wrong things, searching for escapes. She confessed to taking more sleeping pills than she had been letting on and how she had stopped now. That she was struggling, but knew it was the right decision.

"You don't know how happy I am to hear that, Margie. I know I haven't been perfect either, I mean I'm a lazy bastard sometimes, and I know I spend too much time hiding out surfing the internet. But the last few years have been hard on me," Jack continued. "I've missed you, felt shut out of your life. I hope you'll let me in now."

She regretted the time and energy she had squandered on Stevie, and as such she had hardly wasted a single thought on him since. Sure, she had liked the attention she got, but the reality of it was Jack had tried to give her attention too, she just hadn't accepted it. She didn't know how he had put up with her, yet by some miracle he was still there. And now she pulled him towards her in increments. She found herself spooning him at night, curling up behind him and cradling him when he slept, and she knew he felt it by the way his body relaxed into hers, little spoon curved around big spoon, her face close to his hairy neck.

She opened up to him about her difficulties with motherhood some days, and it felt good to admit it out loud. He helped her find the humor in frustrating situations. She discovered a companionship that she hadn't known she'd needed, as did he, and their conversations became more meaningful. She expressed to him how she missed the meds and now wrestled with sleep every single night and he offered support, especially in terms of an ear; she would talk and talk and talk into the wee hours, eventually putting them both to sleep. Turns out he had things to say too—worries, fears—and by sharing their anguish it was diffused, absorbed by the other's body, into the other's bones. They talked the way real couples do, she supposed. She had grown up thinking the world was rigged against her, and only now realized that together they could create their own little world, a world in which—up until now—she had not been very involved.

They decided to put up the Christmas tree the following weekend, a couple of weeks before Christmas instead of waiting until the last minute, or skipping it altogether as they sometimes did if they were going to celebrate at his parents'. Struggling to straighten the ratty old plastic branches, the whole family unanimously decided to trash it and get a real tree. Jack knew of a tree farm outside of town that he drove past on his way to one of his clients. So they all packed into the Manscaping van, the children's excitement palpable. The kids were drawn to a large tree, slightly crooked, imperfect.

"This is the best Christmas ever!" Oliver kept repeating in the car.

"It's not even Christmas yet, you dope." Aimee said.

"But, but, it's the best *tree* we've ever had, and the best thing about it is that we all picked it out together, isn't that right Mom?" He searched her eyes, always looking for approval, always wanting everyone to be happy. What often came across to her as insecurity, she now saw could be interpreted as loving. She made a mental note to try to be more like him.

She had never had a real tree growing up. Her parents' fake tree was the worst, with its spindly branches, some rubbed bare by the time she was in high school, decorated with cheap plastic ornaments. She remembered being embarrassed when the neighbor kids had seen the sad tree, and by the sparse presents underneath it. But she commanded herself to let the thought go; why did she need to continue to dwell on it when she had a family of her own now? Because of their lack of it growing up, she supposed she had always thought that money could buy happiness. But this year they too would have a light Christmas as they tackled her debt, yet she felt closer to her family than she had in ages.

When the last string of lights was wrapped around the bulky branches and they plugged it in, Margie thought it looked spectacular. But what she loved most was the smell of pine that filled the house, which she breathed in each morning as she sat drinking her coffee, consciously, purposefully, literally sniffing the air and savoring the scent.

With the kids out of school on Christmas vacation, she had promised to take them to the Kimbell Art Museum, all the way in Fort Worth. Katie had mentioned it housed one of the best collections in the Southwest and Margie had never been there. She hadn't even been to the museums in downtown Dallas for that matter. She didn't know anything about art but thought it would be fun. Aimee was good at drawing and Oliver was a creative child. They would have their own private field trip on a Saturday while Jack was finishing up a landscaping job.

So she packed a picnic, and they all got ready for their big day out. Aimee was picking at Oliver all morning, forcing Margie to lash out at her. She was still obstinate lately, smarting off, arguing back about everything. But Aimee's mood improved on the drive with each passing mile. She was chatty, asking questions about what the museum and the art would be like that Margie couldn't answer.

"We'll just have to see when we get there," she said.

Upon arrival, Margie was disappointed. The museum was much smaller than she had expected, the grounds less grand. She actually thought the building was kind of ugly, but she kept these thoughts to herself. Instead she read a placard aloud under the arched entryway.

"See, even the architecture is famous," she said.

Once inside, the walls weren't crammed with art like she anticipated. The pieces were spread out more sparsely, giving them room to breathe, she supposed, making her cringe when she thought about the multilayered collages smothering the walls in her own house until recently. She saw that sometimes less *was* more.

They made their way from painting to painting, taking them all in one by one. The kids were quiet, and she couldn't tell if they were ultra bored or extremely engaged. In fact she couldn't decide if she was bored— some of it she certainly wouldn't consider art. Margie worried that she wasn't really "getting it" at all and that it was somehow above her head, out of reach like so many things. Then again, what did it matter? She was spending time with her kids and they could all become cultured together.

"You can draw better than this," she told Aimee, looking at a painting that she read was by Miró.

"Totally," she said.

Moving from room to room, they talked about which paintings they did like.

"This one's pretty," Aimee said.

"That one is really neat," Oliver added.

But it wasn't until they got to the room that Margie read was the Impressionism section that she was really moved by the art. She studied each painting and wondered how the individual blobs of paint, loose, almost sloppy, could come together to create a scene, to capture it perfectly. She tried to learn the artists' names so she could tell Katie. Munch, Cézanne, Matisse, Degas, Picasso!—these were her favorites. She looked closely at the paintings, leaning in over the ropes, nose inches from the canvases. Margie jumped when an alarm went off. Realizing that it was indeed she herself who set it off, she made a face at the kids and they snickered. Forced to take several steps back, she noticed how the different perspective changed the art dramatically. She kept stepping backwards, in such a trance she nearly bumped into other guests, a few feet at a time until she looked at the paintings from across the room. Now they were almost as crisp as photos, but more vivid, the light trapped in vibrant color.

When she moved closer again it broke apart; she couldn't get over how up close they were nothing more than individual brush strokes. Blobs, really. She stared at an image of a mother and daughter on a pier that seemed to splinter into a million shards of color but always came back together again to make a whole, suspending a moment in time. She stood there a long while, until Oliver finally tugged at her arm saying he was hungry. She stared a moment longer, trying to freeze the image on the canvas of her mind.

That night, probably inspired by the mother-daughter scene, Margie wandered in and sat down on the corner of the bed in Aimee's room while she was busy organizing postcards from the museum on her dresser. Oliver was watching TV with Jack. Margie realized it was rare for the two of them to be in one place like this, and as such it felt awkwardly intimate. In fact, it was rare for Aimee to be in the room without Oliver, to have any space or time for herself.

"What do you think about turning the storage room upstairs into your own room?" Margie asked, breaking the silence.

"*Really?* That would be *awesome*. No, it would be beyond awesome, it would be *amazing*."

They talked about decorating ideas for a long time, Margie welcoming her thoughts for once. Then without warning, Aimee shifted to a more pensive tone.

"Mom, what were you like when you were my age?"

She had to think about it. She was not that appreciative and she complained a lot. She remembered being insecure, moody and mischievous.

"I guess I was a lot like you. Not as creative though, and not as smart. I got mostly B's and some C's while you get mostly A's and B's.

"But were you popular?"

"I was kind of middle of the road: not in the top clique for sure, but maybe the next one down. But I got along with lots of the kids, the band nerds, the honor roll students, the art kids. I guess that was the good thing about it. The top clique were so snobby that they stuck to themselves and never got to know any of those kids."

"I never thought of it like that before. That's how I want to be too. Middle of the road like you."

That night Margie slept better than she had in ages. But in the following days, she continued to look at herself, not always liking what she saw. While at times she felt she was becoming more comfortable in her own skin, other times she felt stripped and laid bare. Like she had shed an outer layer, molted, reminding her of the locust shells she used to find sticking to the trunks of pine trees, claws still digging into the bark while the new bodies up and crawled out. She knew what she had she crawled out of, but what vile creature, translucent and raw, had she uncovered underneath? Yet she would have to nurture that new being until it became strong and healthy enough to carry her into this new phase of life.

Although she felt totally exposed, she hid her worst secret, protected it in order to protect the family. She had decided she would never tell Jack about the affair.

She and Jack made love on Christmas Day, in the afternoon, while the kids were at a neighbor's house showing them their new toys. She liked that phrase, making love, and it did make her love him even more. But more importantly, she would continue to make herself love him.

Turned out, Jack had a secret too. But it was a nice one, unlike her own. Emerging from bed naked, he walked across the room and reached into his dresser drawer and brought out a small box. She unwrapped an even smaller jewelry box inside, and when she snapped opened the case, a scrap of paper was folded and folded again into a tiny triangle. She unfolded it to see his messy, manly handwriting, all architectural angles: *A Trip To (the real) Paris For Two.*

"Oh, *sweetie!*" she beamed. "Are you *serious?*"

"I was in the middle of researching this trip a few months ago when I found those goddamned receipts. Can you freaking believe that?" He explained how in the middle of searching for plane tickets he ran across the doctored receipts, dumped in the computer's trash but not deleted.

Margie didn't know whether to laugh or cry. She felt it was definitely too soon to laugh—but he smiled, and they would laugh about it years later.

"You really are a mess, Margie. You're a handful. I swear to god sometimes I don't know what to do with you."

"Keep me?" Margie said with a demure smile. It really was a question. But with the way things had been going she felt pretty confident about the answer.

"You're a keeper alright," he said with a wink. "But you know, after that, I put the trip out of my mind. It seemed hopeless, totally pointless. Not just the trip but connecting at all. But after the last couple of months I think maybe we can make it happen next fall if we play our cards right. Maybe it would be good for us."

"Oh, it would be *amazing.* I mean not just the Paris part but taking a trip just the two of us. We've never done *anything* like that! It could be like sort of a second honeymoon." She couldn't even think where they had gone on their first honeymoon. Oh yes, she recalled their rushed trip to San Antonio. "Do you really think we can afford it?"

"Margie, there are some things in life that are worth it, worth fighting for, and I believe our relationship is one of them."

To Margie's surprise, he mentioned wanting to go to the Luxembourg Gardens. Had he discovered the horrible bubble bath, she wondered? Margie cringed but didn't ask. When he said he had come across the park while doing a google search, her shoulders relaxed, and she realized it was just a wonderful coincidence. For the first time in her life, Margie considered herself lucky. Not about the possibility of the trip, but about the possibility of having Jack, of keeping him.

Suddenly in the spirit of gift giving, she remembered a surprise she had for him. Where in the hell had she put it? She jumped up, threw on her nightie, and ran out of the room, leaving Jack bewildered. She rushed back into the bedroom and dug frantically through the closet, then felt around under the bed, outstretched arms flailing this way and that. She hadn't thought about it in months with all that had been going on. She now ran around the house searching for her car keys. They weren't on the key hook; they never were. She found them on the counter and ran to the car.

There it was, the brown bag, rolled to the far corner of the trunk. She had never even taken it out, the taxidermy chipmunk and all it represented! She worried it would be beat up and badly injured from being tossed around back there all this time. She opened the bag and unwrapped the layers and layers of tissue paper to find it unharmed. The relic was still perfectly preserved, and she looked at it a minute more, staring into its glass eyes before rewrapping it. She remembered being called "Chipmunk Cheeks" in junior high. Now she wondered what was so wrong with the nickname anyway as they were quite adorable creatures, certainly the cutest of the rodents.

She raced in the house and placed the crinkled bag in his hands.

"What in the heck? Where in the world did you get this little guy?"

"I got it in Paris. Paris, Texas, that is. I totally forgot about it! I just loved his expression and thought it would look nice standing on your desk. I mean, I know your office is small and overcrowded already, so I hope you have room for it."

"I'll *make* room," he said, finding her hand and squeezing it.

EPILOGUE

January, 2068

Marjorie Moore was hunched over her computer checking Facebook, which had been abandoned by all but the oldest generation, now nicknamed Deathbook by the youngsters, and appropriately so, thought Margie, as her friends had indeed been dying off left and right. But it was still one of her favorite pastimes, her hands knotted and skinny like branches hovering over the keyboard. Her forearms were so covered in age spots it was the tiny spaces between the splotches that jumped out. Out of habit, she began typing a post until her shaky, arthritic fingers failed her and she called out to her dictation app to take over.

How did her frail, feeble body feel so heavy? Gravity seemed to have a stronger and stronger grip on her, pulling her harder toward the earth, and she knew it wouldn't be long until it pulled her down below, enveloping her at six feet under. Her neck was stiff, her bones ached, her muscles all but atrophied. But her silvery white hair was perfectly coiffed and still stylish, at least in her mind.

The room was not much to look at, sterile and small, a far cry from fancy. The bottom third of the walls were covered in clinical pale green paint left over from an earlier era, buckling and peeling in places. The small space had an unfinished quality due to budget cuts: a bare bulb hung overhead without a fixture, the cushionless chair to the side of her bed with one faulty leg was never replaced with a new one as promised.

Yet she found it comfortable enough and did the best she could with what she had to work with. She'd always had taste, of that she was sure. The four walls that surrounded her were plastered in clippings, in the type of messy collage sometimes indicative of the insane. Yet at ninety she was still sharp as a whip, or so people said.

But the montage was of people, memories, and moments—not products. Some of the clippings had ripped edges, torn from magazines: a beautiful bouquet, a beagle with big brown eyes, a photo of the Florida Coast, and of course, a photo of Jack and her standing in front of the Eiffel tower. Some were cut from newspapers and others were plucked from albums, with a spattering of brightly colored crayon drawings taped to the mix, from her three great-grandkids.

There was the carefully cut article, now aged and yellowing, from the sports page of the *Prairie Mound News* of her grandson, when he'd finished first in three races in the regional track meet, breaking records. If that didn't beat all, and she had been there in the stands to see it, cheering as loudly as anyone. There were handwritten letters, real relics, and various awards, for good citizenship, the winning pumpkin at the state fair, most improved player. A photocopy of Aimee's Masters degree—in psychology—was framed in a corner, space purposely left around it to show its importance, near an old family photo of Oliver and his brood of four kids when they were young.

One person was absent from Margie's collage; she found having photos of her father hanging around unsettling, so they were kept in a dresser drawer. She hadn't wanted to get rid of them entirely and knowing they were there, tied in a neat bundle for her to flip through when she so desired, brought her some amount of comfort.

He had been killed in a car wreck before seeing his grandkids graduate from college, long before they married. He was at fault, probably, pummeling into a deep ditch on the side of the road, his pickup frozen on its nose in the process of flipping over. It was eleven at night so most people assumed he was drunk. Others had sadder, more sinister theories since it was a road near home he had navigated while intoxicated almost all his life. But her mother didn't really want to know—and no one else cared enough—to request an autopsy. Her mother had died soon after in her sleep, no longer having anyone to worry over.

Her dear Jack had passed away ten years ago, from cancer, and her nightstand was cluttered with photos of him. She had wondered how she would survive that year—and every day since his death—but somehow she did. Simple joys and individual moments were the only thing that got her through that time, and sometimes they had been few and far between. She had been honing this skill since middle age, but ironically, at such a ripe old age she'd had to force herself to see the world again through the eyes of a child, to fill herself with childlike wonder in order to survive.

Sometimes the smell of honeysuckle in the summer heat would be her savior. Other times picking a blackberry straight off the vine would redeem her, feeling the texture of its little kernels with her tongue before crushing them to release the sour-sweet flavor. Or sitting in her rocker, a gentle breeze blowing through the pines at dusk releasing their scent might deliver her. A sunbeam on her skin, even through a window, could feel sacred. The taste of vanilla bean ice cream: simply divine. Her faith in humanity could be restored by the warm smile of her daughter or the soft touch of her nurse sponging off her sweaty forehead.

Until a few years ago, she had lived with Aimee all the way out in California and that had been grand, an absolute delight. As her health began to fail, when she needed constant care, she had come back to her roots to be near Oliver, and they had all chosen an old folks home called Golden Acres—ironically sitting on very little land—not five miles away from the trailer park where she'd grown up. The family had joked that she had ended up right where she started, yet Margie had travelled a greater distance than any of them really knew. She had learned a long, long time ago that the where isn't as important as the who or the what. Besides, her two children, six grandchildren and the three little ones visited her often, and those were moments to cherish indeed.

Her friend Katie was still alive, still healthy—and still driving—and when she came by they talked and gossiped for hours. She still lived in the same house in their old neighborhood, but was alone now. Sometimes she snuck in a bottle of red wine along with a tray of ice cubes stolen from the communal kitchen, and they nursed it in the garden, sipping slowly from plastic cups.

And of course she had her extended network of friends and family on Facebook. Though some old folks were afraid of it, Margie loved technology. While actual devices had gotten smaller and smaller and she had to make the type setting larger and larger, it didn't matter, since all she had to do was push "project" to see the images floating in front of her, bringing photos to life out of thin air, so real she often reached out to touch them before she could stop herself, which she found herself doing now.

Just then her dear friend Julia popped her head in, barely supported by her veiny neck and thin frame.

"Marjorie Moore, will you please get out from under that silly computer and join us in the lounge for Scrabble? You missed it last week and we missed you. Besides Christine and Mona are playing and you know those two are an absolute hoot."

"Now Julia, how can you call this beautiful young woman right here silly?" she said, projecting an image of Aimee's daughter, a writer in her twenties, standing on a rooftop surrounded by a sweeping skyline. She zoomed in until it nearly filled the room. "Just up and moved to New York City at the age of twenty-seven. Can you even imagine, I mean only in my wildest dreams…"

"Oh she's gorgeous alright, looks a lot like you. But why don't you get yourself up and come into the rec room. Bring the laptop with you if you must," Julia said with a wink.

"Well I'll sure try. My dang hip gave out again last night, this one here, and I took quite a tumble. But I feel alright today. I guess you could call me a real hipster the way they've been giving out left and right. I'll just bring along some artisanal coffee and some kale." Here she let out a laugh so hearty, shaking her frail body so hard and ending in a coughing fit, that Margie thought if she wasn't careful that might surely be the thing that finished her off.

Margie shifted her electronic bed up to the sitting position. She realized her walker was too far away to safely make it to her wheelchair and called her nurse, searching her side table for her lipstick, applying it generously.

Once comfortably in her chair, she rolled into the rec room and up to her friend Nick, an absolutely ancient gentleman, and flashed him her pearly whites. Nick's lifeless face lit up.

"Looking sharp, handsome fellow," she said squeezing his arm, barely more than a bone beneath his baggy sweater. His head was beyond bald and as dented as a walnut, and she rubbed it three times as always, saying it brought good luck. But in truth, it reminded her of her dear Jack.

ACKNOWLEDGMENTS

Creating art is an act of faith. When I read this phrase in *The Artist's Way* by Julia Cameron it resonated with me—so much so that I wrote it on a sticky note and stuck it on the wall above my computer, reminding me daily to believe in myself, believe in the work, and to have faith that it would come to fruition. But that strength of resolve wouldn't have been possible without all the people who first had confidence in me and have encouraged me throughout the process.

I'm endlessly grateful to my husband, Niklas Andersson, a true life partner who has been fully supportive of my writing endeavors from day one. One of my most trusted readers, he's an excellent editor and an opinionated and honest critic who understands big-picture concepts. And he gave me the same priceless, if simple, advice when I was nervous about performing my first public reading ten years ago that he gave me upon the release of this, my debut novel: the hard work has been done, now is your chance to just have fun with it and enjoy it.

Many thanks to Naomi Rosenblatt of Heliotrope Books for loving and championing the novel, for seeing the potential in the book. Working with her has felt like being part of a team as she's guided me through the publication process, patiently answered countless questions, and generously shared her expertise and insights.

I'd like to thank my mentor Madge McKeithen, who was my first creative writing teacher at the New School, for her continued, thoughtful guidance and her love of language—it was contagious; it infected me with an unstoppable drive to write. And her class spawned a writers' group that evolved into decade-long, dear friendships that I am thankful for, including Kera Yonker, who did a fantastic job editing and proofreading the manuscript, Felice Neals, and Olivia Dunn, an invaluable early reader.

I'll never forget the other early readers to whom I'm indebted: Monica Bidwell, Michelle Sandquist, Alison Restak, Jennifer Liu, Jill Woodward, and Lizzie Fetterman, a diverse group who offered their input—and more importantly—their enthusiasm. And an extra special thanks to my sister, Corie Woodard, who devours books like food; she read several versions of the book in full, always an eager and observant reader.

I want to thank Candy Schulman and Sue Shapiro, New School professors whose help, advice and companionship went beyond the classroom. I'm forever grateful to Adam Langer and Sandra Newman, two of my inspiring instructors at the 92 Street Y, where the book was born and developed, as well as to the writers in the workshops who have read various sections and chapters. To the person who said in their notes: "I know I will see this novel in the bookstore one day,"—thank you. These small words of encouragement scribbled in the margins do make a difference.

Lastly, a great big thank you to my friends and family for always being a comforting and energizing presence: to my NYC "family" who are always crowding into the first rows at my readings; to my three good-natured siblings who always pick up the phone; and to a plethora of kind relatives spread out across the country. And especially to my mom and dad who have always supported me fully, not only in writing, but in all of life's adventures. They have had my back in whatever I wanted to pursue, from studying abroad to backpacking through Europe, Africa and South America alone, from moving to New York to taking my first writing class—all of the things that have made me who I am. I thank you, and I love you.

Writing and publishing this book has been a wonderful journey—and thanks to all who have come along for the ride—as I, like my character Marjorie Moore, continually strive to find my purpose, to live up to my potential, and to be fully present in the moments of my own life.